THE BREATHLESS SUMMER

In 1851 seventeen-year-old Erica Curtis and her two older brothers visit the Great Exhibition in Hyde Park. After seeing the illustrated trinket and tobacco boxes on display at the Crystal Palace, Erica is keen to make them instead of the clay pipes by which the family earns its living. The trinket boxes are a great success for Erica, but her young man makes it clear that he doesn't want her to carry on with the work she adores. Although he has asked her to marry him, Erica thinks she loves another...

THE BREATHLESS SUMMER

THE BREATHLESS SUMMER

by
Mary Minton

Magna Large Print Books
Long Preston, North Yorkshire,
England.

British Library Cataloguing in Publication Data.

Minton, Mary
    The breathless summer.

    A catalogue record for this book is
    available from the British Library

    ISBN 0-7505-1163-X

First published in Great Britain by Severn House Publishers
Ltd., 1996

Copyright © 1996 by Mary Minton

Cover illustration © Len Thurston by arrangement with
P.W.A. International Ltd.

The right of Mary Minton to be identified as the author
of this work has been asserted by her in accordance with
the Copyright, Designs and Patents Act, 1988

Published in Large Print 1998 by arrangement with Severn
House Publishers Ltd.

Magna Large Print is an imprint of
Library Magna Books Ltd.
Printed and bound in Great Britain by
T.J. International Ltd., Cornwall, PL28 8RW.

Chapter One

London 1851

Erica Curtis was angry. Their mother always treated them as children. She was seventeen, her brother Edward eighteen and Charles nineteen.

Charles had once said, 'It makes life easier to give in to mother.'

But this was different. It had nothing to do with work. It was pleasure. Here they were in the kitchen with their Uncle John wanting to take them all to the Great Exhibition at Hyde Park and her mother refusing to allow them to go. It was the most wonderful treat that had ever been offered, with her uncle paying all expenses.

'No,' her mother said, tight-lipped. It would give them a feeling of wanting to rise above their station. 'We earn pennies, not pounds.'

'Faith, you must understand that this exhibition is for all classes.' Their uncle spoke gently. 'People will come from all over the world, the rich, the middle classes and the lower classes. This year, 1851, will be a year to remember for possibly centuries.'

'And what makes it so special?' Faith's tone was dry.

'For one thing, the building is magnificent: it's made all of glass, and is on three floors. They've named it the Crystal Palace and it's built in Hyde Park. They even have trees growing inside. There will be products from all over the world. The Queen, Prince Albert and other members of the Royal Family will be there. There will be cheap excursions, hundreds of people are coming from Ireland. It really ought not to be missed.'

'No—' their mother began but Erica broke in.

'Mother, will you please listen to Uncle John. He has a lot of common sense.'

He was a young uncle, only twenty-six; the boys and Erica regarded him as an elder brother.

Charles added, 'I agree with Erica. I feel we should have a say in this. Why should we be denied this pleasure when uncle is prepared to pay for us all. We've slaved since Father died to keep the business going. You took Erica away from school at twelve years old. She's now seventeen and she spends her days and evenings making clay pipes. What fun has she had out of life? None.'

Erica saw the flush of anger on her mother's face.

Edward spoke up. 'And I agree with Charles. It's only one day out of our lives. I don't think we should be denied when it won't cost you a penny, Ma.'

Faith flared up. 'You're talking as if I was bleeding you to death. Why do you think I try to save? To give you all a chance in life.'

'What chance?' asked Edward.

Their mother's head went up. 'I won't be able to go: I have the Baxter's washing to be done and I certainly won't let them down. And don't forget this: your uncle isn't all that wealthy. It's his wife whose money he's spending.'

The three children turned slowly to him. He was not in the least disturbed.

'I did not marry Hesther for her money. I loved her once. I simply wanted you and the children to have a treat. When *we* were children we led terribly dull lives. There were no treats whatsoever. I thought our lives together as brother and sister might have softened you, Faith, but I see it hasn't. I won't take the children unless I have your consent and, willingly given.'

Their mother sat for a while in silence then she said, 'I give my consent and, give it willingly, but I won't go. I do want to do Mrs Baxter's washing on the usual day.

The children can tell me all about the Exhibition when they come back.'

And she would not be moved in her decision, would not let a customer down, explaining that Mrs Baxter would no doubt find someone else to do her washing and would not come back to her.

The children knew that every penny counted in their lives and were silent.

Their uncle stood up and said, 'Well, I must be going. I shall see you all in a week's time.'

Although he was smiling there was a sadness in it. Erica began to wonder if it was because her mother had refused to go to the Exhibition with them or, if Uncle John's wife was to blame. They had never known that it was their aunt who held the purse strings.

Their mother stood at the door talking to her brother and while they talked, Erica gabbled excitedly to Charles and Edward about the Exhibition. She had heard two people talking about it a few days ago but never had she imagined in a thousand years that she would get the chance of seeing it.

'Just think,' she added, suddenly dreamy, 'At last I'm going to visit the centre of London, see the big shops, the buildings all the people.'

She came back to earth.

'I can't understand Aunt Hesther keeping her money from Uncle John. He made clay pipes before he was married and it was *she* who encouraged him to give up the work. She considered that making clay pipes was beneath her station. I should imagine that he might start a business again.'

Charles said, 'He has suggested that he would like to work with us and I'm willing.' And Edward and Erica agreed that they were too.

'I remember seeing Hesther when I was a child,' Edward said. 'She was different then. Not exactly pretty, but there was something about her. She was shy. Now her tongue, according to Uncle John, is always going ten to the dozen. He told me last week that he's thinking of leaving her.'

'Leaving her?' Edward and Erica echoed.

'So he says, but he wouldn't get a penny from Hesther.'

Erica gazed at him. 'I always thought that a man took over the money a woman had, once they were married.'

'So did I but there must have been a clause in the will. Hesther hands it out to him in small quantities. Uncle John's a gambler. Perhaps that's why.'

'A gambler!' Erica and Edward again exclaimed together.

Charles nodded. 'I imagine that's why

13

she's so tight with him. No one is going to fritter away Hesther's money.'

Faith came into the kitchen and the chatter ceased.

'Well,' she said, tight-lipped again, 'you do have work to do this evening, so you'd better get on with it.'

The three of them went to their allotted task, without saying another word: Charles and Edward to the workshop in the back and Erica to a corner of the kitchen where she packed the finished clay pipes.

Erica thought about her life. She had never known her father. He had died in an accident when she was a year old. Her mother would never discuss him. The boys didn't know much about him and Uncle John said it was an unhappy time and it was best not to talk about it.

They had apparently lived, in those days, outside London, and had then come to live in their grandfather's house on the edge of Lower Clapton, not far from Hackney Marshes.

Erica had been her grandfather's favourite and she had adored him.

He too had made pipes and taught the boys all about them. Her grandfather had made moulds that put fancy patterns on them and as a child she had drawn pictures of the patterns.

She had also drawn faces of people, men,

women and children and her grandfather had been full of praise of her drawings.

'This child is a born artist,' he had said one day with pride. 'She'll go a long way when she grows up. It's an inborn gift. Not one that can be taught.'

Unfortunately, her mother had always tried to stop her doing drawings. One day she had said, 'You'll have to learn to help with the clay pipes. Drawings are a waste of time. If I find any I shall burn them.'

Erica had told her grandfather this and he had said to her softly, 'Keep on with your drawings, my darling. Find a good hiding place and don't tell anyone else about them.'

She had found a good secret place under the staircase, and they had built up over the years and improved.

When she and the boys were still young their grandfather used to take them on a Sunday to a cottage where he had once lived on Hackney Marshes. A friend of his had taken the cottage and they told the children exciting stories of things that had happened in the old days. They were told of big parties in the White House which was in line with the cottage: of people in evening dress and gambling through the night, some losing large sums of money and others making a fortune. But the most exciting thing was learning that the great

15

robber Dick Turpin had once lived in that particular house at one time.

The boys thought of it as adventure but Erica was dreamy about, it thinking of all the beautiful gowns and lovely jewellery.

As the children grew up, however, their mother insisted they were taught how to make clay pipes and the visits to Hackney Marshes had ended.

Erica's grandfather had died from a heart attack when she was eleven and she had been broken hearted. If her mother found her in tears she was told sternly to dry her eyes and get on with her work.

There was a farm a short distance away where a family had left and another family moved in. The people who had left had been unfriendly but the new family came to make themselves known to Mrs Curtis. Although Faith did not welcome visitors she took to the Todds right away and it made a difference to the lives of the Curtis family.

Mrs Todd would bring eggs, an apple tart. Sometimes they got a couple of rabbits and when her husband killed cattle, there would always be a tasty piece of beef.

Although Erica enjoyed making the clay pipes and putting them in the moulds. She felt at times that she needed something different to do, but had no idea what.

16

Now she began to wonder if there was something at the Crystal Palace that might give her an idea of something to do. After all, people were coming from all over the world to show their goods. Excitement rose in her again and she felt she could hardly wait for the day of going to the Crystal Palace in Hyde Park.

After a few days Faith said that all three of them must go to the second-hand clothes shops to get clothes for the day. John had insisted she take money to get them. Her attitude showed her disapproval of this.

They went that evening to the little shop in Lower Clapton. They spent over half an hour there, which their mother indicated was far too long, but all three were satisfied with what had been bought.

Erica had come out with a long, simply cut white cotton dress with thin blue lines to it. There was also a jacket to match in case it was cold. The hat she bought was a blue linen bonnet tied with white ribbon. She also chose a pair of white shoes. The boys chose lightweight grey suits with white shirts and straw boaters and black shoes.

They were all delighted with their bargains. Faith had said the clothes must all go back to the shop after the visit to the Exhibition was over, but all three were adamant. Their uncle had paid for them

17

and they would keep them. Things might change soon and if they acquired a shop they would need to be decently dressed.

Faith, who had looked forward to having some money to be put aside was annoyed, but gave in to their decision, thinking it looked as if she would never again have any say in their lives. But of course they were growing up. They could all get married. Not that any of them had done any courting, but it could happen. And what would happen to her then? At that moment she could not contemplate such a thing happening. She would tackle it when it came along.

A few days later John arrived with a small van, which a friend had lent him, at seven o'clock in the morning, to take them to Hyde Park.

'The boys can sit at the front with me,' he said, 'and you, Erica, can sit on cushions in the back. The floor is covered with straw and there's a cover over that.'

She laughed. 'I would have sat quite happily on bare boards.'

Her mother reprimanded her. 'Don't be silly, girl, you'll have to keep that dress decent.'

Charles turned his head and gave her a wink. She winked back. Then they were away, all of them waving to her mother and she waving back, looking,

Erica thought, a little forlorn. Well, her mother had had her chance and refused it. It was her own fault.

Erica thought that her uncle had called rather early for them: the Royal Family were not opening the Crystal Palace until half-past eleven, but she soon came to realise, once they were on the roads, all the stops and traffic jams there were.

There seemed to be hundreds of people walking along the roads and pavements and there there were vehicles of every description, carts and horses, and Hansom Cabs. People were shouting good wishes to others. Children and grown ups alike waved small Union Jacks and there was such a lovely feeling of jollity.

It was quite a journey but no one seemed to mind.

When they eventually reached the West End, Erica was full of awe at the beautiful buildings, all flying the Union Jack. And when she saw the thousands of people that were going down the road to Hyde Park she felt tears come into her eyes. All going to see the Queen and her husband the Prince Consort. How lucky they were, and they had their Uncle John to thank.

There was a constant noise of people shouting, and there were police everywhere but everyone, although boisterous, was well behaved.

It was actually half past ten when they did arrive at Hyde Park and what a wonderful spectacle it presented.

It had started to rain when they first left but now the day was bright and the sun shone on the vast glass building that was the Crystal Palace.

Uncle John had explained there were three floors, each one was twenty feet high and on each floor were different products.

They stayed on the ground floor wanting to see Queen Victoria, Prince Albert and some more of the Royal Family arriving, but it was not until later in the day that they saw them. They were hemmed in then by the crowds and everyone was shouting hurrahs. Some of them waved handkerchiefs but many of them waved their small Union Jacks. Erica wept with joy, just to be there and knowing they were near.

The crowd moved and they moved with them and could hear The Queen make her speech, and then Prince Albert made his speech and everyone there, Erica was sure, was greatly impressed.

There was singing from six hundred voices (according to Uncle John) of Handel's Hallelujah Chorus, then choir boys began to sing, (two hundred of them), and it was so beautiful that Erica was sure almost everyone was weeping.

A band was playing as the Royal Family followed by dignitaries walked along the building but the deafening cheers were so loud that it could hardly be heard.

Uncle John said they would find their way to the various products and might get a chance of seeing the Royal Family leave later on. He smiled. 'I know you'll be wanting to see pipes that come from all over the world.'

The three of them were very much in favour of this.

There was still a big crowd and they had to edge their way in to see the various products.

Commentators talked about the enormous size of the building, which, they said was 1,851 feet in length from East to West and 406 feet from North to South and stressed that the like of this gorgeous glittering structure, glowing with colour, had never ever been seen before.

Everyone agreed with this. The framework of the building was light blue picked out with orange and scarlet and every storey was adorned with flags of all nations.

The Exhibition was a revelation to many people. Some had never seen a railway train. Machinery of any kind was a novelty. And here were beautiful materials, silks and satins and velvet and fine material that was like a wavering mist when displayed. There were Indian silks, black mantillas from Spain and intricate weaving machinery from France.

They saw the Koh-i-noor diamond which brought breathless murmurs as it sparkled in the light. There were also rough diamonds, before they had been cut and polished that looked like coarse stones.

In another section were statues, many of them nude, which attracted a gaping attention. Charles and Edward tried to hustle Erica away but she refused to be moved.

'They're classical,' she said. 'Where else could I see such things?' Uncle John nodded to her brothers and they released her.

'This is an experience for all of you,' he said. 'You never know in life when you need to know about these things.'

In every section they had to edge their way in and it was Erica who first saw the pipes. She pushed her way through this time and gazed in awe at the display. There were English pipes of course, but there also pipes of all descriptions from Germany, Hungary, Bulgaria, France...the countries were endless. One man in France employed seven hundred workers. 'Seven hundred,' breathed Erica softly. If only she could have a small shop and have three or four workers.

There was a rack with long-stemmed pipes, some so long they would touch the floor and all the pipe bowls were masterpieces of carving or had tiny country scenes painted on them.

Someone suddenly caught her arm. It was her Uncle John. He seemed breathless.

'Erica, don't ever run away like that again. If Charles had not just caught a glimpse of you, we could have been looking all over the place for you.'

'Oh, Uncle, I'm sorry, I saw these pipes. Just look at them. They're from a dozen or so countries. Aren't they beautiful? Look at the paintings and the carving and the polish. Those over there are made of wood.'

The man in charge of the section said, 'Yes, they're made of meerschaums and it's becoming a very popular wood for pipes. The name meerschaums is German, which means "sea-foam". The substance itself is composed of prehistoric, microscopic sea creatures and is composed of silica, magnesia, carbonic acid and water. It is only found in one area of Turkey, where it occurs deep underground.' A big group of people had gathered round him now.

'The material itself is soft, lightweight and porous. Properly treated it is easy

23

to handle. Meerschaums pipes have been transformed into animals, gods and free-form designs. Now I don't want to keep you too long, I know you have so many other items you want to see, so please feel free to take a brochure, which will explain it all in more detail.'

Erica, Charles and Edward, pleased with the talk came away with a handful of brochures and judging by the remarks, many people wanted to make meerschaums pipes. John had had to drag them away, with a promise to return when the number of people thinned out.

They talked of nothing else but meer-schaums until they came to some beautiful, delicate porcelain, porcelain so fine one could almost see through it.

There were crystal wine glasses of every description, silver cutlery, some exquisite vases, a number of huge ones with wonderful pictures painted on them.

There were fine pictures and oil paint-ings, some of which Erica could not quite make out, but knew they were very expensive. They also saw fine English china, Minton and Crown Derby, dinner sets and tea sets.

Their uncle also took them to see mechanical items, but although Charles and Edward were interested, they bored Erica and she longed to go back to the section that dealt with pipes.

John then decided it was time to have something to eat and it was not until they were all sat down with lemonade and sandwiches in the café that they realised just how tired they all were.

In spite of being tired, however, they talked non-stop of all the things they had seen already. Erica had a feeling of living on the edge of a different world.

The food and the rest put them back on form again and once more they were looking at clothes from China when there was a sound of shouting and cheering and to their delight the Royal Family were coming towards them.

They were lucky enough to be in the front line and to Erica's joy The Queen raised her hand acknowledging the crowd just as they were passing. Erica was not the only one weeping.

She saw the handsome Prince Albert and two of the children, Bertie and Vicky, as their parents called them, Vicky holding her father's hand and Bertie holding his mother's hand. Vicky was dressed in lace over white satin, and wearing a small wreath of pink wild roses in her hair. She seemed very shy.

When the retinue had passed Erica closed her eyes. What a day. How could she describe it to her mother?

It was six o'clock that evening when they left and they were back home at nine. Again, although they were tired out, they all told Faith about their wonderful, wonderful day.

She said quietly, 'And I could have gone. Mrs Baxter cancelled the washing. She was going to the Crystal Palace.'

'Oh, no...!'

John said, 'I shall take you one day, Faith. You just can't miss such a wonderful occasion.'

'Do you know, John, you've all described it so well, I don't think I need to go.' A faint smile touched her lips.

Chapter Two

Erica had not slept very well, having dreamt most of the night about Hesther, of all people. She lay thinking about the day that Hesther and John had been married. None of the family had been conscious then of feeling like the poor relations. It was when they were home again that they became aware of it.

Edward had said, 'Hesther was all right when they came from the church, but later

I felt she was trying to keep us all in the background, away from her wealthy friends.'

At first Erica had been too taken at the luxury of the house and the beautiful clothes of the guests. And she had enjoyed the food. It was not until they got home that it had occurred to her how they had been kept as much as possible from the wealthy folk. They had been put in a corner where servants had brought delicious titbits.

John had kept coming to ask if they were all right and they had told him yes, and understood that he had to try and mix with all the guests.

It was the only time they had been in the house. It appeared that John had married a bit of a tartar.

He had brought Hesther to their house once or twice since, but they had never stayed long. Poor Uncle John. Why had he not noticed before then how unpleasant Hesther could be?

None of them had known until now how tight she was with her money.

Erica put Hesther determinedly from her mind and concentrated on the Exhibition. In a few minutes she must get up. It was nearly half-past six. What a splendid day yesterday had been.

What she wanted to know was whether

Charles and Edward would still be keen to start making meerschaums pipes? She hoped so. She would welcome a change. But, of course, it was like anything else, they would have to learn about it.

And there would be no talking about it first thing in the morning. Her mother was always in a bad temper at this time of day. There was a sudden bang on the door and her mother shouting, 'It's time you were up, it's turned half-past six.'

Erica flung back the bedclothes and sighed. Another weary day to face.

The boys were already at the table and eating their porridge. Her mother brought Erica's porridge in and banged the bowl on the table.

She found herself thinking, not about pipes, but of snuff boxes. She had seen them among the exhibits and thought what attractive trinket boxes they would make.

An excitement stirred in her as designs began to form in her mind.

How amazing. There were round snuff boxes, oval ones, square ones, some made of wood, some of bark, others made of copper. Some had beautiful scenes on them, others were carved. Had she actually taken all this in yesterday?

Her mother who had finished her breakfast said, as she got up, 'We'll have to get started. And don't forget

28

that you all have to make up the work you missed yesterday.'

Erica would have to speak to Charles and Edward about it some time although she doubted whether they would be interested. They wanted to change to make meerschaums pipes.

Charles and Edward came in from the shed. Charles looked around him. 'Where's Mother?' They both seemed excited.

'She's in the scullery. Why?'

Edward said, 'Do you know what she was doing yesterday? She dealt with all that clay soaking and fashioned pipe bowls and, put them ready to go into the kiln this morning.' He called out to his mother and she came in drying her hands.

'Yes, what is it?'

The boys told her what they had found and her cheeks flushed. 'Well, I thought it would help to get your number of pipes ready.'

'Ma, you're great,' Edward said. Charles also thanked her. 'It was good of you, Mother. We were both dreading having to start this morning. I think we'll have to try and get you to the Crystal Palace.'

Her mother protested that she couldn't afford it, but the boys both said, that they would afford it.

Faith kept protesting but Erica noticed that there was pleasure on her face and, tears in her eyes.

Well, she thought. It was almost as if her mother loved them all. This made her feel she could not put her idea over to the boys about her change of plan. Not yet, but in a few days.

It was not until the Saturday evening that her opportunity came when Charles said, 'I still feel half dead after going to the Crystal Palace. But I think now that we've fulfilled our order that we'll tackle meerschaums pipes.'

Edward agreed, saying, 'I wouldn't think they'll take any more work than making the clay ones.'

'Don't forget they're made of wood. Totally different work altogether. But we're going to try.'

At this moment Erica made up her mind to approach her change of item. 'I don't want to make pipes any more. I want to concentrate on trinket boxes.'

Both her brothers looked at one another then stared at her. 'Why trinket boxes?' Charles asked.

She told them how the idea how come to her suddenly, then added, 'And no one can change my mind. I want to own a shop one day.'

'Don't be ridiculous.' This was from Edward. 'Girls don't own shops.'

'But I will, because it takes a woman

to know what a woman requires. I shall start small, but I'll build up and have a bigger shop in time, selling cosmetics of every description.'

Edward raised his shoulders. 'For heavens sake come down to earth. Be content that we are earning some money. We're sticking to making pipes and that's it.'

Charles held up a hand. 'Now just a minute. Erica has as much right as we have to make a change in our lives. We will make our meerschaums pipes and she will make her trinket boxes.'

Edward protested. 'No, I won't agree. We've always been a threesome and I feel we should stay that way.'

'I'm doing what I want to do, Edward, and nothing will change me.' Erica spoke firmly.

Edward was furious. 'You're a cheat! We taught you how to draw and now you want to go off on your own.'

Charles grabbed hold of Edward, and shook him roughly. 'Don't you dare call Erica names! You are the cheat. It was she who taught us. She's a natural artist. Grandfather recognised this when she was six or seven and was doing paintings.'

Erica was shocked at the trouble she had caused. She sank on to a chair and covered her face.

Edward's anger was short-lived. 'I'm

sorry, Erica, forgive me. It was the shock of losing you.'

'I'm to blame. I wanted my life to change over night. I'll go on making the pipe bowls. Some day I'll try my hand at the trinket boxes.'

'No, Erica.' Charles spoke gently. 'You must try this new venture. It's learning things early that's important. Edward and I want to experiment with the meerschaums pipes. We'll start with them next week, experimenting at first and if successful—' Charles glanced out of the window. 'Get moving, Mother's coming. We don't want to upset her.'

'No, of course not,' Edward replied. 'We'll talk about this again.'

Faith came in, slitting open an envelope. 'The postman's been. It's from John.'

She pulled out a single sheet of paper, scanned it, then looked at them, dismay on her face. 'He's leaving Hesther. Oh, dear. I think he's doing the wrong thing. He'll have no money. Hesther will stick to it, I know.'

'Is Uncle John leaving her, or has she asked him to leave?'

'He's leaving her, says he can't stand any more rows.' Faith looked at the letter again then raised her head. 'He says he'll call and see us, perhaps in a couple of days when he's decided where to go. Oh, my goodness, sometimes we think we're badly done to, but to separate in a marriage. That's terrible.'

'It's not as if there's any room here. We haven't even a sofa he could sleep on,' Edward said.

'He wouldn't want to stay here,' Faith said, shaking her head. 'I'm beginning to wonder if he...well, if he has another woman somewhere. It does happen.' She folded the letter, replaced it in the envelope and got up. 'Well, we'll know what's happened in a few days. We have our own worries.'

Charles ventured, in a gentle way, 'I know we have our own worries, Mother, but I would be willing to let Uncle John have my bed and I'll sleep on the floor until he finds somewhere to stay.'

'Oh, no you won't. John has been reckless with the money he's had from Hesther. He shouldn't have gambled. It's his own fault. I don't want him to get settled in here and have to feed him. We can't afford it. Don't, and I repeat, don't think you're obliged to give up your bed because he took you to the Exhibition. He wanted company.'

Even Edward objected to this. 'No, Ma, in all fairness I'm sure Uncle wanted to give us a treat. If you had come with us you would have known this.'

'Well, I didn't,' Faith snapped. 'And that's all I'm going to say. He finds himself a place to live. Now, you all have jobs to do, get on with them.'

Charles and Edward went out to the shed. Erica sat down to her work.

While she was working she wondered about her mother. She had worked hard the day before to do what she had done. Did she love them? She had never shown it in any way, had never kissed them, or given one of them a cuddle. It was strange. Erica supposed she could love them. Some mothers did love their children and show them in small ways that they were loved. A woman could yell at her children all day and then at bedtime give then a kiss and a hug.

Just after they had finished their dinner their Uncle John called. His manner was defiant as he explained about leaving Hesther.

'It was simply impossible to go on living with her. She ranted on about all my faults, abused me for not saving the money she gave me.'

'Why didn't you?' Faith was in no way sympathetic.

'I don't think you have any idea how much she allowed me. Four pound a month, that was what was handed over to me!'

'Four pounds? I don't believe it.'

'You can believe it. It's true enough,' he replied, a bitter note in his voice. 'Why do you think I started gambling? I hoped to win enough so other people would never know what went on and think I was mean with all my money.'

'Uncle John, I always thought that a husband took over his wife's money when they married.'

'I understood this too, Charles. And I must admit I didn't like it and was determined that Hester should share it. What a shock I got when I found it was all tied up but the four pound a month she was going to allow me to have.'

'But it's by law that a husband takes over the money.'

'Apparently not. It's too complicated to explain it all, but her first husband had arranged all this before his death. By the time it was all explained I was beginning to think that I was lucky to get four pounds a month!'

'I think it's terrible,' Edward said. 'And I would add that you're well rid of her. What are you going to do, where will you live?'

'With an elderly woman who will rent me a room for two shillings a week. She says she's sorry but she can't cook for me. I won't starve. That allows me eighteen shillings a week for food. The gambling has to stop.'

'I'll do your laundry,' Faith offered. 'That's no problem and we can give you a meal now and then.'

'No, I wouldn't even consider it. You have enough to do with your money.'

'I never dreamt that you only had this amount. It's terrible. Really terrible. And you took the children to the Exhibition.'

He smiled. 'That was a treat to me as it was for them and I will still see that you visit the Exhibition too. I did have a smallish win last week and have put this aside so that you too shall have a treat.'

'Forget it. Keep what money you have, you'll need it.'

'When you have a free day, you shall go, dear Faith. That is a promise.'

'And now I shall find you something to eat. I bet you haven't had any dinner.'

He said no, but that he was not hungry.

But as soon as she had warmed up the broth that was left for the following day he agreed that the smell was appetising and she must stop tempting him.

The way he ate proved to them all that it had been a while since he had eaten.

He thanked Faith for it and said that he would now go and see if he could find a job of some kind.

Charles said at once, 'Edward and I were

36

thinking of trying to make meerschaums pipes instead of the clay ones. If you would care to join us you would be more than welcome. Not that we could pay you at first, but once we've mastered it you can share with us.'

John accepted the offer at once. 'I would like that. I was more than interested in hearing what the man at the Exhibition had to say about meerschaums pipes. The whole system of course, is different. They're handmade. We wouldn't need the kiln any more. I'll find out who will help us to get the whole system organised.'

'We'll have to keep on with the clay pipes for the time being.'

'Yes, of course, possibly for a number of weeks. Could be months.'

Charles nodded. 'First of all we must find out if it'll be worth it. Money comes into it. The man at the Exhibition said that the meerschaums were made of root wood and that it was lighter to handle and easier to work with, but added that they cost more to make.'

'Naturally,' said John. 'Look, I have some friends who are going to the Exhibition tomorrow. I'll get them to ask at the pipe section and get all the details.'

Erica's spirits lifted. If Uncle John came to work with them she would be more free to make trinket boxes. Her luck had changed. This new world she had entered seemed to be ready made for her.

John's friends came back from the Exhibition with good news for them. The man at the pipe section gave them explicit details of the making of the meerschaums, told them where to buy the tools and also told them of a firm who would be willing to buy the pipes, if they were up to standard. He was also told that the pay was good.

'Splendid!' declared John. 'They'll be up to standard all right, by the time we've mastered the methods.'

They all worked hard and Erica took an interest in them too. A piece of the root wood had to be cut up first into pieces the size of the pipe, then there was shaping by hand. They also had to get used to the new tools.

Erica found it lovely light wood to handle. After shaping a piece it had to be lightly sand-papered. Then polished. They kept on experimenting, but it was six weeks before they were getting near to perfection.

Working with her Uncle John seemed to change Erica's life completely. He could be amusing and really seemed to be much happier than when he had been living with Hesther...

It was he who suggested waxing the

bowls, which gave a final touch to them.

Not only were the meerschaums pipes lighter, but they gave a sweeter taste to the tobacco.

Erica found herself thinking that with this wood she might be able to do some light carving on them. But not now, later, these pipes had to be accepted first.

They were still making the clay pipes, of course, and Erica had taken advantage on a Saturday evening when they broke off work at seven o'clock, unless there was anything particularly urgent to be done, to try her hand at making trinket boxes.

Charles, Edward and her uncle always spent the evening walking for exercise and her mother visited Mrs Todd at the farm.

She sawed some up into sizes she felt would be required and sandpapered them smooth. By the next Saturday she knew exactly what she was going to make.

By the following Saturday she had three in her mind: an oblong box, an oval one and a circular one. They would all have lids. She sawed the pieces, glued them together and was well pleased with the result.

Next week she would decide which would need filigree carving and which were to be painted.

By the following Saturday she knew the

oblong one would be the one to be carved and that the other two would be painted.

It took a month to complete them, but she was delighted with the result. The next one she wanted to make would be a taller, two-drawer trinket box. What she needed was some more wood.

There was plenty lying about on Hackney Marshes, The barges brought loads of it that were collected and piled on to deep wagons.

They were into September when the menfolk returned with the smell of beer on their breaths. Erica, knowing her mother's dislike of beer, said, 'You had better eat a piece of bread each or you'll have Mother after your blood.'

Her uncle beamed at her. 'She won't have any objection in this case, we've just met a man who told us he wants all the meerschaums pipes we can make.'

'No!'

'Yes,' declared her brothers, both with broad smiles on their faces. 'Isn't it great?'

They were laughing and dancing around when Faith came in.

'And what's going on here?' she demanded.

They told her and she was overjoyed too. Then they all sat down and discussed the situation. It would mean them working doubly hard because they dared not give up the white clay pipes yet until the meerschaums had been bought and paid for and another order given.

Erica saw an end for the time being to doing any more trinket boxes, but she could be working out designs while she was working on the pipes.

They were all drained by the time the meerschaums pipes were approved and paid for and another order given, but it was worth it. It meant that more meerschaums pipes could be made now that the clay ones were out of the way.

As her mother said, 'Well, at last, we shall have a little extra money to have a treat now and again. This Sunday, we shall have a piece of beef to roast.'

'Three cheers to old England!' declared Edward. 'Roast beef and Yorkshire pudding. What a feast! The only time we taste roast beef is when Mr Todd kills some beasts.'

John said smiling, 'Well I shall be the one to supply this beef for Sunday,'

'No, you won't,' Faith spoke firmly. 'It's our treat to you. You've done enough for us.'

'You still haven't been to the Exhibition. Perhaps next week.'

'Forget it for the time being, you all have work ahead of you. That's the most important thing at the moment. You'll be working only with the meerschaums, not the clay pipes. It's all right experimenting but doing it all the time... Still, if you don't experiment, you don't learn anything.'

Erica thought how true this was and felt suddenly determined that she must go on experimenting with her trinket boxes or she would lose her touch. Should she ask for time to work at them? No, this was impossible at the moment. But once they were in rhythm with the meerschaums then they would have time off again on a Saturday evening.

It was Charles who reminded John that the Exhibition would soon be closing. 'It closes in October.'

'So, it does. Faith, come what may I shall take you to Hyde Park next week.' He turned to Erica, Charles and Edward. 'Your mother worked hard the day I took you to the Exhibition. Now you must work hard on the day we are out. I shall make up time when I get back and in the evenings before then.'

Although Faith kept protesting that it was foolish to go to Hyde Park when there was so much work to contend with, they all talked her into it. She was going and that was it.

John laughed, 'We can get in for a shilling each on special days. What's more the Queen could be there too.'

Faith had worn black since her husband had died. The coat and bonnet had not been worn since the funeral. Erica suggested to her mother that she wear a coloured scarf. She refused, but gave in to wearing a white collar on her one good dress and did eventually agree to Erica putting a pale pink artificial rose on the side of her bonnet. Erica had bought the rose for a penny from the second-hand shop.

It was surprising how much better Faith looked with those two extra items. It gave a lightness to her.

The morning she left with John to go to the Exhibition she looked even better still with her cheeks flushed with pleasure. John drew her arm through his and said brightly, 'Well, we are leaving. Don't expect us home before midnight!'

Charles Edward and Erica all agreed it was lovely to hear her mother laughing.

They waved them away and settled down to work, all of them wishing they could have gone with them.

Later in the day there was a loud knocking on the front door. 'Who on earth?' Erica said aloud as she got up to answer it.

It was Uncle John's wife, Hester...a very angry wife.

'I want to know,' she demanded, 'why my husband takes a woman from this house to the Hyde Park Exhibition. I am his wife, I should have gone with him if that's where he wanted to go.'

Anger rose in Erica. 'I don't know how you have the nerve to stand there and make such a statement. Uncle John left you because he couldn't stand any more of your tempers. Look at you now, eyes flashing, your cheeks an ugly red. It was his sister, my mother, who went with him to the Exhibition, a woman who's never had a treat in her life. She's worked eighteen hours a day, while you have lived in luxury, never wanting for a thing, never had to earn even a penny.'

Erica made to close the door. 'And don't you ever dare come here again with your complaints, you with your thousands of pounds and giving a pittance of a pound a week to your husband.'

Hesther put a foot in the door. 'Please listen to me. I...I love my husband I want him back.' There was a plaintive note in her voice.

'You're too late. He wouldn't come back to you, not even if you went down on your bended knees. You've made a fool of him, a laughing stock and no man could put up with that. Just take your foot away before I slam the door.'

Hesther drew her foot away quickly, but was still moaning on when Erica had slammed the door shut. Erica leaned back against the door and tried to get calm again. The wretched woman. It would probably take her half an hour before she settled back to work again. She was trembling in every limb.

Charles and Edward had been out in the back, but they both came in to hear what all the shouting had been about.

When Erica told them all that had taken place, Edward was angry too, but Charles said he felt sorry for Hesther. What a miserable life she must lead. Yes he knew she deserved to be told how badly she had behaved, but the thing was, she couldn't help it. It was her nature. Erica should be pleased that she had had to work for her living and understood the value of money. Poor Hesther had no idea of the value of it.

Both Erica and Edward stood staring at him, then Edward began to laugh. 'You should be a con man, Charles. You would make a fortune. I suddenly find myself feeling sorry for the woman.'

'Well, I don't,' retorted Erica, 'and, what's more, if Uncle did decide to return to her, Hesther's bossiness would still continue. It's the way she's built.'

And no amount of gentle talk from

Charles would make her change her mind.

When John and Faith returned from the Exhibition, Erica knew by her mother's manner, that things had changed in her that would stay with her for the rest of her life.

Although she was full of excitement there was an air of dreaminess that had never been there before.

'When I think of all the wonderful things I've seen today,' she said, 'I thank the Lord that I'm alive. I saw our Queen and her handsome husband the Prince Albert. And no one can take that image from me.'

John laughed. 'Your mother wore me out. I was nearly on my knees at times, feeling I hadn't an ounce of strength left, but Faith urged me on, saying that I might never have another chance again of seeing so many wonders. Incidentally, it wasn't clay pipes or any other type of pipe she wanted to see. It was furniture—'

'And carpets too,' Faith interrupted. 'Oh, those exquisite silken carpets, the colours. I've never seen anything like it. Also the furniture, chairs gold-framed, so fragile looking yet quite strong. The seats were covered with patterned velvet or silk brocade in the most delicate shades. These, believe it or not, were the kind used every day in big houses. There were

46

some wonderful chandeliers in silver that held a hundred candles. Just imagine. A hundred! There were also the most fascinating lamps, in all shapes and sizes and colours. There was also wafer thin china and cut glass ware. So exquisite and the glass carved by hand.'

Erica noticed that everything her mother raved about were household items, no mention at all of having glanced at even one pipe. There were tears in her mother's eyes when she said to John, 'I can't thank you enough for giving me this wonderful treat.' A smile touched her lips. 'I'll have to pull myself together and get down to some work tomorrow. Now, I'm ready for bed.'

But it was nearly another hour before Faith could be persuaded to retire.

Erica went upstairs to see her into bed and no sooner did her mother lay her head on the pillow than she was fast asleep. Erica kissed her mother gently on the cheek then went down stairs, realising afterwards that it was the first time she had ever kissed her mother.

Would this bring them all closer together?

Chapter Three

Erica and her brothers decided they would not mention to their uncle about his wife's visit until a few days later, Erica pointing out it could ruin that particular day of the visit to the Exhibition for her mother and her uncle.

When Erica did pluck up the courage to tell him about about his wife's visit he was not as angry as she had expected him to be.

'Typical Hesther,' he said, 'wants to keep me under her thumb, but the moment she thinks I might be escorting another woman somewhere she wants me back. I'm sorry to disappoint her but I shall never go back. Not even if she promised to share her wealth. I've discovered, too late, it seems, that living and working with relatives is much more rewarding than living in a small mansion, with a bad-tempered woman.'

'Are you sure you're doing the right thing?' Faith asked. 'Life can be trying at times, living on a pittance.'

'A pittance that is growing, Faith,' John spoke softly. 'We'll make a name for ourselves. It might not be this year, or the next or, even the one after, but it will come. And how proud we shall be.'

Faith gave a little sniff. 'I would be delighted if we could make another ten shillings a week.'

'Ten shillings?' John chuckled. 'That's just a pittance. Let's talk in pounds. Oh, yes, you can smile. It will come, without doubt. We eventually, will be employing a large staff.'

Charles and Edward began to laugh. 'I think it helps a great deal to have an optimist like you working with us,' Charles said.

Edward nodded, grinning broadly. 'I can see myself in the future smoking a cigar as I stroll between two lines of workers. What a lovely thought.'

Faith said a little dryly, 'Why two lines of workers? Why not six or eight lines?'

'Why not twenty?' This from John who was also grinning broadly. 'It doesn't cost anything to dream.'

Erica dreamed a lot these days. Her mind was always on her trinket boxes and she had made three more. Two were circular. One was painted with emerald green enamel paint and decorated on the lid with a narrow pathway around the edge, made of tiny pieces of crystalised rock, which she had picked up from a path in a field when she was a child and kept, because she had thought they were so pretty.

Some were the colour of rubies, some amethyst, others aquamarine and the rest clear crystal. She put them right around the edge, meeting at a stile where two children in bonnets and crinolines were climbing. She had spent a great deal of time doing their faces and had captured a look of mischief on the faces of both.

Around the lower part of the box were leaves and pieces of twig. In the lamplight the crystals sparkled. Erica felt it was the best box she had made so far.

The second circular one was done with ivory enamel, the edge was gold and in the circle was a young man and a woman, who were walking under a bower, with trailing pink roses. The box itself had roses and leaves around it. Erica thought of this painting as 'The Lovers' and felt romantic about it.

The third one was heart-shaped with flowers of every description covering it. Some day they would be for sale and although she longed to show someone her work she kept them hidden in a box under the stairs.

Also in the box were coppers she was saving. It was not her mother who paid her a shilling every week, but her Uncle

John, who thought that she, like her brothers, should receive a wage now that the meerschaums pipes were doing so well.

Her mother said that Erica's wage would pay for her board and lodgings. She didn't need any more. She had heard her mother and her uncle arguing, but her mother was adamant and saying that any clothes she needed would be bought for her. She had no need for anything else.

At first Erica had refused her uncle's offer but had eventually taken it when he said softly, 'You'll need a little money to decorate your trinket boxes.'

She looked at him quickly. 'You knew I was making some?'

'No, just guessed it. I see you scribbling designs now and then and see them going into the fire. Take care that no one else sees them.'

'Oh, thanks, Uncle, yes I will in future.'

'You'll find your little niche in time, my love. Never doubt it. You have a rare talent. You could be an artist.'

'I want to make trinket boxes. Some day I hope to have a little shop on my own.'

'I'll help you all I can when that time comes. Perhaps by then your mother will change towards you. She dreams too since going to the Exhibition.'

Erica felt moved by his words. He

seemed so understanding. What a pity he had not married the right woman. She was glad he had remained firm and not gone back to Hesther. She certainly did not deserve him.

Later, Erica's thoughts had her wondering if she would ever marry? She had known one or two boys but her mother had never allowed her to go out with anyone. When she was sixteen she had been rather taken with a certain boy but her mother had told her to forget about boys, she had a job to do and she must concentrate on that.

That night Erica found herself thinking about the Crystal Palace. She often thought about it but usually it was about all the wonderful things she had seen. This time it was what her Uncle John had told her about Prince Albert.

He said he had been the instigator of the Crystal Palace being built and that it had started two years before when he visited a friend who had a farm. The friend was not doing too well as he had found it impossible to get the instruments necessary. Prince Albert went to another friend who had a farm and was in the same position.

The Prince found out that the instruments were impossible to get in England. It worried him. He was very much for the working classes and it meant that possibly hundreds of working class men were missing out on gainful employment because of this.

He then thought that there must be hundreds of things that could be made and would find a ready market. Perhaps he could build somewhere to house an exhibition of such things, and all countries could take part.

He talked to Queen Victoria about it and she was all for it.

It was discussed with many top men. Many of them were very enthusiastic about it but there were also many of them against it, saying that the Crystal Palace he had in mind would not be strong enough and that it would collapse and kill thousands of people.

'Prince Albert told them quietly but firmly that his Palace would not collapse and, of course, as we know, it stood up to it beautifully.' Uncle John had concluded.

And Erica found that 'from small things, large things grow.'

She made up her mind there and then that she would not give up her trinket boxes in order to get married.

Every now and again they would be asked to do some special meerschaums pipes. This entailed more work, but they were paid more. Erica always tackled these. She enjoyed doing them. This time they had a larger order than usual. There were three dozen more to be done. One dozen were to be done with churches on them, or painted church windows. Another dozen had to deal with outdoor nature scenes and the last dozen had to have a picture of a lady, in profile, wearing a broad brimmed hat or bonnet and each wearing a low cut gown.

Erica was excited about this and she worked out how the ladies would look. They would all have a different expression and wear a different dress.

All the ladies wore a brimmed hat with a frothy feather on the side, in varying colours. Dresses were in different shades of emerald green, rose pink, and forget-me-not-blue.

What really pleased Erica was the wonderful remarks made by her family and more so when her uncle said, 'You are truly amazing, Erica, every lady has a different expression, one is haughty, one is sweet-faced. This one looks hopeful and this lady has a very gentle look. Oh, and look at this one. She's on the plain side but those delightful laughing blue eyes makes one forget the plainess.'

Erica gave him a beaming smile. 'Uncle John, I love you.'

'How did you make them all so different?' asked Charles. 'I fancy the plain-faced one with the laughing blue eyes too.' Edward said he would go for the sweet-faced one, while their uncle liked the gentle lady.

A friend of John who had called to see him, said with a grin, 'I'll take the sexy one any day. Put an order in for me.'

Faith was shocked and scolded him, telling him not to use words like that, there were women present.

The men all tried to straighten their faces, but without success. Faith shooed them out of the kitchen, telling John's friend that they did not take single orders.

'I'll give you a sovereign for that one with the "Whimsy" face,' John's friend said, still grinning.

Erica hesitated a moment then picked up the one the man had mentioned. 'Right, I'll finish this off tomorrow but don't tell anyone where you bought it. I'll have the sovereign now.'

Her mother made to protest, but John soothed her. 'A sovereign is not to be cast aside these days, Faith.'

She was angry but said no more until the friend had gone, promising to call and pick up his 'lady' the next day.

Then Faith tackled Erica. 'Don't you ever dare do such a thing like that again, my girl.' She held out her hand. 'And I'll have the sovereign.'

'No, mother, you refused it, I took it. As Uncle John said, "A sovereign is not to be cast aside these days." '

'We're a working family, not working singly. Give me that sovereign or you are out of this house immediately.'

'Right. I'll go.' Although Erica was trembling she took off her apron, folded it and laid it on a stool.

Her mother stared at her. 'How dare you behave in such a way! If you leave here you don't come back.' Her lips closed tightly.

'It suits me.'

Charles and Edward told Erica not to be foolish.

'Perhaps I am but I'm doing this work and I think it's more daft to refuse a sovereign for something that I had fashioned. I need more paints.'

'You had only to ask for money for paint,' her mother snapped. 'Don't make that an excuse.'

It had been an excuse and Erica knew she was beaten. Where could she go? What was more she didn't want to leave home. She was part of a team. She knew she would have to hand over the sovereign but she was determined she was not going to apologise for her behaviour. If she did she would always be beholden to her mother.

She laid the sovereign on the table. 'There you are, put it to your hoard, perhaps you'll be a rich woman one of these days.'

The next moment she felt ashamed, especially when her brothers and her uncle objected to her behaviour.

Her mother said, in a defeated voice, 'You will be the rich one, Erica, if that is the way you want to make money.'

Erica was shocked. 'I'm sorry, Mother, I didn't mean it. I was annoyed. Forgive me. Please. I was letting the praise of you all go to my head. I'll try and remember that we are a team.'

Her mother was silent for a moment then she looked up. 'And I shall try and remember that I'm not the boss of the team but a worker too.' She picked up the sovereign and handed it to Charles. 'Put that aside for when we need more paint. I'm going to bed.'

Erica said, 'Mother, don't go without saying you forgive me.'

'Of course I do.' She came back and touched her arm. 'I have a lot to learn too. It will all be forgotten by the morning.'

Erica would have liked to put her arms around her mother, but she was unable to.

'Good night,' Faith said, and left.

'Oh, Lord,' Charles said. 'I hope we

won't have any more do's like that. Is this what will happen now that we try and make progress.'

'No.' Erica shook her head. 'I was to blame. It's just one more lesson to learn in life. I was so cock-a-hoop, getting praise.'

It was another few days before things really got back to normal and then another crisis occurred, a much more important one.

Edward announced that he wanted to get married.

'Married?' Faith said, in a tone that refused to believe it.

'Yes...soon.'

'Oh, my God, she's pregnant, whoever she is.'

'Yes, but I love her. I want to marry her.'

'Well, you can't and that's that.'

Edward was pale. 'I'm going to marry her. Janet's not to blame for the situation. I am.'

'Of course she's to blame. The scheming wretch! Oh, don't get me wrong. You're both to blame. You fools. How could you put us into such a situation? Where are you going to live? She's not coming here.'

'She'll have to, her parents have thrown her out.'

'Well, you can throw her back,' Faith shouted at him.

Charles, who had come in while this was going on said, 'Mother, have pity, for heavens sake. Things like this happen every day.'

'Not in connection with my family. I don't want anything to do with her.'

'The problem isn't yours, it's Edward's, your own flesh and blood.'

'I don't care!' Faith shouted.

'Well I do. I'll speak to Uncle John, see if Edward and Janet can move into an empty room where he lives. All they'll need will be a bed and bedclothes.'

'Oh, so I can feed them, can I? Well, let me tell you—'

'Janet can help with the work. She's working in a boot factory at the moment. She'll learn how to make pipes. She's quick.'

There was a silence and Erica guessed that her mother would not want to lose Edward. 'Very well,' she said at last. 'You can bring her here, but only to work. Not to stay on in an evening.'

'You're determined to make them both suffer, aren't you?' Charles said quietly. 'There's a two-roomed house empty three streets away. I'll go with them and share expenses.'

'Why are you doing this to me, Charles? Have I to suffer for their sin?'

Erica was aware of a break in her

mother's voice. Charles replied, 'You know what Jesus once said about an adulterous woman who was about to be stoned by a crowd. "He that is without sin among you, let him first cast a stone at her." ' Then Charles added, 'And you know what happened,' he quoted, ' "And they, convicted by their own conscience, went out one by one." '

There was another silence, longer this time, then Faith looked up and her eyes were full of pain.

'Very well. I won't make them suffer.'

Erica knew that this was something that would not be over in a few days like the last upset she had had with her mother.

Edward brought Janet home that afternoon, a quiet girl, with big blue eyes that were also full of pain. She thanked Faith for accepting her and promised to do as much work as she could, adding, 'I do pick up things very quickly.'

She was softly spoken and seemed sincere. Erica found herself liking her and hoped they could be friends.

Edward took Janet to the shed and when they came back Janet asked a lot of questions. Both Edward and Charles answered them.

Then Edward said to her, 'My sister Erica is the artist. She does nearly all the paintings and the carving.'

Janet gave a brief smile. 'I hope that sometime I can help with that.'

Erica said, 'I'll give you some lessons, when you're free.'

'Thank you.'

Then on an impulse Erica added, 'You can share my bed until you and Edward are married. I think it will be big enough for both of us.'

Her mother gave her a black look, but made no remark then or later about this.

'That evening when the two girls went up to bed Janet said, 'It was so kind of you to share your bed with me. I do appreciate it.'

'I felt it was the least I could do. I don't know what position I could be placed in the future. But we won't discuss that. Tell me about working with boots. Is it hard work?'

'I found it monotonous. I feel I'll like working with pipes better.'

'I hope so. Janet...don't be upset by my mother's reaction. She's a good mother.'

'She is, just to have taken me into her home. I still can't get over my parents turning me out. They're church people and feel I've sinned deeply. According to them they'll not dare to show their faces when the baby comes.'

Erica was startled by hearing her mother

shout outside their door, 'You go to bed to sleep, not to talk!'

She stifled a giggle then whispered, 'Oh, dear. We'll talk tomorrow, Janet.'

Actually, Janet fitted very well into the family. She picked up the making of the pipes quite quickly. Edward talked about having the banns for the wedding called three Sundays in succession at the church, but she refused, saying that people would know soon enough when she was no longer sitting beside her family. And it was Uncle John who paid for them to have a special licence.

By the end of the following week they were wed, in the registrar's office, with Janet in a dark blue dress and bonnet. They had a cake, also provided by Uncle John and some homemade scones provided by Faith. Janet, who was near to tears several times said she couldn't thank them all for their kindness, especially for Edward's mother's kindness when, for the first time she showed signs of weakening towards the married couple.

Only Erica knew the hurt Janet had suffered by her parents' total disregard of her, and did say one day that perhaps they would acknowledge her when the baby came.

Janet seemed doubtful about it and Erica did not press it.

An affection, in time, developed between the girls and Erica thought it must be like having a sister. She had always longed for one and had never had what she could call a good friend. Her mother had always insisted it would spoil her life. Friends quarrelled, fell out and interfered with their working life. Janet did none of these things. On the contrary, she improved Erica's life. She learned from Janet things she had never been told before. How a baby was made. Janet had been very careful about this.

And the day Janet allowed Erica to put her hand on her stomach and feel the movements of the baby had Erica spellbound.

'It's kicking,' she all but squealed.

Janet put a hand on her lips and whispered, 'You must swear on the Bible that you will never tell anyone else this.'

Erica did so, feeling that some magic had now come into her life. How wonderful that God had allowed her to feel the movements of a baby still in the womb. And it was then that this became more important than owning a shop. She must have a baby some day but it must be when she was married and not before.

Erica had taught Janet to paint small motifs on the pipes but although Janet could manage these she could not paint faces and bring them to life, which to Erica was definitely the most important thing about faces. They had to be 'living'.

Since Janet had come to more or less live with them nothing had been settled as to what would happen when the baby arrived. Janet and Edward were still sleeping at the house where her Uncle John slept.

Erica, knowing it would not be sensible to speak to her mother about this, mentioned it to her Uncle John.

'Mmm, yes,' he said, rubbing his chin. 'I've been thinking about the same thing myself. Do you think it might be a good idea to suggest getting a larger house to rent so we can all live in it?'

'No, I don't. Don't forget that this is Mother's house. Has been since she was married. She would feel that she was being pushed out.'

'I look at it a different way, love. Your mother can't have everything her own way. She's earning a living from all of us. We could all move out and start our own business. How do you think she would feel then?'

Erica stared at him. 'I don't know you any more, Uncle John.'

'You have the wrong idea, Erica.' He spoke gently. 'I want what's best for all of you. The only money that Edward can earn is by working with the pipes. Must he go on in the way that he and Janet are living when the baby is born? Of course not. They haven't a piece of furniture in the bedroom, apart from the bed. Nor is there room for any. Would you like to live under such conditions if you were married and had a baby to bring up?'

'N-no.'

'Then what would you do about it?'

'I don't know.'

'Imagine yourself in Janet's position.'

'I would never be in that position.'

'Erica, you've never been in love,' John spoke sadly. 'None of us know what is facing us in the future.'

Colour stained Erica's cheeks. 'I think I know now what to expect if such a thing were to happen.'

'So, what do we do about Edward and Janet? Do you think that the baby deserves to suffer because its parents got themselves into trouble?'

'No, I...I don't know what else to suggest.'

'Charles is on my side. Would you be willing to back us up?'

'I would like to, Uncle John, but I'm sorry, I can't. I must see my mother's side. She has to be the one to give up her home without anyone trying to dissuade her.'

'You're right of course. I won't say any more.'

'Uncle John...I do agree with you too, but I do think that Mother would be very hurt if she thought we were all on the side of Edward who did get Janet into trouble. I never thought of Mother as having any feelings for us until the time you took her to the Exhibition. She did a tremendous amount of work that day. I feel now she does love us all. As for Edward I think that he should be approached about his wife. He could at least ask Janet's parents if they would have her home to have the baby.'

'Would you tackle him?'

'Yes, of course.'

'Right, I'll leave you to it.'

It wasn't until later in the day that Erica managed to get Edward on his own and have a word with him about his wife.

He said, 'I'm worried about Janet. I've been five or six times to her parents' house and although I know they're in, they don't answer. I wrote a letter and asked if she could have the baby at home, but they didn't even answer that. She has an aunt and an uncle but when I wrote to them they said they were unwilling to interfere with such a trouble. It would cause a rift between the two families. Then they asked if my parents would let her have the baby at their house. They obviously don't know the position I'm in.'

'Well something has to be done,' Erica persisted. 'Uncle John suggested that Mother move to a bigger house but—'

'No,' Edward said, 'Ma, wouldn't want to do that. I know that Uncle John suggested it but I just couldn't ask her. She has a right to her own house. I certainly don't want Janet having the baby where we are at present. It would be terrible. I'll try and think of something else. Leave it with me.'

But nothing occurred to him and Christmas was drawing near. Janet was expecting in March.

A week before Christmas a cart drew up and two armchairs were delivered. John had bought them at a second-hand shop near the market. 'They're in fair condition. I thought that Faith and Janet would have a bit of comfort in an evening.'

Faith and Janet thanked John and he said, 'Think nothing of it.' Then added boldly, 'I wish I could think of somewhere that Janet could go to have her baby. Her parents don't want her, neither do her aunt and uncle and she can't stay alone in the house where she and Edward sleep. Miss Thomson is out most of the day and evening.'

Erica found she was trying to hold her breath when her mother said, 'As a matter of fact I've been thinking of that and I did think it might be wise to move to a bigger house. I was going to mention it. There's one just become vacant on Hackney Marshes. Mrs Todd was telling me about it. It's a cottage, but it has two attic rooms. What do you all think?'

There was complete silence for a moment then all of them were talking together. Yes, it seemed a good idea... Yes, why not...? The money that John and Edward were paying Miss Thomson would help with the rent...Erica said she thought it an excellent opportunity...

Then they were all laughing and John was saying that if the house was suitable he could afford to buy a little more furniture. Erica said she had a few shillings put away, they could buy a second-hand carpet for the living-room.

There were all sorts of plans, then Charles said, 'Don't you think we had better go and see it before it's snapped up?'

Faith shook her head. 'I'm going alone. I shall make the decision. If I like it we'll have it, if not, we'll look for somewhere else.'

Faith went to look at the house. When she returned, in spite of them all waiting with bated breath, she took off her bonnet and coat and put the kettle on before saying, 'Well, we have the house and it's in reasonable condition. I need a cup of tea then we'll all go and have a look around it.' The next moment they were all laughing and talking.

'Before we go,' Faith said, 'I had better tell you that it's going to take a lot of work to tidy it up.'

The chatter stopped immediately.

'It's in reasonable condition, but it stinks to high heaven. It's worse than any farmyard. The floors are covered in filth. The tenants did a moonlight flit, leaving a month's rent owing.'

'It's a wonder Mr Todd let them owe rent when they were like that.'

'But he didn't know it was in that condition. Someone paid the rent every week at the farm and he is a busy man. Then they began making excuses about the rent. They were waiting for some money to come to them. The last he heard from them was when they called to say they would get the money the next day. That night they vanished. How they did it without anyone hearing them packing furniture he had no idea. He soon found out. They had taken his horse and cart.'

'Oh, Lord!' said Edward.

'Heavens above!' declared Charles.

'Mr Todd will soon find them.' This

69

was said by John and it was said with conviction.

Faith said, 'Well, we'll soon know. Who wants tea?'

Chapter Four

The house was certainly in an appalling state. Once the door was opened the women put handkerchiefs to their noses and looked from one to the other. They stepped gingerly inside. The hall floor was caked with dirt.

'It'll need a scraper to get this off,' declared John. pulling a face. Charles and Edward didn't say a word but their expressions showed disgust.

Faith squared her shoulders. 'It's nothing that a good scrubbing won't put right. Mr Todd talked about putting lime wash on the walls, but the walls will have to be washed too. Thank goodness we've just about finished the orders. I want us in here by Christmas.'

'Impossible,' declared John.

'Not with all of us working. It shall be done. Now, let's take a look at the downstairs rooms then we'll go upstairs. You won't know this place when we've got all the muck off. I would have started scrubbing tonight but I think we had better get the order finished first.'

There was a living-room, kitchen and scullery downstairs, three bedrooms on the first floor and two attic rooms. All the rooms were larger than the ones they now had. By the time they had been around them all their spirits had lifted again, even though the whole house had a terrible smell. Faith said, 'A good old scrub and before long it'll smell as sweet as honey. I feel we're lucky to get it.'

They all agreed with this. Edward said to Janet, 'I'd like to bet, when we all get settled in the new house and the baby's born, your parents will want you back home.'

Janet replied softly, 'I wouldn't go, Edward. I've been happier here than I've ever been in my life.'

He put his arms around her and gave her a hug. They never kissed in public, but Erica was touched by the gesture.

The whole house had been scrubbed by the Saturday and even some of the outside walls had been washed. John said he would pay for wallpaper for the living-room and the main bedrooms. He also said he would buy some limestone for the other rooms.

John, with Faith's approval, bought blue paper for the living-room and also bought some blue linoleum for the floor which matched and, when Faith had bought some second-hand rugs the room took on a cared-for look, which pleased them all.

It was not until they slept in the house that they realised how noisy it was.

The cottage was not very far from the river, and men on barges that arrived there, were always shouting to other men unloading, causing a constant din. John said, 'We'll get used to it, one does after a while.'

Christmas Day was a day which was usually no different from any other day for the working people, except that they got up early to go to church.

The family were all up at six o'clock and did some work before leaving.

Janet, who refused to go on account of being cold-shouldered by her parents, said she would stay behind and see to cooking the rabbit, which had been given to them by Farmer Todd. His wife had given them a Christmas cake. Both gifts were very much appreciated by them all.

Faith told Janet, when they came back, that her parents ignored them.

Janet said that such a position no longer worried her, but Erica knew that Janet worried in case the vicar would refuse to christen the baby because they had not been married in church.

72

John told Erica that some vicar would christen the child and that she was to tell Janet not to worry about it.

There were no presents on Christmas Day, there never had been, so it was not something that anyone missed. Having the house spotlessly clean really meant something to them all.

In time, John said, the house would be fully furnished.

January and February were freezing cold months, with heavy showers of snow and icy underfoot. Janet said she only hoped the weather would improve for the birth of the baby. The midwife lived a distance away and she did have four other births that month.

Faith said that even without the midwife, Mrs Todd had said that she had brought a number of children into the world and would help out if necessary, which was a consolation.

Janet carried her baby well and although she got very tired she continued to work with the pipes.

At the beginning of March the weather changed, but in the middle of the month the weather was boisterous again. There were terribly high winds and deluging rain and on a wild night Janet started her pains.

Edward set out to get the midwife but had to come back because the river had overflowed its banks and the water was rushing over the road.

He was in a terrible state. Should he ask Mrs Todd if she would come? 'Of course,' Faith said and scolded him, saying that this was not the time to go to pieces. His wife was having the baby, not him.

It was John who went for Mrs Todd. She came right away and she and John fought the storm. By then Janet was in a bad way.

Mrs Todd, after examining Janet, told Faith that it would be a breech birth, but they were not to worry, although she had not handled a breech birth herself, she knew how to deal with one.

Erica, having overheard this, felt panic. Janet had explained about a breech birth saying that the baby's legs came first instead of the head and had added that it was one thing she had dreaded as most of these babies died. Surely a doctor was needed, Erica thought. When she mentioned it to her mother, Faith gave a definite no. Mrs Todd would manage to bring the child safely into the world.

Edward had gone into the next bedroom to Janet to be near in case she called to him and had persuaded Charlie to go with him.

74

Erica worried when she heard the cries of Janet and sought advice from her Uncle John who was the only other person available. He said he would explain the situation to Edward. But Edward said he did not dare interfere and Charles for once was on his side.

John came down in a temper. He agreed with Erica. It was important to let the doctor know. He had instruments to help bring the baby into the world. He lived on this side of the river. He would go and see if he would come. He would take full responsibility.

John put on a sou'wester with a hood that jutted over the forehead and was tied with strings. Erica went to the front door with him and the wind was so strong that she had a job to get the door shut and to slide in two bolts.

She was at the window in the hall but was unable to see how far John had got, all that was visible were pieces of branches of trees that were being swept along by the wind. Would the doctor venture out on a night like this? He used a pony and trap for his visits. Would the pony be able to stand up to the gale? She went back to the living-room then crept up to the bedroom and listened. All she could hear were groans from Janet and a wild screaming, which had Erica aching for her. After a moment she knocked on the door and asked if they would like a cup of tea.

Her mother shouted, 'Go away and stay downstairs!'

There was a panic in her mother's voice and Erica was glad that John had gone for the doctor. Pray heaven he would come.

She became angry as the minutes sped by. She was seventeen and had as much right as her mother and Mrs Todd to be there with Janet. Why were things like this kept hidden from a girl until she was married and then found out? Janet had told her that she had had no idea what it was like to fall in love with a man or her emotions being so strong as to give in to his love making. Nor had she any idea how a baby was made. Another girl, a married friend had told her about babies and how they were born. Janet had added drily, 'My friend was very worldly wise, but then she had five sisters all older than herself.'

When Erica heard Janet screaming she wanted to run upstairs and burst into the room and tell her that her Uncle John had gone for the doctor. But instead she hurried to the hall and peered out of the window again. The same scene met her gaze. Bits of branches of trees being bowled along by the gale.

Then she tensed as she saw two men come into view, their heads bowed as they battled their way forward. Thank the Lord, it was the doctor and John. She had the door opened when they reached the house. Neither of them spoke when they came in. John bolted the door and nodded towards the stairs. They went up and Erica heard her mother say, 'Oh thank goodness you've come, Doctor.'

John came downstairs and they went into the living-room. He took off his sou'wester and took it into the scullery. He did not say a word for several minutes when he came back into the living-room. He looked grey.

'I don't think I've ever experienced being out in such weather before.' Then he said, 'Where's Edward and Charles?'

'In their bedroom. Edward wanted to be near Janet. Charles went up to be with him. I think that Edward was ashamed at letting you go for the doctor.'

'I think you're being a bit hard on him, Erica. I think he did want to be near Janet, in case things went wrong.'

'And I think you're being too kind to him,' she answered sharply. 'Janet needed help. Not someone to sit and hope next door.'

There were some groans and cries of pain and Erica gripped the arms of her chair. 'I won't ever want a baby. Not after this.'

'You will, Erica, you will. All this will be forgotten when you get married.'

A man might forget, Erica thought, but she would never forget Janet's torment, her pain.

Every ten minutes seemed an hour, then there was an agonising scream and both of them got up. 'Oh, God!' Erica exclaimed. 'How much more pain has Janet to endure?' Then there was the sound of a baby crying and not long afterwards Edward came rushing downstairs.

'We have a son,' he shouted, tears streaming down his cheeks. 'Oh, Erica, oh, Uncle John, I can't believe it.'

Erica hugged him then drew away. 'How is Janet?'

'She's going to be all right. Ma told me, but I can't see either of them for another ten minutes or so. I can't wait.'

It was nearly twenty minutes before the doctor came down. He said to Edward, 'Well, young man, you can go up and see your wife and baby, but it must be a quick visit. Your wife needs some sleep.'

Edward was away like a flash and Faith came down. She thanked the doctor for his work, then thanked John for going to fetch the doctor.

John said, 'I too, thank the doctor for

coming but it's Erica you should thank for suggesting that the doctor should be told about the case.' He turned to the doctor. 'I would like to settle up with you, Dr Grant. You deserve a medal for turning out on such a night.'

He gave a brief smile. 'I've been out in worse weather. I was once nearly lost in a huge amount of snow.' He became serious as he turned to Faith. 'Your daughter-in-law will need a lot of attention. I've left some medicine and I will be here in the morning.'

He picked up his bag and John said, 'I'll walk back home with you, Doctor.'

'There's no need, the wind has died down.'

They stood listening and there was only the sound of an owl hooting. 'Get that young man away from his wife and child. She must rest. I'll be in tomorrow morning. Ah, yes, and I must say, no more visitors until the morning.'

Faith hurried upstairs. John and Erica went to the door with the doctor and were amazed at the change in the weather.

Everywhere was silvered by a full moon.

The doctor bid them good-evening and when Erica and John went back to the living-room Edward was grumbling that his mother would not allow him to stay with his wife and baby.

John said, in scathing tones, 'You'll never learn, will you, Edward? Your own sense should tell you that your wife and child need rest. They both could have been dead had it not been for Erica urging me that Janet needed a doctor.'

Charles, who had come downstairs said, 'Don't be too hard on Edward, Uncle John. He went through torment too.'

'Not the torment his wife went through. None of us have to see Janet and the baby until the morning and, not until the doctor has been.'

'Yes,' Edward said, in a low voice. 'I don't have much sense, do I? Janet is my life and now so is our baby. He's marked on either side of his head with the forceps.'

Mrs Todd, who had come into the room said, gently. 'The doctor had to grip his head to bring him down. That will wear off. He's a lovely child, over eight and a half pounds. I thought I knew everything about babies but I had never dealt with one in a breech birth. One is always learning.'

She stood a moment then said, 'I offered to sit with your mother tonight and she accepted. I did wonder, now that the wind has died down if one of you would let my husband know I'm staying for the rest of the night. We can take turns catnapping.'

Charles said that he would go and went to get his coat.

She thanked him when he came back and he said, 'I've done nothing, Mrs Todd, except sit with my brother. I'm glad I've been able to do something. Thanks for all you've done. My mother would have been lost without you.'

Mrs Todd went back upstairs, Charles left to go to the farm and Erica, with Edward and her Uncle John sat in silence for a few moments. Then Erica said, 'I don't suppose I'll sleep tonight but I'm going to bed. I'll be resting. Probably I'll be able to relieve my mother tomorrow.'

Edward said he was going to sit up and John said, 'I'll keep you company, in case you have an urge to go and take a look at Janet.' Edward was silent and Erica wondered if that had been in his mind.

Erica heard Charles return then heard no more. Her sleep was uneasy but she woke at five o'clock and got up. Charles and her uncle were fast asleep in the two armchairs, each with a blanket over them and Edward was asleep on the sofa, also covered with a blanket.

She decided to go back for another hour. It was seven o'clock when she roused the next time and she dressed and went downstairs. There was a lovely smell of bacon cooking.

John greeted her brightly. 'We didn't want to wake you, but we're glad you're up, now that the breakfast's ready. Your mother came down to say that she and Mrs Todd had had some tea during the night but asked if some breakfast could be taken up and left outside the door. They're keeping strictly to the doctor's orders that no one is to see Janet or the baby until after he's been. I should think he'll be here early.'

'How are Janet and the baby?' Erica asked.

'Janet isn't too well,' Edward said, sounding disgruntled. 'I want to see them both.'

John's attitude changed. 'You will do as the doctor said, Edward, and that is an order. And, if there's any more grumbling I shall lock you in a bedroom. Now please shut up.'

Edward sank back in his seat. 'It's all right for you. If it was your wife and baby—'

'If it was I would have more damned sense! Are you going to shut up?'

'Yes!' Edward shouted.

'Right, then we'll get the breakfast served.'

Farmer Todd had done them proud. He had been over at half-past six and left some bacon and eggs.

John laid a tray for Faith and Mrs Todd while Erica cut some bread and, after John had brought two plates of bacon and eggs and one boiled egg from the oven, he carried the tray upstairs, knocked gently on the door and called softly, 'I'm leaving your breakfasts, Faith.'

Faith opened the door, took the tray in and closed the door without a word.

There was a silence, a long silence as they ate their breakfast and before they had finished the doctor arrived. He greeted them, remarked it was a better morning and went upstairs. Faith had the door opened and he went in.

There was a long wait during which Edward paced the floor, then the doctor came out looking grave. Faith came downstairs with him, they were both talking quietly and Erica's spirits sank to zero.

Then the doctor turned to them, 'Well, our patient is doing quite well. She's still sleepy.' He turned to Edward. 'Your baby is splendid, sleepy too. When you go up don't attempt to keep either awake. That will come later. You can all visit today, but only for minutes, and I mean minutes. I shall call again this evening. Good-day.'

Faith saw him to the door and Edward was away, taking two steps at a time. John called, 'Edward, for God's sake, stop behaving like a child!'

He stopped, said sorry, and took the rest of the steps slowly.

Faith came back and hurriedly followed him up, saying, 'I hope he has the sense to treat Janet gently.'

It was not long before Edward was down again, greatly subdued.

'The baby looks fine,' he said, 'but Janet looks terrible.'

When Erica went up, Janet did not look as bad as Edward had made out. She was only half awake and whispered, 'The baby's lovely.'

Erica had a peep in the cot and saw that the doctor was right: the baby was sleepy too. He gave a small cry and his legs curled up. Mrs Todd said softly, 'He has a bit of wind, bless him, but that will pass. Janet fed him this morning without realising it, but her colour is returning. I reckon they'll both be grand in a day or two.'

The bruises were obvious on the baby's brow and Erica, loving the child already, felt she wanted to smooth the bruises away.

When Erica went downstairs Edward was slumped in a chair, hands over his face. She said brightly, 'I don't know why you're so depressed, our Edward. How did you expect Janet to look after what she's been through?' She looked up. 'Charles, you can go up now.'

When Charles came down he echoed Erica's remarks and Edward perked up a little. John then went up and by the time he had come down Edward was smiling. 'Oh, Lord,' he said, 'I'm such a Job's comforter. I won't be after this.'

It was days before Janet was up, and it cost her an effort to try and be cheerful. She said she felt so weak, but was assured by the doctor that she was making excellent progress. The baby had lost some ounces but was now making them up again. He had clear blue eyes that were constantly searching and his plump little hands twisted and turned. Edward said, with pride, 'This lad will soon be talking.'

Faith bathed him night and morning and Erica only wished that she could be there, but there was work to be done. They were all a little behind and had to work late to catch up.

Mrs Todd called every day to see how Janet and the baby were. She never came without bringing some thing, even if it was a loaf of brown bread. The farmer would send a couple of rabbits now and again and at odd times there would be a piece of beef, or pork or lamb.

Erica began to long to make her trinket boxes again and did start, but did not get very far. There seemed to be so much to do with the extra members of the family. Erica, her mother and Mrs Todd were always knitting for the baby and Mrs Todd had said that she could lend Janet's baby a christening robe if she did not wait too long to have the baby christened. Her daughter had weighed under six pounds when she was born and had been a sickly child until she was a year old.

Erica knew that Janet had put off the christening, hoping her parents would relent and accept the baby, but they stayed away and ignored notes that Janet had written to them. In the end she decided that she and Edward must go and see the vicar and ask if he would christen the baby.

He asked only one thing, that when the child was old enough would they allow it to come to Sunday School. They both made a promise that they would, and each promised it with a hand on the Bible.

And so the date was set that the baby would be christened in six weeks time.

They were all going to church for the christening and by the time they were ready Janet was trembling. Supposing her mother started calling her names, a whore or something? She wouldn't be able to go through with the christening.

It was Uncle John who talked her into it. Her parents wanted nothing to do with them, so why should she have anything to say? The vicar would not allow any name-calling in his church.

Janet was calmer after that. The day was sunny but cold. The christening robe just fitted the baby. Another two weeks and it would have been tight on him. He was growing every day. He was to be christened Andrew Jonathan; the name Andrew was not after anyone and Jonathan was after Uncle John, who was to be one of the godfathers. Charles was to be the other one and Erica was to be godmother, which made her feel very proud.

The baby was wrapped in a shawl which Faith had made, and had bootees which Mrs Todd had made.

John had said they would sit at the back away from Janet's parents and she seemed reasonably calm.

Erica was surprised at how full the small church was, never thinking it would be because of the christening.

The vicar's sermon was about children and how important it was to bring them up in the right way, to the word of the Lord, who said, 'Suffer little children to come unto me.'

The whole family were moved by it.

They were all aware of Janet's parents who sat stiff-backed in the front row, as always.

Mrs Todd came with three of her children and sat in front of Faith and her family. Janet seemed calmer than ever and returned their smiles when they sat down.

When the service was over Janet's parents passed them, heads up, staring straight ahead. They shook hands with the vicar as they left but not a word was spoken. Erica could see them waiting to speak to other people as they always did, but to her surprise not many people came out of the church. Then she was aware that one or two were turning around and giving a smile to Janet. She glanced quickly at Edward and he whispered, 'They're staying for the christening.' He was smiling. Janet's eyes were full of tears. So were Erica's.

There must have been thirty people who stayed and when the christening was over they all congratulated Edward and Janet and remarked what a beautiful child the baby was. One or two of the younger women whispered to her, 'Serves your mother right.'

It was a joyous party who went home to their christening cake and a drop of wine. Mrs Todd had given them a bottle and as John said, it was one of the best christenings he had ever been too.

Edward grinned. 'The first one?'

Charles smiled. 'There'll be others.'

Chapter Five

The days, the weeks and the months sped by and they were all so busy that Erica had never had any time to make any more of her trinket boxes. She did, however, jot down any ideas she had, and would put them down in a little book she kept for the purpose.

Janet worked as hard as anyone else but would never allow any one but herself to bathe Andrew. Faith longed to bathe him and so did Erica. Faith told her one day that someone else must bathe the baby. What if she were ill at any time?

'I won't be ill,' she told them firmly. 'I want that privilege because something tells me I won't be able to do it for very long.'

Faith and Erica glanced at one another then both stared at Janet. Faith said, 'What has put that idea into your head?'

'I knew it the day Andrew was christened. My mother put a curse on him. I ignored it, but I know every day that it's getting stronger.'

Faith took Janet by the hand and said, in a slightly shaky voice, 'Come and sit down, Janet, and tell us all about this. I know that some people have this curse.'

'It was there the moment I saw my mother in church. Although she never spoke to me there was something telling me this. A voice was saying, "Take care of your son, you will not have long to be with him." '

Faith said gently, 'It was your state of mind, Janet.'

'No, I was calm once I knew that so many people had stayed in the church for the christening. I could not have been happier. It was during the following morning when I was bathing the baby that the voice began again. I was so enjoying bathing him, I truly love him, and I was greatly surprised when the voice repeated what had been said in the church.'

Faith asked Janet if she had ever heard her mother talk about anything like this.

'Oh yes, she told me once that she came from several generations of witches and I was to do as I was told or she would put a curse on me. I was young at the time and a little scared of this. I told my father about it and he said, with a solemnity, unlike him, that this was so. My mother did come from witches.'

Erica came in then. 'Did your father seem scared of your mother?'

'I asked him and he said no, but then he explained he never did anything to upset her. He added, "I have nothing to be afraid of." '

'So did you always obey your mother?' Erica asked.

'No, I was naughty like other children and this was not mentioned again until I told her about the baby and that Edward wanted to marry me. She told me that I could have the baby aborted or leave the house. She was absolutely adamant about this. I told Edward about it and the rest you know. Never once did my mother mention anything about witches and it was not until I was in the church that I heard the voice and I know I have to pay the price sometime.'

Erica felt icy shivers go up and down her spine. 'Have you told Edward of this voice?'

'No, and I don't want him to know. I want my baby to live and with the help of both of you I'm sure no harm will come to him. Will you do this for me, Faith? Erica?'

They both said that of course they would, but both insisted that Edward should be told what was on her mind.

'No,' Janet spoke firmly. 'I love him dearly and I don't want any harm to come to him. Please promise that you will never tell him.'

Faith and Erica promised, and then Janet said, 'I feel happier now, knowing that I shall still have some time to spend with my darling baby.'

Janet left them then and Faith and Erica talked for ages about this problem. In the end they both accepted that Janet's mind had been turned in some way during the birth of Andrew and settled that they would put it from their minds.

This, as it turned out was easy. Spring burgeoned into a beautiful summer and by August Andrew was the most lovely child. Erica felt she could watch him for hours. Edward had made a circle of wooden spokes to enclose him and after Janet had laid an old piece of blanket on the grass she would take pipes and paint them outside. The baby played with wooden toys that each of the men had made. Andrew would try and pull them apart and grumble in his way when he couldn't manage. He would toss one aside then pick up another which received the same treatment.

Erica would often pop out to have a word with him and his face would light up with a smile and he would hold out his arms to be picked up. Janet never refused him and Erica could have played with him all morning, talking to him, and Andrew would talk back in his own gibberish and Erica would say, 'Well!' and 'Would you believe it?' and Andrew always laughed as if he knew it was all just fun.

She always gave him a hug and a kiss before leaving him and wished that she could spend more time with him.

Mrs Todd always wanted to take Andrew for a walk in his pram but Janet always went with her. They all loved him at the farm and would have had him there all day if Janet had allowed it.

Andrew grew into a sturdy child, and by the following summer was toddling all over the place, chatting away to himself in his own language.

He loved to see the cows and one had to keep hold of him or he would be among them. 'Angers moo-cows,' he called them lovingly.

One morning Janet and Erica were crossing the marshes with each of them holding the toddler's hand, when an elderly woman carrying two bags of shopping collapsed and both of them let go of Andrew's hands to go and attend to her.

Normally the child would have been all right, but a boy with a dog opened the gate and went in. The dog immediately began harassing the animals and Andrew ran forward, crying, 'Moo-cows!' and the cattle stampeded out. In horror both Janet and Erica started running.

But they were too late. The cattle were tramping Andrew down.

Janet screamed, 'Witch!' and fainted.

People came running from all directions and Erica never saw the trampled body of poor dear little Andrew. All the family suffered from shock.

Janet never spoke a word. She looked grey and had no life in her. Edward kept saying over and over again that he would kill her parents, they were responsible. Janet had told him about the witchcraft the day before.

'I tried to talk her out of it. She had said that the witchery was very close and she was sure that she would be the one to suffer. She *is* suffering but it's our darling boy who's dead.' Tears rolled down his cheeks.

John talked gently to him, telling it was not witchcraft, but was one of those terrible things that happen in life. But nothing he said made any difference. Edward was still intent on killing her mother.

Faith said sternly, 'And if you did kill her, what would you achieve? You would be arrested and hung and then Janet would have two deaths to deal with. That isn't going to help her, is it?'

After that he never mentioned witchcraft again.

But the people in the village did and no one knew who had told them. Nor did anyone know the boy and the dog. He had vanished into thin air.

On the day of the funeral everyone who could manage to come did. Janet's parents did not show up and when a few women went to the house they said it was empty, they had gone, vanished, no one knew where.

It was a moving service at the church and there was hardly a dry eye when the vicar quoted the words, " 'Suffer little children to come unto me." '

For the first time Janet raised her eyes and whispered it.

That evening she said, 'I do at last have a feeling that Andrew is in heaven. God would not allow him to go anywhere else.'

Janet did not recover quickly, but every day she seemed to be a little better and every day she took wild flowers to the small cemetery and put them on the grave.

No one mentioned Andrew's name in her presence and it was not until the following spring before she would talk about him.

Erica began to make her trinket boxes

of all shapes and sizes again. She made diamond-shaped ones and very tall boxes with five and six drawers for trinkets. She made some in half-moon sizes and some that opened out with small drawers on either side. She experimented with making circular ones with divisions in them and a lid to cover them. No trinket box was ever carved or painted alike. John was very taken with them and asked why she did not want to sell them.

'Because,' she said, she wanted to start with a large stock.

'I suggest you sell them,' John suggested. 'You will need money to start a shop. With your talent you should start in the West End of London.'

Erica explained that if she started to sell them now someone else might take over. She wanted her very own shop.

During this time, John was always talking about getting a divorce, but he never seemed to get around to it. Was it that he still loved his wife? Hesther had made several attempts to get him to come back to her but each time he had refused, the last time rather vehemently, stating that he would never ever go back to her.

There was a man, a friend, of Mrs Todd, who had asked Erica to walk out with him, but she had smiled and said she was working every evening. So she stayed away from the farm and Mrs Todd wanted to know why.

'We used to see you nearly every day,' she said, 'but now it's about once a week. Why?'

'I'll be honest with you, Mrs Todd. Your friend Frank keeps asking me to walk out with him and I just haven't the time.'

Mrs Todd chuckled. 'You make time, girl. I'll have a word with your mother. You work too hard. Frank's a very nice person and hard-working.'

Erica laid a hand on her arm. 'Don't say anything to my mother, Mrs Todd. She says I work too hard, but I want to work. I'm hoping to open a small shop sometime.'

'How splendid. I wish you luck. But do go out with Frank.

'You'll like him. He has good manners. There won't be any Shenanigans where he's concerned.'

Erica decided it was best to accept Frank's offer. Once was not going to do any harm. She could tell him of her future plan. That would surely end him asking her out.

Her mother and Janet showed interest that Erica had been asked out. 'You've become a recluse,' Janet said. 'It's not right that you should be constantly working. You need a change.'

Faith made no comment.

At the farm Frank had seemed lively and like the other boys had teased her. When they were out walking, however, on the Tuesday evening, Frank seemed shy and had little to say.

They walked along by the river and Erica realised how much she had missed of Hackney Marsh. There were a line of mills, and further along the bank were some trees. They stopped there and Frank talked about the purity of water after the filtering beds were put in. 'The water filters through sand,' he said and Erica thought how boring it was.

Then he said suddenly, 'Actually, I'm thinking of going to America.'

She turned to him. 'Why there?'

'It's a big place. I know it's slave labour, but I can make more there than in England.'

'Are your parents agreeable to this?'

'I haven't any parents, they died in a cholera epidemic.'

'Oh, Frank, I'm sorry. I didn't know. Who brought you up?'

'An aunt, and she's been kindness itself to me. Unfortunately offering to care for me stopped her getting married.'

'How terrible. Why?'

'Her fiancé said he didn't want to bring up another person's child and then added that actually he didn't really want children at all. This was apparently a great shock to Aunt Minnie, but I didn't know about this until I was nearly fourteen. I was due to leave school and my aunt wanted to send me to a boarding school. I told her I wanted to work and was awkward about it. A friend of hers told me her life had been spoilt by her determination to look after me.'

'You must have felt awful.'

'It brought me to my senses but Aunt Minnie. told me that she was glad that her fiancé had said that he didn't want children. She would have hated to find this out after they were married.'

'It was a pity though that you missed having a father.'

Frank smiled. 'I have three uncles who kept me in line.'

'Good. And so you went to a boarding school?'

'No, my uncles were in business together and I went into an office there. I hated it and ran away. I was brought back and given a sound thrashing for giving Aunt Minnie so much heartache. That was when I really grew up.'

'So what happened then?'

'I went into a boot factory and I liked it. I found I wanted to make things. I was there until a month ago when it closed down. Then Mr Todd offered me a part-time job on the farm until something else came up.'

Frank gave her a broad smile.

He was easy and natural and Erica realised he was more attractive than she had at first thought. He was tallish, well-built and had a lovely smile. She wondered how old he was. About twenty-three or twenty-four?

She knew he had been told about her work and talked about her ambition to open a small shop in the city and sell trinket boxes.

'It's something I've wanted to do for a while, but since Uncle John took Charles, Edward and myself to the Crystal Palace Exhibition the urge has become much stronger.'

He glanced at her and his expression was serious. 'But surely that is man's work?'

'Why?' she demanded. 'I make the boxes so surely I have the right to sell them?'

'I think you have, but would your customers accept you? You should have a man to sell your goods and you to make them.'

'Perhaps you think that you should sell them?'

'Me?' He laughed heartily and she was annoyed that she had said what she had. 'I couldn't sell a loaf of bread.'

'Anyone can do anything if they make their mind up to do so.'

'I don't agree with you. A man who would be a manager in a shop would have to be educated, dress smartly and would have to know all the ins and outs of trinket boxes. Am I right?'

'Yes, but I'm not planning to have a manager. I shall be the owner and sell the goods. If I can't I shall marry and settle down and have children.'

'So you've got it all worked out.' He spoke quietly. 'I don't wish to be rude, but I don't think you would be interested in me. You seemed a different kind of girl when I met you at the farm. I thought you would be fun to be with.'

'And I'm too dedicated to my work, is that it?' Erica's anger was so strong she more or less spat the words out. 'Well, I think it might be best to go back home before you become contaminated by me.'

He laughed softly, 'Oh, you are funny after all.'

'I'm not trying to be funny,' she snapped.

'I know, that's what I like about you.'

'Like?' A smile slowly appeared. 'I understand why you think I'm funny. I have a cheek really, stating that I would get married. Do you know, you are the first man I've walked out with.'

'I don't believe it.'

'It's true. My mother was always on to me, saying there was work to be done. I became used to it and never thought of my life in any other way.'

'And now?'

'Now that's something that will need a great deal of thought.'

'So, while you are thinking about it will you walk out with me, once or twice?'

'Mmm, I suppose so.'

Then they were both laughing.

Erica found Frank quite an educated young man. He talked about Queen Victoria and Prince Albert, and how Albert had been looked down upon until the Crystal Palace had come into being.

'Now,' he said, 'he's being praised for the work he's done. He's never stopped and there was a vast amount of paperwork to be seen to. I admire him.'

Frank talked about other countries. She knew about New York and about the Statue of Liberty, but knew very little more. He talked about the vast number of people from different countries who now lived there and said he thought he would be doing the right thing in emigrating.

'Are you sure?'

'At the moment, yes. As sure as you are of running a shop.'

'But you know nothing really about the work.'

'I do. I have a friend out there who keeps me in touch. It's worth the work, he said.'

Erica found herself hoping that he would stay in England. She was enjoying his company and, by the time they returned home she found herself thinking he was a man she could love.

Which, when she analysed it, knew how crazy it was. How could she fall in love with a man she had walked out with for the first time?

What was more she didn't want to fall in love. She wanted to have a shop and sell trinket boxes.

When he brought her home he asked if he could see her the following night and she suggested the evening after, adding, 'I don't want mother to get worried.'

'Worried?' He seemed puzzled. 'Surely any mother would be pleased that her daughter had a young man to walk with.'

'Not *my* mother. She's the business head of the family. Don't get me wrong. I don't know what we would have done without her. When we needed a larger house she found one. My mother is a worker.'

'So, I'll see you on Thursday evening.'

'Yes,' Erica said, doing a little dreaming.

Chapter Six

The next day Erica tried to stop thinking about Frank, but every now and then she would pause in her work and go over something he had talked about.

Then her mother scolded her saying, 'Going out with that young man from the farm hasn't done you a bit of good. Every now and then you're wasting time, day-dreaming and there's no room for that in our work.'

Erica felt a rise of anger. 'Don't become a slave driver. You talk as if I must be working every blessed minute of the day. Well, I'm not doing it. If I want to stop working for a couple of minutes I'll do it.'

'But it's not a couple of minutes it's nearer five. And if you stop for five minutes ten or eleven times a day that's nearly an hour's work lost.'

Erica stared at her. 'I can't believe it. At the most I've stopped four times and definitely no longer than two minutes. You've become a slave driver. Yes, a bloody slave driver!' She threw down the meerschaums pipe she was busy carving.

'You can get someone else to do the job.'

'Don't you dare use swear words in this house!'

'I won't in future because I'm clearing out this minute!'

Janet came in and wanted to know what was going on. They both tried talking at once with their own version and both were shouting. It brought the men in.

It was some time before it got sorted out, and then Charles said, 'This is all ridiculous. It's got to stop at once.'

'It'll stop,' declared Erica, 'because I'm leaving.'

John said in his quiet way, 'Before you leave, can we have the story told sensibly?'

Erica told her story first, saying that she had stopped perhaps four times to think for a moment and her mother told her she was losing nearly an hour's working time.

John turned to Faith. 'Is this true?'

'Yes, well, perhaps I exaggerated a little, but I only wanted to point out how work could be wasted by day-dreaming.'

Edward said, 'Ma, if a girl can't day-dream for a few minutes she may as well be dead.'

'And I agree,' said Charles.

'So *I'm* at fault!' shouted Faith. 'That's right. All of you be on her side. I'm in the wrong. But if the work isn't done on time what would you have to say then? It's this Frank man from the farm that's at fault, filling her mind with day-dreaming.'

'So that's the problem,' John said. 'The young man from the farm and you couldn't bear the thought of your daughter having a young man. Well, I'm surprised at you, Faith. I thought you would have been pleased.'

'I am. Oh, what's the use. I may as well keep my mouth closed.'

'No, Ma,' Edward said, 'we should all say what's in our minds, but for heaven's sake don't twist it to suit you. Why don't you admit you were in the wrong? We've all been too keen to let you be the boss, but I feel those days are over.'

She looked from one to the other in alarm. 'Don't take that away from me. It's all I have left.'

'You have a family,' Charles said softly. 'A family who've worked damned hard for you, Mother. If you want to go on running it you've got to forget treating us all as if we are poor relations.'

Tears rose to Faith's eyes and she said, 'I've been a fool. I'm sorry, Erica, for saying what I did. I don't want to lose you.'

'You won't lose me, Mother, not if you behave sensibly. I have to say this. None of us want you to be always watching us.

106

We make a good team and want to go on making it. Shall we forget it and get on with our work?'

Faith got up and dabbed at her eyes. 'Yes, it's nearly dinner time.'

Erica would have liked to have put her arms about her mother but was afraid she might push her away.

Janet had not spoken a word when they had all been together but when she and Erica were alone, she said, 'The trouble with your mother is that she's jealous, Erica. I realise now I would have been dreadfully jealous about Andrew if he had grown up. I made the excuse for not letting anyone bathe him because of the witch's curse. I do believe he was killed by her, but I was also jealous. I have learned a lesson about jealousy. Edward wants me to have another baby and I said no. Now I can say yes.'

Erica put her arms around Janet and hugged her. 'So good has come out of bad. I have learned something too. Not to let myself think about loving someone unless I've a long time to think about it.'

Janet smiled. 'I think you'll know when you meet the right man.'

The quarrel had not made Erica stop wanting her shop but it did make her think about marriage and she realised that it was impossible to try to plan both.

Marriage would have to be sacrificed for the time being. When she had that settled she would hope to have a husband who would understand her need to own a shop. And, who would want children.

When they met on the Thursday, Erica and Frank walked further round the river bank. There was a constant movement of barges.

They talked about many things, then Frank suddenly said, 'Oh, I've just remembered, I haven't told you that my friend who went out to America wants to come home. I had a letter from him yesterday. He said the work just about killed him. The trouble is he hasn't any money to get him home.'

'What will he do?'

'Another friend and myself are sending his fare to him. He's not a man who grumbles about work.'

'So, what are you going to do now?'

Frank rubbed his chin. 'I'm not sure at the moment. Something else will come along.'

'You're an optimist.'

'Probably.'

Erica felt disappointed. He didn't seem to have any ambition. She wished that he could have been more ambitious. Still, if that was the way he wanted his life to be, it was not hers. She had thought it would be nice to have a husband, one who would understand how much she wanted to be married, but who would also be agreeable that she wanted to set up business. And, proving by what he had said previously, that was not exactly in his mind. She had better finish with him.

As soon as they arrived at the front door her mother called, 'Is that you, Erica?'

She wanted to snap back, 'Who did you think it would be?' but she called back, 'Yes, it is.'

To Frank she said, 'Parents. Honestly.'

'I'd better go. Would you be willing to meet me again on Saturday evening?'

Erica wanted to say no, because she thought it should end, but found herself saying, 'Same time?'

'Yes. Splendid. Good-night.'

Erica sighed and went into the living-room.

Her mother and Janet were packing pipes. Janet smiled and said on a cheerful note, 'Enjoy your walk?'

'Yes, it's a lovely evening and Frank is a very interesting companion.'

Faith said on a dry note, 'They're all interesting when they're courting.'

'Frank and I are not courting. We're just friends.'

'That's how it seems to be but it's

different when you're married.'

Erica studied her mother. 'It's strange but I always thought you loved Father.'

'Who said I didn't?' Her mother's voice was sharp.

'It sounded as though you didn't, just now, but there, we are not going to have another row.'

John, Charles and Edward came in, carrying boxes. 'This is the lot,' John said, then added, 'Oh, hello, Erica, I didn't realise you were back. Did you enjoy your walk?'

'Yes, very much. It's a lovely evening. By the way, what time will the man be calling for the pipes in the morning?'

'Seven o'clock. We had another extra-large order at the beginning of the week.' This from Charles. 'But they expect them completed in the same time.'

'If we get up an hour earlier in the mornings we'll be able to manage them. Or work an extra hour in the evenings.'

They settled for doing extra time in the mornings.

The following day one of Mrs Todd's children dropped a note to Erica the following morning from Frank, saying he would be unable to see her for a few evenings, they were busy at the farm. He would let her know when he was free again.

She shrugged. It was perhaps just as well. A good way of finishing it.

But when three evenings had passed and there had been no word it niggled at her. He could have let her know that he wanted to finish it...

Another week went by and he never came near, and when Mrs Todd asked her when she was coming to the farm she made the excuse that they were so busy with the meerschaums. Perhaps next week she would be over.

Then one day she overheard her two brothers discussing Frank, saying he was a fool not to take the job that had been offered to him. He did want to go to America and he might never have another chance.

Her heart began to pound. So this was the reason he had not contacted her.

Erica decided to ask her Uncle John about him. He would tell her.

'Frank? Yes, he's still working for the Todds but he has the chance to share a business with a friend of his in Durham.'

'Durham? What kind of business?'

'A market stall, I believe, selling men's wear.'

'He's not very ambitious, is he?' she said drily.

'I think he is. He does have a shop

in mind later. Start small and rise, is his idea.'

Two days later Frank called at the house and asked if she was free to have a walk with him. 'I'm leaving in a week's time to go up North and I would like to have a talk with you before I leave.'

She said, 'Yes, how about eight o'clock tomorrow evening?' She changed her mind. 'I think this evening would be better.'

'Fine. I'll explain everything then. Must get some work done here before I go. See you.'

He strode away and Erica found herself thinking he really was a handsome man, so well-built and with a determination in his step.

Erica was not a patient person when waiting to know some thing and was ready a good twenty minutes before Frank was due to call. Not that she wasted the twenty minutes. She busied herself doing some carving on a pipe. But as soon as she caught sight of him coming from the farm she was ready at the door.

'You're prompt,' she said.

He grinned. 'One of my good points.'

'And what are your bad ones?' she teased.

'They're secret.'

They took the road to the belt of trees where they sat down and went through the business of why he was going to Durham.

'A friend of mine had a brother who had this market stall. Unfortunately, he was a drinker and a gambler. He died very suddenly and his wife paid for the stall and ran it for a few weeks.'

'So, his wife has taken over?'

'No, she's full of aches and pains and had to give it up. She asked her brother-in-law if he would take it over and he said yes, he would, if he could get a partner.'

'And you are to become his partner?'

'I am. You sound disappointed.'

'Yes, I think I am.'

'Don't you think it's better than becoming a slave in America?'

'Strangely enough, I expected you to get to bigger things in time.'

'Such as being a manager of a factory.' His tone was scathing.

'No, you're exaggerating. Just well, someone a little further up the ladder.'

'Erica, you have big ideas for yourself. You want to be an owner of a shop before you've even worked in one.'

'Don't you see, I wouldn't be able to get a job selling trinket boxes. It's the only way I can start.'

'Well you start your way and I'll start mine.'

He sounded peeved and Erica asked

him in a reasonable tone, what exactly they would sell.

'Everything for the working man: trousers, shirts, socks, underwear, caps, hats, handkerchiefs.' He smiled. 'Some to wipe your nose with and others to carry bait in. We are also going to try and sell a better class of goods as well. A lot of people come into Durham from outlying villages to buy food, and some of the better class come as visitors, to view the cathedral. And they naturally have a look around the town.'

'Now I get down to it I think you show a lot of common-sense. I can see you opening a store in time.'

'So now I'm in favour?'

She wanted to tell him that he had always been in favour but simply said lightly, 'Of course.'

By the time they had returned to the road home Frank had all but talked her into accompanying him to Durham and renting a shop. Erica, however, would not be stampeded into it. She said she would certainly give it some thought.

'That's all I want,' he said softly. You might wonder why I stayed away from you for so long, Erica. The thing is, I know I'm in love with you. I don't expect that you have fallen in love with me, but I do hope you will, in time. I shall see you before I leave, but I don't expect an answer at once.' He paused then said, 'Good-night, Erica, pleasant dreams,' and hurried away.

So...he was in love with her. Erica walked slowly, deep in thought. It was too soon. She liked him, liked him very much, but she was not sure about love. And would she want to go to Durham? She had set her mind on having a shop in London. It would have to be London to make a living. There might not be many sales in a small place.

There was also the fact that her mother would not want her to go with Frank.

At that moment Erica had the feeling that she was tied with a rope to her mother. Would she ever be free?

Chapter Seven

Her mother wanted to know all that Frank had to say. Erica told her briefly about him going to share a market stall at Durham and Faith said, 'Well, let's hope he makes a success of it. I can't imagine him getting very far in life. He changes his mind too often. One minute he is going to America and the next, sharing a market stall.'

Erica forced herself to speak calmly. 'I

think he's behaved very sensibly. I think he and his friend will do very well.'

'With a market stall? You have more faith in him than I have. I hope you'll forget him when he's gone.'

'I won't forget him,' she said, then added, 'We might even get married one of these days.'

'What? You don't know what you're saying. He'll never make anything of himself. You've got a good living here, you don't need to get married.'

Erica stood staring at her. 'Do you expect me to remain a spinster and spend my life carving and painting pipes? You do, don't you?'

'It's something you're good at.' It was said grudgingly.

'You get most of the benefit,' Erica snapped. 'And do you expect Charles to remain a bachelor?'

'There's plenty of time for him to get married.'

'You were married when you were seventeen. Why didn't you remain a spinster and stay on at home?'

'Because your father asked me to marry him. He had a reasonable job.'

'So it was all right for you to get married, but not us? No, you want every penny we can make. You'd bleed us all dry so you can add to your little haul.

Well, I can tell you now, I'll get out of here as soon as possible. I shall probably go North to be near Frank.'

She stormed upstairs and fuming, flung herself on the bed. What a fool she was, staying at home so her mother could add to her hoard. Later the tears came. She would go North with Frank. She would at least be able to keep what money she earned.

There was a gentle rap on the door and Erica, guessing it was either Charles or John, sat up and brushed her hand across her eyes. 'Come in, the door's unlocked.' Her voice was shaky.

Her Uncle John came in. 'So, Erica my love, what is all this upset about? Your mother said you want to leave and go up North with Frank.'

'My mother obviously did not tell you the true story.' Erica spoke bitterly. 'She wants every penny out of us all to build up her little hoard. Well, I'm going to clear out and make my own way. I'll go to Durham and try to find a small shop.'

'And do you think you can make your trinket boxes and run a shop at the same time?'

'I can try. There won't be a rush of people coming in.'

'I know you have made quite a few, but just think it all out. Supposing they all sold

117

in the first week? What then?'

'They wouldn't.'

'Why not? They're a different class of people who go to Durham. Frank won't be able to help you in any way. I suggest you stay and go on making some money so you will have a bigger supply of trinket boxes. Even then you will need some help. As a matter of fact Charles and Edward and myself were talking about making a change. We would like to go to London and open a business, and a shop. You could join us.'

Erica flared up again. 'Oh, no. I want to be on my own. I know what I want. I don't want to be part of a big team. And what about Mother? Is she going to be left on her own?'

'Of course not. She will live with us and we will take care of her.'

Erica laughed harshly. 'And do you expect her to go meekly with you? She has to be the boss.'

'I'm afraid it's time for your mother to start to rest.'

'She wouldn't do it!'

'I'm afraid she will have to, Erica.' John spoke gently. 'Your mother is a sick woman. The doctor told us the other day that she must stop or she will kill herself. She has, unfortunately, a cancerous growth, but it's too far gone to operate.

Her aim was to get as much money as she could, then share the money among the three of you.'

Erica looked at him in wide-eyed distress. 'Oh, God, why didn't she tell us?'

'Because she didn't want any of you to know about it. Believe me she wants you all to stay with her as long as possible. When you were talking about going North I knew I had to tell you.'

Erica put her hands to her face a moment then let them fall. 'Thanks, Uncle John. I think that Charles and Edward have a right to know.'

John sighed. 'Yes, I think so too. I'll tell them later and explain that she didn't want any of you to know because, well, because she didn't want any of you to worry over her. She does suffer quite a lot of pain.'

'The dreadful things I called her. May the good Lord forgive me.'

'Don't blame yourself, you didn't know.'

'I should have known. I should have known she was in pain. Does the doctor give her anything to ease it?'

'Yes, some pills.'

'Thank goodness for that.'

John went to the door. 'I'll tell Charles and Edward. We shall probably all have a talk later and stop your mother from working.'

'She won't listen. I know that.'

'We can but try.'

Erica sat a long time going over everything and wishing that she had been kinder to her mother, wished she had not said such awful things to her. But then her mother had never been able to show any of them any affection. Nor had she been able to show any affection to little Andrew. Yet Erica could tell by the look in her eyes that she had loved him.

Was it too late to show her any affection now?

She got up and went downstairs. The kitchen was empty.

Erica felt suddenly forlorn. There had been so many changes in her life. And soon there would be another one. Where would they all go when their mother was no longer with them?

Ten minutes later John came in with Charles and Edward and they were all sombre. Charles said, 'Uncle John's been telling us about Ma. What a dreadful thing, and neither Charles or I knew.'

'I didn't either,' said Erica. 'What we have to do now is to try and make it up to her.'

'I doubt whether she'll let us. Fools that we were not to realise it.'

'How could we?' asked Erica. 'I never even noticed when she must have been in pain at times. The trouble was that we were all concerned with ourselves.'

'Where's Janet and where's Ma?' This from Edward.

'Janet went to the farm for half an hour. I should think that Mother probably went upstairs. But she won't be in bed, she wouldn't go without saying good-night.'

They talked about her among themselves then Janet came in from the farm. When she was told about Faith she said, 'I knew there was something wrong with her but when I asked she went out of the room without saying a word. She's a lonely soul. I grieve for her.'

Ten minutes later Faith came down. She simply looked around the door and said, 'I just wanted to say good-night to you all. Don't stay up too late.'

John called, 'Wait, Faith, we all want to have a word with you.'

'Tomorrow,' she answered in a voice little above a whisper.

'No, now,' John spoke gently and he went to the door and brought her in.

It was easy to see that she had been crying.

John put her in the big armchair. 'I had to tell them, Faith. They had to know. I think it's sensible.'

She looked up, tears swimming in her eyes again. 'What is there to say? I'm dying and that's it.'

Erica went over to her and put her arms about her. 'We all care, Mother. I'm sorry I was so sharp.'

'It's all right.' Erica felt her mother's arms moving but they did not go around her. She wished they would.

'You're right, we must be sensible. It's something we all have to face sometime.' She drew her fingers across her eyes. 'I had hoped you would all go on working here until I'm...'

She was unable to speak. John said, 'Of course we'll stay, but you are to rest, Faith. You know what the doctor said.'

'I'll stop working when I have to and not before. I still have some strength left.'

'Which you are going to save,' Charles said.

They all echoed his words, but they knew as they said it that Faith would do as she wanted. She got up then, saying they could talk about it some other time.

Three days later Faith was dead.

The family were shocked at the suddenness of it. Faith was nearly always the first one up. Erica went upstairs to wake her and knew by the peaceful look on her face that her mother had gone. She knelt by the bed to thank the Lord that he had saved her from any further suffering.

John went for the doctor, Janet went to

the farm to let them know and Charles, Edward and Erica talked quietly about their mother, with Edward repeating several times, 'How good to know that she didn't suffer any more pain.'

After the doctor had seen Faith he said, 'I have a letter for you all, which she wanted read after she had died.'

He brought it from his pocket and handed it to Charles.

Charles' hand was trembling as he opened the envelope. He unfolded the sheet of paper, then started to read.

' "My dear children,
    First let me say that I loved you all, always have done, but found it difficult to express it. Please forgive me for this." '

Charles paused to blow his nose and tears welled in the eyes of the others.

' "I so much hoped to leave you sufficient money to get yourselves established in business. But the Lord decided that there was to be no more.
    What I have left should pay for my funeral and get you started in a small way in business. You are all hard workers and should be successful.
    God bless you all,
                    Your loving mother." '

The doctor said, 'I have the key to the box which holds her savings. The box is under the boards in her bedroom. It's covered by a rug.' He handed the key to Charles saying, 'It was her wish as you are the eldest. Oh, yes, and I have a note for her brother John, not to be read out.' He handed it to him then said he must be going. He would see them later.

Janet and John stayed behind to see the doctor out while the others went up to their mother's bedroom.

The rug was beside the bed. Charles pulled the rug back and they all stood staring at a piece of wood which had a small iron ring inset to open it. He looked from Edward to Erica who both nodded and he raised the piece of wood.

He lifted out a wooden box and all stood a moment before he opened it.

Erica had it in her mind that there might be thirty or forty pounds but they all gasped when they saw the number of sovereigns. Charles said in a voice little above a whisper, 'There must be three or four hundred sovereigns here.'

'It's impossible,' Edward said, 'Ma couldn't possibly have saved so much money.'

'What about Dad?' Edward asked. 'He must have left it.'

Erica shook her head. 'His parents weren't wealthy.'

Charles pulled on his lower lip. 'But they did have money. I remember when I was quite small Mother shouting at Father to ask his parents for some money. They have it, she said, and you are their only child.'

'We were poor when we were young,' Edward said. 'I know there were times when Ma struggled to make a meal.'

'But why have all this money and struggle to make a meal when there was no need to?' Charles queried.

Erica nodded slowly. 'I think I know why. Because pride wouldn't allow her to touch the money.'

'It could be.'

They counted the money and there were four hundred and fifteen sovereigns.'

'That's over a hundred each,' declared Edward in an awed voice. 'We would soon build up a good business with that amount.'

Erica had gone through three stages at seeing the money. At first she had been awed, then a little excited, but now she felt thwarted, and wondered why.

Was it because there was no longer a purpose in making the trinket boxes? She had enjoyed struggling to get each one made. Now she would be able to buy in some already made.

No, she would go on making them. That was her aim: to sell goods that she had made herself. The money would be useful to get herself a small shop in London. She must work on her own or there would be no feeling of achievement.

She was about to tell her brothers this when Edward said, 'Well, at least the money will give us a good start. We'll have to have a look around London, see what we can find and then—'

Charles got up. 'I think this should be discussed at another time. Our mother is lying dead in her bedroom.'

Erica and Edward got up too. 'Yes, of course,' Edward said. 'I do think however, that allowances should be made. None of us has handled this much money before. It doesn't take any respect for Ma away from us.'

Charles nodded his agreement and before they went downstairs he said that only Janet and their Uncle John must know about the money. Erica and Edward agreed.

John and Janet who had been sitting talking looked up as they all came in.

Charles told them straight away about the money and they looked dumbfounded. 'We won't discuss the amount at the moment, but of course we shall have to discuss what we are to do after the funeral.

Don't please tell anyone else.'

John and Janet agreed.

Mr and Mrs Todd came from the farm. Mrs Todd was very upset. 'Your mother was the only real friend I had,' she said. 'She'll be terribly missed.'

It was she who saw to the laying out while the men went to register the death and arrange the funeral. Erica was surprised at the number of people who called to offer solace and by the evening she felt drained.

It was not, however, until the next morning that Erica realised what a loss her mother was going to be.

They had an order to see to and they had to go on making pipes and seeing to their decoration. Later, she was glad they had something to occupy them.

Janet saw to the making of the dinner and was helped by Mrs Todd who said it would be strange at first without their mother but that time would help.

The one thing that did help Erica was recalling the peaceful look on her mother's face. She had never seen her mother looking peaceful before then.

On the day of the funeral there was a surprising turn out of people at the church and quite a number followed on foot to the cemetery. She thanked them silently for their respect.

About thirty people came to the house and had tea and cakes.

When everyone had gone and only the family was left they were all silent for a while, then John said, 'I was surprised to see Hesther at the cemetery. She made no attempt to speak to me.'

Janet said, 'I saw her and was glad she didn't speak to you. I had more respect for her. I thought she looked older than her years. I felt she regretted being so mean to you.'

'I would never go back to her.' He paused then went on. 'I don't know if this is the right time to tell you all but your mother left some money to me.'

'I'm glad,' Erica said. 'You were her only brother. I felt you should have been included in what was left to us.'

John sighed. 'This is difficult. She asked if I would let you know who it came from.'

They were all alert, unable to think who it could possibly have come from.

'Your mother, apparently, had an illegitimate child.'

They were all startled. Edward muttered, 'Illegitimate? Good God. Who was this man who put her in this state?'

'He was an educated man who owned an engineering factory. Your mother was a nanny to his children. She too was educated and there developed a feeling between them. Then she became pregnant and her parents refused to keep her at home. She already knew your father and he offered to marry her.'

'So I was the illegitimate child,' Charles said bitterly.

John shook his head. 'No, it died.'

'What about all this money, where did it come from?' Edward asked.

'From the man who made her pregnant. He paid her an amount every month on condition that she never made his name known.'

'Poor Mother,' Erica said. 'What she must have suffered and only Father knew about it.'

'But he never knew about the money. This was something she kept secret until she died.' John sighed again. 'So that's her sad story,'

'It's tragic,' Erica said, 'because she was never able to show any of us affection yet she loved us all.'

'I suppose she wanted to pay for her guilt,' Edward said.

'And why we benefited from it,' Charles spoke quietly.

No more was said about it that night but Erica wept over her mother's sadness in life. How different if would have been if she had married for love. Her dedication had been to make sure that her family had money to help them with their ambition, even to deny using some of the money when they needed it to help them with food.

Erica felt like a lost soul, restless. She needed her mother, they all needed her. If only things had gone on without this happening. But it had and she must face up to it.

None of them were getting as much work done. The man had been once to collect the pipes and when they were not ready he said he would call two mornings hence.

They worked that day until the early hours of the morning and were up again at six. That day they never stopped and the goods were packed at midnight.

The man left another order but Charles said they must have a day's rest. It was foolish to work themselves to a standstill, especially after the trauma of their mother's death.

Edward said, 'If Ma had been here she wouldn't have allowed us to stop.'

'But she isn't here,' Charles snapped. 'We must do as we wish.'

Erica said, 'I think we must have some guidance.'

This started a row and it was John who brought it to an end. He spoke in his quiet way, 'I'm sure this is one thing that your mother would not have allowed to go on. We must work in harmony, otherwise the business will be doomed. I suggest we have a rest this morning and work no more than two hours this afternoon. Are you all in agreement with this? It will get us started again.'

They accepted it and they all apologised to John. This must never happen again.

Erica who had developed a headache went upstairs to lie down.

How easy discord could happen. They must all control their tongues. If her mother had known about it how unhappy she would have been. The trouble was they needed a boss. Would Charles and Edward be willing for Uncle John to fulfil this need? She would ask them later.

In another few minutes Erica had drifted into an uneasy sleep. When she awoke later Frank was on her mind. Had she been dreaming about him? When was he going North? Tomorrow? She must see him before he left.

She flung back the eiderdown and got up. She felt unsteady and hoped she was not sickening for something.

There was a tap on the door and Mrs Todd looked in.

'Oh, you're up, Erica. Frank's downstairs, he's leaving in an hour and he wanted to say goodbye.'

'What time is it?'

'Nearly twelve o'clock.'

'What, I can't believe it! I thought at the most it would only be half an hour since I came up. I'm glad Frank came.'

Although Erica had felt ill moments before, she seemed to recover.

Frank got to his feet when Mrs Todd and Erica came in.

'I hope I didn't spoil your sleep, Erica.'

'No, I had just woken up. I'm glad you called, Frank. I would have been sorry to have missed you.'

'You know I wouldn't have gone without seeing you.'

Mrs Todd said, 'I'll leave you two to have a natter. I've brought a pan of stew for you. Your Uncle John and the boys have gone for a walk. They said to tell you they won't be long.'

'Oh, Mrs Todd you're spoiling us.'

'I'm not, it's the least I can do.' Then she went out.

Frank said softly, 'Have you made up your mind whether to follow me to Durham, Erica?'

'It's impossible at the moment. I can't leave the menfolk to manage on their own. Mother is a great miss.'

'She must be. I wanted to come and say how sorry I was to hear about her death.

It was so sudden and Mrs Todd suggested that I leave it until later.'

'That's all right. It was sudden. Are you looking forward to going to Durham?'

'Very much so. I feel sure it's a good move. My friend is looking forward to having me there. I think we'll make a success of the venture.'

'I'm sure you will.' There was a silence and Erica couldn't think of anything more to say, which seemed silly after they had talked all the time when they had walked out together.

'Erica...' Frank leaned forward. 'Never forget that I love you. Perhaps later you may feel you want to break away from the family.'

'Not for some time, Frank. It's difficult to explain. Mother left a letter for us all. In a way it binds us together.'

Erica wished that her mother had not made it so difficult to part. It was the money that bound them together.

She had felt quite rich when she knew about it. Now it seemed all wrong. The money should free her, give her the right to do what she wanted with it. Some of it would help Frank with his business. She suddenly wanted to go with him. They could make a life together.

But almost as soon as she thought this she knew it would be wrong. Her mother had sacrificed her own life so that she could leave them comfortably off. It had no doubt been in her mind all these years to keep them together.

She said, 'I do hope some day I shall be able to come to Durham to see your stall and the cathedral. We shall both try and get established.'

'I'll miss you, Erica.' There was a sadness in his voice. 'But I musn't be greedy. You have your work to attend to and I have mine. We will get together in time, I know it.' He got to his feet again. 'I shall write and let you know how I get on.'

'I'll write too and let you know what we decide to do.'

'I must go. A friend is giving me a lift in his cart to the main line station.'

He came to her and taking her in his arms put his lips to hers. An emotional, mysterious feeling in her body made her respond to his kiss and in the next moment he was kissing her passionately and she realised she was really and truly in love with him.

Erica felt breathless when she drew away. Frank gazed deeply into her eyes. 'We need each other, my darling. Come to me soon.'

She nodded. 'As soon as I can.'

'That's a promise?' He backed away then

stopped. 'I wish I didn't have to leave.'

'But you have to, your friend will be waiting for you. I'll—I'll write to you.'

He came back, gave her a quick kiss and a hug and hurried to the door. At the door he turned and his smile was heart-warming. He raised his hand then was gone.

Erica ran to the door and watched him striding over the field. At the barn he looked back and gave her a wave, then he was lost to her.

She stood for a while then she went back into the room and sitting in the rocking chair rocked gently to and fro.

Her world had changed again. Frank loved her, she loved him. She would have to be with him. How could she now exist without him?

Janet came in. 'So what happened?' she asked gently.

Erica brought the chair to a halt. 'I'm in love, Janet.'

'With Frank?'

'Yes. He wants me to go to Durham...as soon as possible.'

Janet came to her and sat down. 'Erica, you must think this over very carefully. Your mother divided the money between you and Charles and Edward, expecting you would work together. Is it fair to them if you leave now?'

'Janet, is it fair to Frank and to me to be parted for heaven knows how long?'

'Has he spoken of marriage?'

'Not today, but he has previously.'

'Frank has a business to build up. He'll need money to build it up.'

Erica shot up in the chair. 'That's a mean thing to say. He told me he loved me before Mother died. And anyway, he won't know about the money.'

'I'm not being mean,' Janet said gently. 'I'm trying to be sensible. He is starting a new business so he won't have money to spare for you both to get married and you won't be able to start your work until you are settled in a house. Feelings for one another are strong in young people. You could get careless and become pregnant. What then?'

Erica jumped up and walked to the window. 'We wouldn't get careless.'

'Your own mother did and can you think of anyone less careless than she would be?'

Erica realised that Janet was right. She would be doing wrong to pack up and rush to Frank because she had suddenly found that she was in love with him. What was more she was under an obligation to stay with her uncle and her brothers.

Her shoulders went slack. 'You're right, of course. I'll write to Frank and let him know.'

'If he loves you, really loves you, he'll be prepared to wait.'

'Yes, I'm sure he will.'

Erica, however, was not so sure about Frank waiting. There would be plenty of other girls in Durham to choose from. A depression set in.

Chapter Eight

During the next two evenings there were long discussions between the family about what their plans would be, but nothing was actually settled until the third evening. Then it was decided that John and Charles would go to London and see what the situation would be in starting a new business in the West End.

Erica had had a letter from Frank praising the situation at Durham, saying how taken he was at being in partnership with his friend. He was staying with him and his brother's wife until they found accommodation for the two of them. It was not until he had repeated every item they would be selling before he asked Erica if she had made up her mind about coming to Durham.

'Perhaps it would be advisable to wait a while,' he said. 'It's a big step to take. Not that I don't want you here. I long to see you, but I don't want you to feel homesick.'

He concluded, 'I love you, my darling, long for you, but I also want the best for you. Bert's sister-in-law is crippled with arthritis, but she would be willing for you to stay with her for the time being.'

She wrote to him the next day, explaining that in fairness, she would have to stay with her family for a while.

She explained that her Uncle John and Charles were going to the city to see about accommodation for starting a business there and she was honour bound to go with them, if they did find what they wanted. After all, she was the main one to do all the painting work. She told him she was delighted he was pleased with the stall and wished him every success.

She signed it simply, 'with love, Erica.' And ached afterwards that it had ended in this way. It was her first love affair and how quickly it had ended, realising now how tied to her family she was. How could she let them get started in the city then walk out on them, depriving them of her work?

John and Charles were up at five o'clock
and the family with them, all wishing they
could have been going too. Mr Todd had
a small wagon and ran the two men to the
station.

After that, the rest of the family were
on tenterhooks. What would John and
Charles be doing now? Had they found
any premises to look at? Uncle was the
only one who had been to that part.
He said that businesses often changed
hands. Not the very important businesses,
but there was movement. He did warn
them, however, that they would not have
much choice getting into the West End,
a shop and a house would be much too
expensive.

Erica was so anxious to get to the city
that she said they would take anything to
get started.

John and Charles had reckoned that they
would be back home no later than ten
o'clock, and Mr Todd took the van to
meet them. He came back without them
and also came back at eleven o'clock alone.
It was not until half-past twelve that they
all arrived.

Both John and Charles looked drained.

Edward said, 'Just tell us one thing.
Were you successful in getting a place?'

John answered. 'All we've come back
with is a promise of a shop on the

Tottenham Court Road and a house in a road off it.'

'What do you mean by a promise?' Edward asked.

As eager as Erica was to know the result she said to her brother, 'For goodness sake let the poor souls sit down and have a cup of tea.'

Janet made it and poured it.

Not another word was spoken until John and Charles had drank some tea then John said, 'That was good. Now we can tell you what happened.'

John and Charles between them told of the hours of walking they had done without having seen one place that was empty and, how they were beginning to despair when, by one of those off chances that happen in life, they met a man in a teashop.

Charles said, 'The tea-room was packed and a man asked if he could squeeze in at our table. It was a table for two but he had found a stool and was standing smiling at us. Uncle John and I moved closer and he said, "Thanks, I was just about dying of thirst."

'Uncle John told him that we were too and in the next breath told him of our search. The man said, "Strange that. My uncle is wanting to move from his shop to a larger place and has been promised something. He's waiting to hear."

140

'Uncle John and I were immediately alert and asked where his uncle's shop was. He told us it was small but it was on Tottenham Court Road, a very busy road and there was a house that would be empty too if he moved. It was in a side street.'

'This must have been exciting,' Erica said.

Her uncle took over. 'Indeed it was. It was an antique business and this man's uncle had done so well he wanted to get on to larger stuff and needed the space.'

'And did you go to see him?' Edward asked, almost bubbling over.

'We certainly did. Unfortunately,' John paused. 'It's the waiting that's the problem. The man who has the bigger shop wants to go into partnership with someone else who is waiting for his decision. A little complicated I'm afraid.'

Charles said, 'But I feel that the antique man is honest. He has promised faithfully to let us know if it comes off.'

'What about the house?' asked Janet. 'Did you see it?'

'Yes, his son took us there. It's in decent condition. There a living-room, a scullery and three bedrooms.'

'Well, I learned one thing today.' John tugged at his ear. 'I do believe there will be other people wanting to move and can't find what they want. If this does not come off, Charles and I will go again to the city and spend two days there.'

He stretched and stifled a yawn. 'Now I think it would be sensible if we all went to bed and talked some more about it tomorrow.'

They were all tired the next morning and not a great deal of work was done. Because of that, they were all in bed early that night and were themselves again the following day.

A letter came from Frank by the afternoon post saying, he quite understood how Erica felt, but he would wait patiently for the day when she would come to Durham.

A week later they heard from the owner of the antique shop that he now knew that the larger shop was his and, if they would care to come to London, at their convenience, the deeds could be settled.

There was a lot of shouting and dancing around and trying to fix a date.

John held up his hand. 'Just a minute, there's a P.S.'

'What does it say?'

'It asks would we leave it until the following Tuesday to come to London as they, themselves, have some signing to do.'

There was a sudden silence and in that

silence Erica knew what she wanted to do. She wanted to go and visit Frank in Durham.

When she told them they all stared at her.

John said, 'To stay?'

'No, oh, no, just for a weekend. I want to see Frank again before we go to London. I can stay with his friend's sister-in-law.'

'What's the purpose?' Edward asked.

Erica took a deep breath. 'Well, let me put it this way. We are all bound together. I, as much as all of you. We want to have a shop. I hope, however, some time, to get married and I want to know what Frank's stall is like, so that when he writes I know about it. I want to see the cathedral. I want to see where Frank lives. Is that too much to ask?'

Her Uncle John said quietly, 'You do know that it's quite a journey to go to Durham.'

'Oh, for heaven sake, Uncle John, don't you start treating me as a child. I shall go directly there. That's no problem.'

'You can't go directly there, Erica.'

'Of course I can. There's a new line that goes from London to Scotland. I read about it somewhere.'

'You might have read about it, but that line isn't opened yet.'

143

'*No*, it isn't,' Charles said. 'Lord knows when King's Cross station will be opened.'

'Charles is right,' John spoke gently. 'You would have to go from Maiden Lane station and from there you would only get as far as Doncaster.'

'Doncaster?' Erica exclaimed.

'And then you would have to go to York and then Newcastle. From there you would have to go by coach to Durham. It could be a whole day travelling. The trains on that line travel, at the most, twenty-five miles an hour.'

'Oh,' Erica said, and sank on to a seat.

'You would certainly have to have someone travelling with you,' declared Edward. 'You couldn't go by yourself.'

Erica's head shot up. 'Why couldn't I? As I told Uncle John I am not a child.'

'But you haven't done a long journey, Erica.'

'So now's the time to start. I'm sure I won't be the only one on the train wanting to go to Durham.'

'I'm surprised that Frank didn't tell you about the trains,' Edward said.

'He doesn't know I'm about to visit him, does he?'

Erica had set her heart on going to Durham and she was near to tears.

John, aware of this said, 'We'll get you there, Erica, don't worry.'

At this a babble of voices broke out. This was crazy... It could be another time... There was no need for Erica to go now...

John held up his hand. 'There *is* a need for her to go now. She wants to see Frank. As she says she's not a child, she does a man's work and is an adult. I shall give her some of my own money so she can travel by coach from Newcastle. And I shall give her enough in case she has to stay overnight in Newcastle. Is there anyone who objects to this?'

There was silence.

All the excitement had gone out of Erica, but with her uncle's fight for her to get her there, she felt only love and gratitude towards him.

She said, 'I shall enquire about trains tomorrow and then send a telegram to Frank.'

The following morning she learned that the stops from London were Peterborough, Boston, Lincoln, Retford and then Doncaster.

From there she would have to board a train that went to York and Newcastle.

The next thing was to draft out a telegram to Frank. She said: *'Coming to Durham tomorrow. May be late. Will come to your address.'*

Back came a reply: *'Brave girl. Delighted.'*

Erica began to feel a strange excitement. Was it love?

All the family went with her to the station at Maiden Lane, all seeming to want to make up to her for their remarks of the day before.

Edward said, with a grin, 'You will promise to come back?'

'I give you all my word. I'll be back on Sunday night.'

'Don't rush,' Janet said. 'Have an extra day or two.'

'No, I want to be back to hear about the shop.'

A lady came on to the platform. She was well dressed and she sat on a seat.

Janet said, 'I wonder where she's going to? I think I'll ask her.'

Before Erica could stop her Janet was away. They all watched the two women talking then the well-dressed woman got up, smiling and came over to them.

'I'm going to Newcastle,' she said, in a soft cultured voice. 'And I would be delighted to have Miss Curtis's company.'

She introduced herself as Mrs Tyson and John introduced the rest of the family to her.

Mrs Tyson did say that if the train was very late Miss Curtis could stay at her home overnight and travel by cab the next morning to Durham.

The family were relieved at this, and they stood chatting on the platform until the train came in.

It worried Erica that Mrs Tyson would be sure to travel first class but she got into a third class carriage where a young couple had just sat down.

Erica had put her bags on a seat when an older couple with two small girls got on. 'Any seats?' the man asked.

'Oh, yes,' Erica said, 'I'm just going to say goodbye to my family.'

She stepped down on to the platform and there were hugs and kisses and good wishes before Edward said, 'The guard is closing the doors, Erica, don't forget to come back.'

'I won't.' She stood at the window waving until they were out of sight and feeling near to tears.

She blew her nose and sat down next to Mrs Tyson, who said, 'What a lovely family you have. You are lucky.'

'Do you have a family?' she asked.

'No, my husband died six months ago and we had no children. I spend my time between two very good friends, one lives in London and the other one at Dundee.'

'Looks like being a good day,' said the father of the family.

The young couple nodded. Mrs Tyson

said, 'I hope it stays sunny, but there were a few heavy clouds earlier.'

This seemed to set them all talking for a while, then Mrs Tyson said, 'It will be a good thing when the trains will be going from St Pancras to Edinburgh.'

They all agreed but the father said, 'I doubt it will be for a few years yet.'

They all talked about this and that. The couple got off at Boston, saying how much they'd enjoyed the talk, and so did the family when they got off at Peterborough.

No one got on.

Mrs Tyson, having found out that Erica had not been to Durham before, remarked that she would love the cathedral.

'It's just so beautiful. So much work has gone into it.'

She talked about different parts of the cathedral and Erica was fascinated.

'I detest journeys on my own,' Mrs Tyson said. 'I feel so lucky to be sharing it with you. I have a feeling that you have had an interesting life.'

'Yes, I suppose I have. It's been hard work, but quite interesting really.'

And within minutes Erica started telling her about the pipes they made and how she did most of the paintings and the tracery work on the meerschaums pipes.

She hesitated for a moment after all

148

this had been told, and then Erica told her about the secret trinket boxes she had made and about the family hoping to go to London to start a new business, in a shop.

'How fantastic! How lucky you are, Miss Curtis. To be making so many wonderful things. When you are settled in London I shall have to come to your shop.'

Erica smiled. 'You would be more than welcome.'

She had brought three trinket boxes with her, wanting to give one to Bridget whom she would be staying with, and wanting her to have a choice.

Then she thought, why shouldn't she let Mrs Tyson see them? She might even want to buy one. A bit extra money would be welcome.

Erica told her about them then brought the bag out that held the trinket boxes.

Mrs Tyson was very impressed with them. 'My goodness, young lady, what a talent you have! You are an artist. The work on this trinket box is perfection. The expressions on the faces of the parents and children are so alive.'

The one she was holding was Erica's favourite.

'Could I order one? I could pay for it now and you could send it to me.'

Erica said, 'Have that one. I only brought

the three to give the lady I'm staying with a choice, but she doesn't know anything about them.'

'Oh, thank you.'

A mischievous smile came over Mrs Tyson's face. 'Dare I ask for the spare one for my friend? I know she would love one.'

'Yes, of course.'

It was a three-drawer one and Mrs Tyson was ecstatic. 'My friend loves caskets with drawers in them. Let me pay you for them right now.'

As Erica put the sovereigns into her purse she felt a thrill of pride. She would have to share the money with the family, but this was from her very own work.

She found herself telling Mrs Tyson about Frank and being in love with him, but explained how difficult it was to leave her family. 'I'm bound to them because of sharing the money that my mother left.'

'No, of course you're not. You've done your share. You have a life to live. Your family won't deny you that. I have no family left. Just good friends. I'm lonely. Enjoy yourself, my dear. Life is wonderful when one is young, and a little sad when one is older. Don't miss opportunities.'

'The trouble is,' said Erica, 'I'm the only one who can paint the meerschaums pipes and the trinket boxes. It's difficult.'

'There will be other people who can do this work. There are always experts. Don't sacrifice your life for your family. They won't expect it.'

But they would, that was the trouble, Erica thought. They expected her to stay with them. This was only a small holiday, they would expect her back after her holiday was over.

And yet, was she doing the right thing? Mrs Tyson seemed to have money but she had only friends to love her. No husband, no children.

Erica decided not to think any more about her problem. Things would work out, she was sure.

She watched fields as the train puffed along. They looked sad. It was autumn and there were only a few faded flowers in the hedgerows. The leaves on the trees were turning brown. There were layers of leaves lying on the paths. She could imagine them scrunching underfoot.

Oh, heavens above. She was on holiday for three whole days. She was going to enjoy herself. And as soon as she thought it she felt different, uplifted.

There were a number of people who got on at each station and not all were sociable. Most got on at one station and got out at the next station without having spoken a word.

Altogether, Erica and Mrs Tyson had done a great deal of talking and by the time they reached Doncaster, they were both feeling exhausted.

Both of them had had a few sandwiches earlier and both knew there was a wait of an hour and a half for the York to Newcastle train.

Mrs Tyson squared her shoulders. 'We shall have lunch at the Station Hotel at Doncaster.'

Erica hesitated. Lunch at a hotel would be expensive.

Mrs Tyson said quickly, 'This is my treat and please don't say no. I would be offended after all I've had from you.'

Erica gave in.

It was an excellent lunch and afterwards they went to the toilet, freshened up then sat in the lounge until it was near departure time.

Erica felt ready to face the extra hundred and thirty miles to Newcastle but knew it was going to be late when they arrived. With all the stops they had had it was dark when they arrived at Newcastle and Erica was exhausted. She didn't need any persuading to stay overnight at Mrs Tyson's house.

But she did say one thing, she must let Frank know she would not be arriving until the following morning.

Mrs Tyson sent the telegram from Newcastle station and Erica's eyes felt heavy. She had a job to keep them open. By the time the telegram had been sent Mrs Tyson patted her hand.

'Poor you, I know that feeling. We'll soon be home. We'll get a cab outside.'

There was a line of Hansom cabs waiting, and they were soon on one and driving away.

As tired as Erica was she could not help but stare at all the activity. It was like the middle of the day, all the people and the traffic.

When Erica mentioned it Mrs Tyson said, 'It will be the same at midnight. I live in Jesmond, it's not far.'

Erica had to fight to keep awake. She was aware of passing shops then they went along a road where there were big houses.

They stopped at one with a big elm in the front garden and soon they were in the house where a maid was saying, 'Would you like coffee and sandwiches, ma'am?'

Mrs Tyson looked at Erica and Erica said, 'Dare I ask if I can go to bed? I feel all in.'

'But, of course, my dear.'

Erica was vaguely aware of going up thickly carpeted stairs and into a room that was also thickly carpeted...then her mind went blank.

Chapter Nine

When Erica awoke the next morning she had no idea where she could be. She was staring at a canopy overhead. A canopy?

She drew herself up slowly.

Of course! She was at Mrs Tyson's house. But how had she come to be in bed? She looked around her. What a beautiful room.

Then it came to her. She remembered asking if she could go to bed.

Oh, Lord. Her face burned. How could she have behaved so churlishly? She had been tired, yes, exhausted but...

There was a tap at the door and Mrs Tyson looked in. 'Oh, you're awake.'

'Mrs Tyson, how can you ever forgive me? The dreadful way I behaved last night. I've never done such a thing before.'

She chuckled. 'I've experienced the same exhaustion in the past. Think nothing of it.'

'But you had to undress me.'

'Strangely enough you helped me. You seemed to be asleep, but you undid buttons, and pulled a night-dress over your head and, crawled into bed. Did

154

you sleep well?'

'Like a log. What time is it?'

'Seven o'clock. I knew you wanted to make an early start.' She smiled. 'And so would I, if I had a young man waiting for me. I've hired a cab to take us both to Durham. I shall come straight back, that is, after I've had a look at the cathedral again.'

'Oh, no, you mustn't. I'll be all right.'

Mrs Tyson beamed. 'I'm coming. I want to make sure you get there safely. And please don't say no.'

'You embarrass me.'

'Don't be. I would do the same for my own daughter and I see no reason why I shouldn't do it for you. Please accept.'

'I do, it's just that—'

'Shall I bring you a cup of tea?'

'No, but thanks, I'll get washed and ready and make that early start.'

Mrs Tyson left and Erica was washed and dressed in twenty minutes. The stairs had deep piled carpet and the carpet was the same in the hall. What a lovely house, she thought.

Although she didn't feel she wanted any breakfast, she ate bacon and egg with kidneys and had two slices of toast and could have sat talking to Mrs Tyson but, they had to get ready for when the cab came.

They were ready and waiting at twenty past eight.

Erica said, 'You've been so good to me Mrs Tyson. How can I ever thank you?'

Mrs Tyson laid a hand over hers. 'I should be thanking you. Not only for your company but for your lovely trinket boxes.

'May I call you Erica?'

'Yes, do please.'

'And my name is Lydia. I do hope we can keep in touch.'

'I would like that very much. I shall certainly write to you and give you all my news.'

'That will be lovely. And here is the cab.'

Erica was interested in the elegance of the district and thought how wonderful it must be to live in such a place. She also enjoyed going down Northumberland Street with all its shops, and crossing over at the bottom they went further on towards the High Level Bridge that Lydia had told her about over breakfast.

The bridge spanned the river, which was full of sailing ships, barges and small tugs, with their constant mournful hooting. She would have such a lot to tell Frank. She did hope that he would not be working on the stall this morning.

They moved eventually into the country

and everywhere here looked so very green. It was like spring. The sun was shining.

Lydia pointed out various beauty spots and seemed to be entranced with the countryside. 'Not that I would like to live in the country,' she said, 'I'm a townswoman through and through. My friend will be arriving from Dundee this evening and she is a horsewoman through and through. I find it strange that we should make such good friends when we are so different in temperament. She will come quite happily shopping with me and I will go to horse shows happily with her.'

They travelled beside a river after that and the sun sparkled it. It was so beautiful and quiet.

Erica wondered if she was doing the right thing to want a shop in busy London when there were peaceful places like this where she could perhaps live in a cottage, with a husband and children.

She dreamed of this for a while then suddenly put such thoughts aside. She sat up. She had a family who needed her. They had to progress. She must do her duty. Perhaps in another year when they had become established she could be freed.

Freed? No that was the was the wrong word to use. The family were not trying to tie her down. They needed her help.

And she must give it and not grumble about it.

It was after ten o'clock when the driver stopped, and, getting down, came to the door and opened it.

'We'll soon be coming to Framwelgate, Miss. Do you know where the street is? It's a busy place.'

'No, I'm sorry, I don't.'

'I'll ask someone later.' He climbed up to his seat again. They came to some isolated cottages and farmhouses and as they went along by the river there were thickly wooded parts that went steeply down to the water.

Soon more cottages and work places appeared and before long, the place was thickly populated. Workshops, factories, an unpleasant smell came in at the window. Perhaps there was a leather factory.

Erica felt dismayed. The houses were like slum dwellings. Was this where Frank was staying?

The cabbie stopped and shouted to a group of men, wanting to know where the street was that they wanted.

They directed him, and they went through a number of streets before they came to their destination.

It seemed a huddle of houses but at least some of them had sparkling window panes and their steps were sandstoned.

As the cab stopped, the front door at number six opened and who should appear but Frank.

Erica, excited, had the cab door opened and Frank lifted her out and hugged her.

'Oh, my darling girl, you're here at last!'

Then Frank became aware of someone else in the cab and Erica quickly explained about Mrs Tyson and how very kind she had been.

Frank thanked her and asked her to come in for a cup of tea.

She stepped out of the cab and Frank laughed, 'So you were the person who wrote me the lengthy telegram last night.'

'Yes, I was, I had to make you understand everything.'

She refused his invitation to come in. 'No, I want to have a quick look at the beautiful cathedral then go back home. I have a friend coming from Dundee this evening.'

She turned to Erica and gave her a hug and a kiss. She looked near to tears. 'Now do keep in touch.'

Then she climbed back into the carriage and the next moment the cab moved away. Erica waved until the cab turned a corner. She said, 'She was so good to me.'

Frank put his arm around her waist. 'I can't believe you are here. Come along and meet Bridget.'

At the open door Frank called, 'Bridget, Erica's here.'

The front door opened into a living-room. A woman came forward, smiling. She had a stick and limped to them. She was thin and bony but had a lovely sweet smile.

'How nice to meet you, Miss Curtis.'

'Do call me Erica.'

'Sit you down, I have the kettle on.'

Erica, noticing how difficult it was for Bridget to move around, asked if she could help.

Frank smiled. 'That is something you must never do. Very independent is Bridget.'

'He's right,' Bridget declared and went out.

The table was covered with a dark red plush cloth and on the table was a plate of sandwiches and a plate of cakes.

Frank came over to her and bent to kiss her when they heard the stick tapping. He hurried back to his seat, grinning.

'Help yourself to some sandwiches, Erica. I'll pour the tea when it's brewed.' Erica was not hungry but she took one.

Everything in the room was spotless. It was not only the window that shone but also a mirror on the wall.

'So,' said Frank, 'how did you come to

meet Mrs Tyson?'

Erica explained how she and Mrs Tyson met and how she had been utterly exhausted when they arrived at her home in Jesmond.

'Do you know I do remember asking if I could go to bed, but I can't remember any more. I woke up this morning in this canopied bed and I had no idea where I was.'

Bridget and Frank laughed.

'And it was Mrs Tyson who got the cab for me this morning and wouldn't let me pay for it.' Erica looked at Frank. 'I thought you might be working at the stall today.'

'Bert arranged for an old chap who helps him out at times to come in and cover for me. I could not have been working while you are here, Erica.'

His eyes caressed her. She felt a stirring of emotion.

'We shall go to the market stall first then go to the cathedral afterwards.'

Bridget beamed at Erica. 'You have a treat in store. It's beautiful, really beautiful. You'll fall in love with it.'

'Now then, Bridget,' Frank said in a teasing way. 'She's in love with me.'

'Oh, you men, you think you're so important,' Bridget laughed.

'Of course we are.'

Erica thought how very attractive Frank looked in his best suit. She felt quite proud of him.

Bridget said to Erica, 'You can see the cathedral when you go across the bridge to go to the Market Place. It's hidden as you come into Durham, unless you're high up. Durham is hilly.'

'Yes, I noticed. But it is so lovely and green. I'm looking forward to seeing the cathedral. The lady who travelled with me told me such a lot about it.'

Bridget grinned. 'I don't think there's anyone who can tell you more about it than Frank. He knows every date. You would think he had helped to build it.'

They talked nearly half an hour about the cathedral, during which time Frank told her that they started to build it in 1091 and it took only forty years to build.

'Only?' Erica exclaimed. 'That's a long time.'

'You won't think so when you see it. It's massive.'

Bridget said, 'I suggest you go to the Market Place now. Bert will be wanting to meet Erica. I'll have the dinner ready at twelve and afterwards you can go to the cathedral.'

'Yes, ma'am,' said Frank smiling as he got up. 'Do what the teacher tells you.'

Bridget laughed. 'It's a good job you have me to look after you.' To Erica she said, 'We have a lovely castle too. You'll see that as you cross Framwelgate Bridge. It's just above you at the beginning of the bridge.'

They left then and Erica had a feeling of adventure as they set out.

Erica was surprised at the size of the castle. It stood on a fairly high slope. Frank said, 'Wait until you see the size of the cathedral. You can see it from here.' He stopped at the side of the bridge and pointed it out. 'It stretches from one side of the river to the other side.'

Erica drew a quick breath. 'It's magnificent. Although I've had descriptions of it I had no idea it would be so imposing. How is it that the river goes round it in a horseshoe curve?'

'Nobody knows, my love. An act of God?'

They walked on and turned left down Silver Street and saw some beautiful three-storeyed houses.

Frank pointed ahead. 'That's the market stall at the bottom.'

Silver Street was on a slope and Erica said, 'Durham *is* a hilly place. But there's plenty of lovely woods. How green it all is.'

Erica would have liked to linger as they

went along Silver Street, to study the houses but Frank urged her on; he wanted Bert to know that she had arrived.

'Why?' she teased. 'Did he think I wouldn't come?'

Frank grinned. 'I think so. He was late home last night and didn't know about the telegram until he arrived. We knew the lady must have money by the length of it.'

He paused a moment then went on. 'You'll like Bert. People think he's the typical stall holder, making jokes, but there's a depth to Bert that few people are aware of. He's a good partner.'

'There are some lovely buildings in the Market Place to see. There's the Town Hall complex, which includes the Guildhall, with it's three arched Tudor doorways and balconies behind it.'

Erica said, 'I can hear shouting.'

'It's the people in charge of stalls in the Market. You have to shout to draw the customers to you.'

Erica looked up at him. 'You like the market, don't you?'

'Yes, I do, but I would also like to have a shop that sells better clothes for men. In time I hope to have a number of shops.'

They had come to the stalls and Erica was fascinated and would have stopped at certain stalls had Frank not said smiling, 'There's Bert.'

He was calling to a number of people around his stall, men and women.

'How about a working shirt for your men? They were one and eleven pence ha'penny early this morning. Now they are only one and sixpence.'

A woman laughingly asked, 'Why don't you lend me one and six and I'll 'ave one?'

'Next week, ma'am,' Bert replied solemnly. 'I have to add my bankbook up this week. I've already lent over a hundred pounds to you ladies who are determined to have a bargain.'

This brought a yell of laughter.

One woman asked why the shirts were cheaper than they were early morning and Bert, still solemn, replied, 'Because a fly walked over them.'

There was another yell of laughter and two women bought a shirt each, one saying, 'You deserve to sell them, Bert. It's the only place where I can get a laugh.'

Bert caught sight of Frank and Erica and his face brightened. 'Well, guess who's here. Frank and his lovely lady friend.'

They all turned and greeted Frank. 'Where've you bin, lad... We missed you this morning.'

Bert was about thirty, with dark curly hair and had a tubby figure. His cap was tipped to the side of his head. He said something to an elderly man behind him and came over to Frank and Erica.

He said to Erica, 'Well now, young lady. Aren't you just beautiful? How long are you planning to stay?'

'Until Sunday.'

'Too short. Come behind the stall.'

They went behind and Bert said, 'Hang on a minute, Erica, I'll get you a stool to sit on.'

He was away and came back seconds later with a stool. 'There, sit you down, would you like a cup of tea?'

'No, thanks, I'm fine here.'

The people had obviously not finished with the shirt business. A middle-aged man said, 'It's the God's honest truth, Bert, but the last shirt my wife bought me, not here, was riddled with fleas...'

'You're lucky, mate,' declared another man. 'I've never yet worn a shirt that hadn't washed the floor.' Then he began to guffaw. 'I'll reckon I've won the prize, ain't I?'

'I reckon you have, Stan.' Bert reached up to a line and pulled down a tie.

'Wear that to church tomorrow.'

'I'm working, but thanks. It's a smasher.'

Bert kept talking in between having a

word with Frank and Erica. Then trade slackened off for a few minutes and Bert let the old man take over, saying, with a smile to Erica, 'I could sell you easily.'

Colour rushed to Erica's face and she thought that Frank would have said something to Bert, but he laughed, 'Hands off.' Then he added, 'I think we had better be going. Bridget will have the dinner ready then we're going to the cathedral afterwards. We'll be back again to see how you're getting on.'

'Oh, you'll enjoy the cathedral, Erica,' Bert spoke gently. 'It has a timeless beauty.'

A timeless beauty? Erica began to see the side of Bert that Frank had spoken about. A depth.

Yes, she understood him better. It was just that she was unused to so much banter. She liked him and was glad that Frank was working with him.

On the way back to Bridget's house Frank talked of Bert.

'He's had a sad life. He was engaged to be married, when, three days before they they were due to be married, she ran off with a friend of Bert's.'

'What a dreadful thing to do. Is he still unmarried?'

'Yes, and still in love with Arabella. She has three children and her husband goes out with any girl he can pick up.'

167

'How terrible. Why doesn't she leave him?'

'She has three children to support.'

'Does Bert see her?'

'No, it's against his principles. Perhaps one day he'll come to his senses. There are plenty of decent girls in the town.' He sniffed and began to laugh. 'I'll swear I can smell Bridget's cooking.'

Bridget called from the kitchen. 'Dinner's just about ready. I've cooked a piece of beef and I've made a Yorkshire pudding.'

Frank blew a kiss. 'Just wait, Erica, until you taste Bridget's Yorkshire pudding. It's delicious.'

It brought to Erica's mind memories of her home, when they would have such a meal on special occasions. She was sitting, her mind far away, when Bridget came in pushing a stool on wheels with the dinner on it.

'Here we are. Sit up to the table. Did you enjoy the Market Place, Erica? I hear that a statue of Lord Londonderry is to be made to go into it some time. He's apparently on a bronze horse. Not that I care whether he'll ever be there. Did you see Bert?'

Frank said yes, and they talked about the market place during the meal.

The meal was delicious and although Erica was sure she would not be able to eat anything else she ate the stewed apples and custard that Bridget had made.

She did say she wouldn't be able to eat another thing that day, and had Bridget replying, 'Oh, yes you will, I've baked especially for you: a rice cake, some little iced buns, ginger bread and teacakes, and tea is at four o'clock.'

Frank laughed, 'We won't be back from the cathedral by then.'

Bridget grinned. 'All right, five o'clock.'

'Half-past and not a minute sooner. I want to show Erica other places round about.'

'All right. I shall have a longer rest today.'

They left at half-past one with Frank saying, smiling, 'I have to put my foot down sometimes.'

Erica said, 'Poor Bridget. She needs to be the boss, otherwise life would not be worthwhile.'

'I know, and that's why I give in most of the time.'

When they came to the cathedral, Erica stood looking up at it with awe. Mrs Tyson had told Erica some of the beauty of the cathedral and so had Frank, but neither had prepared her for the architectural work. The high ceiling, which according to Frank was seventy-five foot high, had many curved arches, all overlapping and all made in stone, and he added, 'It was the first building not to use all wood.'

There were tall, massive, beautifully fashioned pillars also of stone, with galleries above. The more Erica saw the more impressed she became.

The backs of the choir chairs were leather covered and at the top of the seats were traceries of wooden carving. And above this was a panel of fine tracery that went the length of the choir chairs and almost to the ceiling, a tracery so fine and with such an intricate pattern that it must have taken many men weeks, months to make.

Erica felt she wanted to cry.

And she had thought of herself as an expert at fine carving. She was nothing compared to the people who had done this screen.

When they came out of the cathedral Frank said, 'Well now, shall we go down to the river and have a walk along the bank? It's not so cold as it was and it is sunny. You'll enjoy it there.' He paused then went on, 'Actually, we have something important to discuss.'

Eric's heart missed a beat. 'Yes.'

The slope was steep and the land thickly wooded.

Frank put a hand under her elbow.

'Now, about our marriage.'

'Do you think we could talk about it later?'

'Why? This seems the perfect time. Look, there's a seat along there. We'll sit down and discuss it.'

When they were seated Frank said, 'Well, can we set a date?'

'No, it's, well...'

She was conscious of the water flowing gently by and it was all so peaceful she hated to destroy the atmosphere of the afternoon. She didn't want to break with him, wanted him to know she still cared about him, but it would be some time before they could talk about marriage.

He picked up her hand and held it firmly and she weakened. Need she tell him now? She could let him think that there would only be a few months delay. No, she must be fair with him.

'Frank, we won't be able to be married soon.'

She told him what the family had planned, pointing out that it was impossible to think of marriage for some time.

'You see, the money was spread equally between us. I made the trinket boxes. I was the one who had the gift of painting them. I also put the drawings on the meerschaums pipes. I can't just walk out on them, knowing they wouldn't be able to get someone to do the pipes and the trinket boxes right away.'

He released her hand. 'So how long would this take? You can't go on making the trinket boxes, not if we are to be married.'

'I know, Frank, but I can't just drop them right away.'

'How long?'

'Say—six months? Give them time to get on their feet.'

He look relieved. 'That's all right. By then Bert and I should be in a shop.'

'Don't forget,' she said, 'that there won't be so many people coming into a shop.'

'I know, we both know the clientele will be different. Bert will be different in a shop. Quite the gentleman. He can put on a good show. Oh, Erica darling, I long for you to be with me all the time. I want to make love to you.'

'And I want you to make love to me,' she said softly, her inside churning and, she experienced little secret aches, but sweet aches affecting her emotions.

He seemed about to take her in his arms then got up abruptly.

'We'll go a little further then we must go back to Bridget's. I don't want to keep her waiting with the tea ready.'

Erica got to her feet. 'I won't be able to eat a thing.'

'You must. She made such an effort to make cakes and scones. Her hands are painful, but for heavens sake don't let her know that I told you so.'

'I promise.' She took the liberty of linking her arm through his. 'Don't be cross with me, Frank. It won't be too long before we shall be together for good.'

'Yes, of course. And by then, as I say, Bert and I will have started a shop.'

Chapter Ten

There was no love in Frank's voice when he said that by then he and Bert would have a shop. But Erica accepted it. He would naturally be disappointed.

Then it occurred to her that he might expect to make love to her anyway. Her brother Edward and Janet had made love before they were married.

But Janet had become pregnant and her parents had turned her out of the house.

No, she would not agree to anything like that.

But thinking of Frank making love to her made her want him desperately. Surely this was all wrong.

They came to a belt of trees and Frank

stopped suddenly and drew her to him. He kissed her, gently at first, then with passion and heaven help her, she responded.

He started to undo the buttons on her dress and this brought Erica to her senses.

She stayed his hand and drew away.

'No, Frank, it would spoil everything.'

'Yes.' There was a catch in his voice. 'I'm sorry.'

He ran a finger gently down her cheek. 'You are just so beautiful, so lovable. I had no right to take advantage of you. You're very precious, to me, Erica. I hate myself for being so weak.'

'Our emotions are a natural thing. I'm just beginning to realise this. I had no idea that my emotions could be so strong. I think I came to my senses when I remembered that a—a friend of mine became pregnant before she was married. Her parents disowned her. I know she still grieves over it.'

'I promise I won't put you in that position, Erica.'

He took her hand in his and they walked on.

They walked in silence for a while then came out into open land again. Frank laughed softly. 'The trees must come in very useful for lovers in an evening.'

Erica looked up at him smiling. 'Numbers must be a disadvantage.'

His eyes held mischief. 'I never thought of that.'

Erica was glad they were no longer serious. She said, 'I've just had a thought. If you would like to help Bert tonight at the stall I'll be all right chatting to Bridget.'

'Oh, that's great, isn't it? You come to spend a weekend with me and now you suggest chatting to my landlady. I'm deeply hurt.'

His expression showed just the opposite, then they were both laughing.

Frank walked the rest of the way with his arms around Erica's waist.

They both went back to the Market Place after tea. It was dusk and lamps were lit, giving a warm look to the scene.

The market was still busy and there were quite a few people around Bert's stall. When he saw them he raised his hand and greeted them. 'Have you come to help me?'

Erica said, a little shyly, 'I did suggest that Frank came to help you, and I could have a chat with Bridget, but Frank said no, you would understand.'

'Of course I do.' He gave her a broad smile then leaned towards her. 'The poor fellow is eating his heart out over you.

175

How long are you staying?'

'I'm going home on Monday.'

'Oh, good, you have all day tomorrow.'

A woman held out a pair of socks. 'I'll have this pair, Bert. I'm sick of knitting.'

'They're just as cheap as knitting your own.'

'Aye, but they don't last as long.'

The woman left with her purchase and Bert said to Erica and Frank, 'So what are you going to do this evening?'

Erica glanced at Frank who said, 'I think we'll go for a walk by the river.'

They left, with Frank saying to Bert, 'See you again, perhaps sometime later.'

'Oh, fine, fine,' Bert replied.

Frank tucked Erica's arm into his and they went around the river.

They walked quite a distance and saw many different houses, nearly all three-storied, some with balconies and all of them being lit by lamps having a mystic look.

Frank took her specially to Old Elvert to show her a house with an old Grecian balcony, from where, he told her, people watched public hangings on the Court Green opposite.

As every street had a steepness Erica was beginning to feel tired.

Frank put his arm around her. 'We'll go back to Bridget's and have a glass of wine.

Bert brought it especially for you coming. He should be home by now and I know he'll be wanting to have a chat with you tonight.'

When they got back Bert had the wine and glasses on the table and was all smiles.

Erica sank on to a seat. 'We've walked miles, but I did enjoy it.'

'A glass of wine, Erica.' This from Bert. 'It'll help to buck you up.'

She laughed. 'I'm not used to drinking wine, but I'll be a devil and have a glass.'

Bert poured them each a glass and Bridget came in. 'Just in time.' She picked up a glass. 'I wish you to so enjoy Durham, Erica, that you will want to come to us again and again.'

Bert and Frank both touched glasses and wished Erica the same.

Erica said, 'I shall certainly come as often as I can.'

She took a drink. The wine was sweet, but heady and she knew she would have to drink it slowly.

'And how did your day end up, Bert?' Erica asked.

'Splendidly. We doubled our amount from last Saturday and we thought that amount excellent.'

'Oh, good.'

Bridget said, 'I shall miss you, Erica.'

'And I shall miss all of you.' They talked for ages and it was nearly two o'clock when Erica began to have a job to keep her eyes open.

Frank noticed it and said, 'It's bed for you, my love. We have all day tomorrow.'

Erica was glad to get to bed and soon fell into a heavy, dreamless sleep.

Chapter Eleven

Erica and Frank spent the next day looking around the other sights of Durham, and in the evening they had the house to themselves as Bridget was out, and Bert would not be back till later.

They were sat by the fire when Frank asked her, 'About our future. What have you in mind?'

'You know my plans. I want to make trinket boxes.'

'But when we marry you would have to give it up, darling. I want a home, a wife and children.'

'And I want a husband and a home and children, but I also want to make my trinket boxes. They're a part of my life.'

When Frank tried to interrupt Erica

went on, 'Look, I was making clay pipes from being a child, we went on to making meerschaums and then I became interested in trinket boxes. I love making them and see no reason why I should give them up.'

'If I have children I want them to have the attention of their parents,' Frank spoke coldly.

'They would have the attention of their parents. Hundreds of women work and look after their children. You would be working in a shop until nine o'clock at the earliest. Later, if you had an awkward customer. How much would the children see of *you?*'

'I'm not talking about how much time *I* would be able to be with them, it's how much attention they would get from their mother. And I know that it would be very little.'

'Because you don't want it to work,' she shouted. 'I don't want to hear anything more about marriage. It's finished. It wouldn't work.'

'No, I don't think it would. In fact I'm sure it wouldn't.' Both Frank and Erica sat silent and the evening looked liked being endless. It was becoming unbearable.

It was Erica who said, 'I think we must find something to talk about.'

'Have you any suggestions?'

'We did talk about my plans but not yours.'

'I can soon give you my plans.'

'Go ahead.'

'Right. Well, Bert and I want to find a shop in a better part of Durham and sell good quality clothes.' Frank sounded superior.

'Wouldn't the fact that you handled a stall in the market put paid to that?'

'No, there are several people who have had market stalls and now handle high class goods.'

'Have you any ambition to end up in London?'

Frank shook his head. 'No none at all. There's too much competition.'

'Will you get enough customers to make your business pay?'

'Yes, I'm sure of that. We shall employ expert cutters and use the best of materials. If a customer is not satisfied with the work we've done, we'll make no fuss. We shall say, "It's quite all right, sir. The customer is always right." '

'And do you expect him to return?'

'Of course and he shall be our customer for life.'

'You are very confident.'

'One has to be,' Frank replied promptly.

'You'll need an awful lot of money to get that kind of business started.'

'We won't rush. We'll take our time.' He smiled. 'Bert is an excellent mimic. He can be a gentleman one minute and a rabble rouser the next.'

There was a long silence then Frank said gently, 'Erica don't let us part bad friends.'

'I don't want to do so, but I'm just as determined as you are to make my way in the world.'

'With children excluded?'

'No, there's no need for them to be excluded. I know plenty of families who have children where the wife works and brings up the children. The children have their places. They are a family.'

'Perhaps I've been too hard. Can we be friends again?'

'I'm willing.'

'Good.' He kissed her on the cheek and they went on talking in a businesslike way.

At ten o'clock Bert came back. 'How did the evening go?' he asked.

'Splendidly,' both Erica and Frank said together.

Then Frank went on, 'We covered quite a lot of business. Got it all sorted out.'

'Business?' Bert queried. Then he grinned. 'Oh, I see. You have to call it something, don't you. When does the wedding take place?'

'It's too early to say,' Erica said quickly.

'You and Frank will have to get your business settled first. And that should take a while.'

Bert looked solemnly from one to the other. 'I do believe you have been talking business.'

'We had to. It was sensible.'

'Who thinks about sense when you're in love?'

Erica, not wanting Bert to believe they had been wasting time, smiled.

'It was a lovely evening, We both thoroughly enjoyed it.'

'Oh, I see.' Bert laughed. 'Right, who wants a hot drink?'

Erica said she thought she would go to bed. They had to be up early the next morning as Frank had insisted he would accompany her on the train to Doncaster. Then she added to Frank, 'I still say it's not necessary for you to travel to Doncaster with me.'

'Say no more. I'm going and that's that. I want you to have a reasonable journey.'

It pleased Erica that Frank was concerned about her and she knew it would help to ease the long journey.

A friend of Bert had lent Frank a small van. They would drive to the station next morning, board the train and when Frank returned from Doncaster he would pick up the van again.

Frank and Erica were up early the next morning, and she said her farewells to Bert and Bridget. After that, they climbed into the van and headed for the station.

On the train they travelled to Doncaster in the company of an elderly couple, their daughter and son-in-law. They were quite a talkative foursome and Erica was sorry they were not travelling all the way to London.

The father owned a shoe factory and all the family played a part in the business. They owned three shoe shops just outside of Doncaster. They had been to a leather merchants in Edinburgh.

Frank and the father and son-in-law talked of money to be made while the women folk talked of style.

The mother and daughter were fascinated that Erica made trinket boxes and told her that they could always find a niche in their shops to sell trinket boxes.

Frank had told the men about wanting to build up a business in men's wear and they tried to persuade him to sell shoes. They even gave him names of firms where he could buy the best.

By the time they had reached Doncaster they all felt as though they were firm friends. They all promised to keep in touch.

When the family left them Erica and Frank talked non-stop about business and Erica ignored the fact that Frank was all for having a big family. 'Just think,' he said, 'how that family are all involved in the business.

'But there,' he said, 'that's for the future. Now we must try and find a family for you to travel with.'

Frank weighed up every group of people who came on the platform and decided on a couple with a boy of about twelve and a girl of about ten.

'I like the way the parents talk to their children. They encourage them to talk, not forever telling them to be quiet.'

By this time Erica wanted to travel with adults. She didn't want to feel she was a child who was unable to travel alone. But before she had a chance to say this Frank was up and chatting away to the small family.

The wife said at once that she would be delighted to have a companion to talk to and when Frank drew Erica forward and introduced her she liked them, the children too.

The saddest part, of course, was leaving Frank and she was near to tears when the time came for the train to depart.

Frank teased her, said he was sure they would be meeting again quite soon, and informed her he would be going to Edinburgh to order shoes.

He kissed her and gave her a warm hug, 'Write to me, my darling,' he whispered. 'You must get on the train, the guard is shutting the doors.'

Within seconds a cloud of steam blotted Frank from her view.

Erica pulled herself together and sat down with the small family.

They were charming people and the children were well behaved but Erica would have liked to go over the past few days she had spent with Frank, Bert and Bridget.

Her family were waiting on the platform when they arrived in London and Erica was aching to know what had happened.

She introduced the small family to them and they thanked Erica for making their journey pleasant.

Erica noticed that her Uncle John slipped some money to the children, which made their eyes grow big. Then they parted and Erica was being asked how she had enjoyed her holiday.

She hesitated a few seconds then said, 'Tell me your news first. I've been dying to know.'

Her Uncle said smiling, 'We shall be moving to the shop and the house, next week.'

'Next week?' Erica exclaimed. 'Absolutely splendid. Wonderful!' Then they were all laughing and talking together.

It was not until the next day that her uncle said to Erica, 'Am I to take it that your weekend was not exactly a success?'

Erica hesitated. 'Well, there were problems. Frank doesn't want me to make trinket boxes if we marry. He says he wants a home, a wife and children.'

'I don't see anything wrong with that.'

'You disappoint me, Uncle John. I've worked since I was young. I love making trinket boxes and want to have a shop and you say you can't see anything wrong with that.'

'Erica, they are two entirely different things. You and Frank would be making a home together. He doesn't want you to be slogging away making trinket boxes. Especially if you had children.'

Anger was rising in Erica. 'You've gone through the mill. You married and you wanted to go on working. And what did you do? Walked out of your marriage.'

'You know why I walked out. Money was involved. Hesther wanted me to be at her beck and call all the time. If I was to divorce her and marry again I would not want my wife to be making trinket boxes.'

'You know there are plenty of families who make pipes. They have children but the children are looked after.'

'Yes, but what happens if the children are ill and the pipes have to be delivered. The children suffer. If the pipes aren't ready when they promised they lose the work. It's as simple as that.'

'So, I don't get married.'

'That's up to you.'

Erica stormed out, feeling that her Uncle John had let her down. She was not going to be trapped into marriage. She would go on making her trinket boxes. Why was the woman always penalised?

After a while she simmered down. It could be months. Could be a year before she was likely to marry Frank. By then she might not want to make any more trinket boxes.

Although Erica could not imagine such a thing happening she was prepared to accept it for the time being. Let things take their course.

She entered into preparations for making the move.

This was something that took longer than they had expected. It was what to take and what to leave behind.

The day came at last and they all travelled in the van with the furniture. They had decided to go to the house in

London first before going to the shop.

Although they all had something to sit on it was not what could be called a comfortable journey. They had packed sandwiches and filled flasks and the men dealing with the removables shared them, grateful to have meat in the sandwiches.

It was late when they arrived in London and dark when they got the house reasonably straight.

All the family slept heavily and were awake about the same time the following morning. John was up first and took cups of tea around. He was cheerful. 'Come on, you lot, there's work to be done.'

It was just after six but within fifteen minutes they were all down for breakfast and they were cheerful too. All of them anxious to get to the shop.

The three men had told Erica and Janet that the shop was small but Erica was disappointed, having imagined it to be a great deal larger.

The door was on the corner of the street and the larger part of the shop was to be for the pipes and everything concerning them. The other side was for Erica's trinket boxes and was quite small. There was a counter on each side and everything would be put on shelves on the walls.

When she complained about this her uncle said patiently, 'But you were told all this, Erica, after we had first seen it. We'll get quite a lot on the shelves.'

'Will you? How many brands of tobacco have you. How many varieties of cigarettes and how many brands of pipes?'

'There's room for all we have,' Charles said. 'The stock itself will have to be kept in the house.'

'Where?' she demanded. 'There are not all that many rooms.'

'Yes, but you haven't seen the cellars.'

'Oh.'

'Your surplus trinket boxes can be put down there too. I should imagine you can get quite a display on your shelves. You can also have a stand of them at the end of the counter. We shall also have a stand on our counter too.'

'Yes,' she said dispiritedly.

Edward became annoyed. 'Oh, for God's sake, Erica, stop moaning! You were all for us getting a shop.'

John said, speaking gently, 'Remember this, Erica. The people who had it before us made a small fortune here with their antiques. It takes time. They're moved to a bigger shop and that is what we hope to do in the future.'

'Yes, I'm sorry I've been such a damp blanket. We'll get the shop set out as soon as possible.'

To the surprise of all of them the shop became quite busy. There was a constant movement of people who passed the shop and quite a number came in and bought tobacco and cigarettes, saying, 'Well, this is useful.' Some stopped to look at pipes and said, they would come again and have another look at them when they had a little more time.

And Erica sold three trinket boxes. One man bought one to keep his tobacco in and two women bought one each for a birthday present for relatives.

'Well,' she said, delighted. 'That was unexpected. I had never thought of one being sold for tobacco.'

'You'll have to get down soon to making some more,' Charles said.

'Yes.' Erica looked thoughtful, wondering if she should start making tobacco boxes. But she did want to serve in the shop. Even making her trinket boxes was going to keep her at home for a part of the day.

Well, she would have to try and work it out, By the end of the week it was not only Erica who was wondering how she was going to supply all the trinket boxes she could make but the men had decided they would only make a small proportions of meerschaums pipes, more expensive ones and order the rest from a good firm.

'There won't be such a big profit, but it looks as if we'll make it up in sales,' said her uncle.

They had all had a walk up the High Street one evening and found that they were well up the road before they found another tobacconist shop.

'So that's the reason,' said Charles. 'We are nearest to the station.'

Edward chuckled. 'I hope we don't put the other bloke out of business.'

'You would like nothing better,' declared his wife. 'How mean can you get?'

'It's business, my love.'

'Your way of business isn't mine,' she retorted. 'It should be shared.'

'And most likely is,' said John in his quiet way. 'Men who've been going to a tobacconist for a long time won't stop going because someone else has started lower down.'

Charles said, 'I'm only thankful that we're doing well. And may it continue.'

There were two cellars downstairs, one large cellar and a smaller one. The men used the larger one for making the meerschaums pipes and Erica used the smaller one for her trinket boxes.

She fashioned the boxes downstairs but finished them off in the kitchen, finding the daylight better for this work than the gas light.

Erica began to worry that she would have to make a lot more to keep the stock up and it was not what she had planned. It was the shop she was interested in and meeting customers.

Then the men took some orders for her, quite a lot, orders given by men who wanted to use them for tobacco.

This is when she rebelled. 'You can buy tobacco boxes.'

'But it's your patterns they're after,' the men stressed.

Erica said, 'I have an idea but I don't know whether it will work. I served a woman a few days ago who bought a trinket box for her sister's birthday. The next day she came in and told me that not only her sister was delighted with it, but her three daughters. The daughters she told me go to art school two days a week and thought that the work on the box was beautiful.'

'So?' John prompted.

'They asked if they could meet me. And I did wonder if this was an opportunity to get some more workers.'

'Could be. On the other hand you won't want raw workers.'

'They've apparently been drawing since they were young. They're all enthusiastic, their mother said.'

'Well, we've nothing to lose. Ask them

to come over one evening.'

The mother and daughters arranged to call that evening.

Erica thought the mother attractive. The girls were all plain and resembled one another.

After they had been there about five minutes, however, she found that each girl was very different. At first she was unable to say why. Then she realised that Emily, who was the youngest and sixteen, talked as if she wanted to conquer the world. Margaret who was seventeen was a dreamer and Angie at eighteen had a purity about her.

They all proclaimed how fascinated they had been by Erica's drawings of people on the trinket box.

'You made them come alive,' Emily enthused. 'Although they were so small each feature was perfect. I would be very happy if I could draw like that. May I ask who taught you?'

'My grandfather encouraged me when I was quite young. He said I had a gift. I suppose it is. I never went to art classes.'

'Would you be willing to teach us?'

'Emily!' Her mother scolded her. 'Miss Curtis runs a business.'

'I would like extra help,' Erica said. 'And would be willing to pay you for what you did. Would you be willing to try?'

They were all excited. Even Margaret seemed no longer dreamy. 'Papa would be delighted. He is always complaining that we are not going forward at art classes.'

'I must say,' Erica said, 'that the work must be of a high standard.'

'We shall certainly work to that end,' declared Emily.

'Could we work at home?' Angie asked.

'Yes, after you've done some lessons here first.'

Their mother thanked Erica for her kindness and said she would see that they all worked hard.

After they had gone, Erica said, 'I wonder if I did right?'

'Well, you won't know until you try, will you? And if they are not all perfect the trinket boxes might still sell.'

Erica wanted perfection and hoped that the girls would achieve it.

Chapter Twelve

The next morning Erica was very disappointed to discover that the three girls showed less talent than she had expected.

Emily featured landscapes. It was countryside all right but fields, bushes, trees and hedgerows were all the same shade of green. There was not even the pink of a wild rose in the hedgerows.

Margaret's work was still-life, featuring the contents of a room. Two kittens were asleep on a cushion on a footstool. The kittens looked like toys and the cushion was colourless. There were other items. On a dressing-table was a brush, comb and mirror set. They should have looked silver-backed, but had no feeling of being silver.

Angie favoured portrait painting, but not one of her characters looked alive.

Erica said, 'I'm sorry, but all this work seems wasted to me. Nothing has any life in it.'

The girls all seemed eager to tell her that this was what both their parents had said. Then Angie went on, 'Our teacher said our work had to be modern if we wanted to get anywhere with it.'

Erica gave a small sigh. 'It might be modern but it's of no use to me. In my work everything has to be natural. It must be alive.'

'And that is what we want ours to be,' declared Emily. 'Your characters are so wonderful. Can you teach us the method?'

'If you all are willing to try, I am willing to teach.'

'Splendid,' they said.

195

It took Erica a good part of the mornings for a week before the three girls showed any sign of improvement and it was Angie who showed the best work. Her characters were larger than required but their expressions were alive.

Emily's countryside scenes had more shades of green, but still there was not the colour of a wild flower in sight.

Margaret was struggling to make objects in a room come to life. She was still working on the two sleeping kittens and although Erica advised that it might be better if she had the kittens playing, Margaret was determined that she could put life into them.

After another two mornings with no improvement Erica said to her, 'You will have to take my advice or fail to be of any use to me.'

'Oh, no! I'm sorry I've been playing around. Really sorry. I'll take more notice of what you have to say. Fool that I am.'

In another two days her kittens were showing signs of life and there was a red velvet cushion on the stool.

Erica praised her and Angie beamed her pleasure.

After this Erica, needing to get on more with her own work, let them take their work home.

They never really achieved the perfection

of Erica but the trinket boxes were being constantly demanded.

Erica was satisfied that she was able to be in the shop more often.

What suddenly surprised her, however, was when her Uncle John said to her one evening, 'Have you noticed how our young men are very taken with the girls?'

'In what way?'

'When Charles is here he hardly takes his eyes off Margaret and when it's Edward's turn to work at home he keeps staring at Angie.'

Erica teased, 'And which girl holds you spellbound?'

John smiled. 'I have my own young lady, but I don't discuss her with anyone.'

'Oh, is that so.' Erica felt suddenly annoyed. 'Well see that our young men don't get involved with the girls. Especially Edward, who is a married man.'

'No, it's all a bit of harmless fun.'

'Don't be too sure.'

'I am sure. They'll have more sense than that.'

'I have heard the expression that where love is, common sense flies out of the window.'

'What's wrong with you? I spoke in fun about it. You're making a mountain out of a mole hill.'

'You made the mountain.'

'Excuse me.' Her uncle was now annoyed. 'I'll go and get some work done.'

He went out of the room and Erica was furious with herself. She was jealous about her uncle having a girlfriend and not telling her. But then why should he? He was not a youngster.

She would have to apologise. They were working together this morning and she did not want any hold-ups.

The three men took turns in one of them spending the morning at home to deal with trimming the trinket boxes, some of them being used as tobacco boxes. Erica went into the kitchen. She closed the door then said, 'Look Uncle, I'm sorry I went on so about our men taking notice of the girls. I know the girls' parents. I think they have all lived a sheltered existence.'

'Well it's time they were unsheltered.' He spoke reasonably. 'We only see the girls for a few minutes. And, you were the one who wanted them.'

'Yes, I know. I was glad to have some help.'

John put down the sandpaper and looked up. 'Erica, why don't you give up the idea of making trinket boxes?'

She stared at him. 'You can't be serious. They're selling very well indeed.'

'You could buy them ready made and

do the painting on them.'

'No, this is my side of the business. I want to make them.'

'You do realise you are spoiling your life,' John spoke gently.

'In what way.'

'Well, Frank won't marry you while you continue making them.'

'I love Frank, but I also love my work. Time will tell whether he will change his mind. I won't.'

'You are quite definite.'

'You don't realise do you, all the years I slaved to make first of all pipes then the boxes. I want to make and sell them.'

'Well, it's your choice.' He smiled. 'Are we friends again?'

'I hope so.'

He squeezed her hand. 'Good.'

Unfortunately, Erica was not at peace. Why had her uncle wanted to keep his girlfriend in the background and not introduce her to them? Perhaps she was a married lady.

No, she was sure that was not the answer. There was no answer and she got down to work again.

When the girls came with their work Erica took them into the sitting-room and not one of them asked about the men.

'I think this is the best one I've done,' Emily said to Erica. 'What do you think?'

Erica nodded. 'I think so too. You have all the lovely greens, the blue sky and the gold of wildflowers.'

Margaret put hers on the table and Erica was delighted about this one too. Everything seemed to have life in it. A tiny dog was standing in front of a little boy, begging for something. Both dog and boy looked alive in the room.

Then Angie set her box down and Erica saw work that was almost as perfect as her own.

She had done a snow scene and there was colour in it. The grey sky was tinged in places with blue, and the blue was echoed in the path of a garden. What was more there were faint tinges of pink in the mounds of snow that lay in places.

Erica gave them all a big smile. 'These are just beautiful. I know too that without any question they will be all snapped up.' She added softly, 'and this means a lot to me.'

'And to us, Miss Erica,' the girls enthused. 'Just wait until we tell Papa and Mama. They will be delighted.'

The next morning Charles was at home and he too seemed enamoured with Margaret and the following morning Edward was just as enamoured with Angie.

This upset Erica. What would Janet have

to say if she could see such a scene? Janet always went shopping in the morning and called at friends she had made. She would have to speak to Edward about this.

When the girls had gone, Erica spoke to Edward saying lightly, 'Don't get any ideas about Angie.'

He looked at her in surprise. 'What do you mean, don't get any ideas about her?'

'Oh, I was just joking. You seemed to be admiring her.'

'I was. I think she's a lovely lass. But a little too young for me and anyway,' he grinned, 'Janet would have something to say if I went soft over Angie. Don't worry. Nothing like that could happen.'

Erica felt relieved. She had been far too serious about the whole thing.

That evening she thought about Frank a lot. He hadn't written to her for about two weeks, but he had said that he would be busy looking for premises for their new shop, she was not to worry.

She realised now that Frank had been the sensible one. She would no doubt have let him make love to her. He had been the one to desist. It was a good job he had. She could have been pregnant now and would be worried sick.

No, things had turned out sensibly and he might, in time, give in to her to have her own shop.

Three mornings later the girls mother, Mrs Lewis, came to see her at home. She seemed agitated.

'I hope you don't mind my calling, but my husband is very worried. Is it necessary to have the girls work so late in an evening? It was after eight o'clock when they came home last night. They left home at six saying it was urgent that some trinket boxes were done that evening.'

Erica's heart began to thud. What had been going on? She said, 'I'm sorry, Mrs Lewis, but the girls were not working for me last night or any other night.'

'Oh, dear.' Mrs Lewis sank on to a chair. 'What happened? Where could they have been?'

Erica spent every morning at home and went to the shop after lunch. She stayed until six o'clock then left when trade had dropped off a little.

The men all stayed at the shop until closing time at nine o'clock. Surely the girls could not have been there?

Mrs Lewis said, near to tears, 'Where could they have been? My husband will be furious with them. They were lying and he and I have insisted that they must always tell the truth.'

Erica's mind was working at double speed. She did not want to lose the girls but she would if she didn't think of some thing quickly.

Then she had an idea.

'Look, Mrs Lewis, I'll make some tea and we'll talk this over while we drink it.'

Mrs Lewis took some persuading but eventually agreed. Erica asked if the girls had ever been out with young men and their mother said, 'Oh, no. We don't encourage it. There's plenty of time for marriage.'

Erica had some slightly intimate talk with Mrs Lewis and asked her how old she had been when she first went out with a young man and discovered that Mrs Lewis had been a bit of a devil when she was young.

She gave a little giggle. 'You might not believe this but I went out secretly with three different young men. I would slip out of the house about eleven o'clock and get back after midnight.'

'Didn't your parents find out?'

Her smile vanished and she gave a big sigh. 'Eventually they did. I spent a week locked in my bedroom and had very little to eat and drink. Then my father told me they had chosen a husband for me. I knew I dare not refuse. But—' she paused then went on softly, 'My husband turned out to be a good man.

He's been a lovely husband and a good father.'

Erica smiled, 'So, shall we concoct a little story? I shall take the blame for them being so late, but I will tell the girls it must not happen again.'

Mrs Lewis agreed with this, then said, 'Will you speak to them in the morning?'

'Definitely. I shall find out what happened and let you know.'

'Oh, good. I must say that my husband has a great admiration for your work and is so pleased that you have taught the girls movement in theirs. I do hope you find out where they were yesterday evening.'

'I know I shall and I do promise once more it will never happen again.'

Most nights Janet was in bed and asleep when the three men came home. And often Erica was in bed too but that night she waited up for them.

They came in quietly and were surprised to see her up.

'So,' she said, 'what have the three of you been up too?'

'What do you mean?' her uncle asked.

'I had Mrs Lewis here today, asking if I needed to have the girls working so late. They left home at six o'clock, supposedly to do some work for me and didn't get home until after eight o'clock. Their parents were worried sick. Perhaps you know what happened to them.'

Both Charles and Edward's cheeks were red. Her uncle looked from one to the other.

Charles said, 'Both Edward and I were to blame. John was not involved. He was out these last three nights. The girls said they wanted to see the boxes in the shop and to ask which ones were the most popular.'

'And you actually let them stay until eight o'clock?'

'They didn't say they were playing truant.'

'I would have thought your own sense would have told you that. You must have realised how sheltered they were.'

'We didn't,' Edward said. 'They talked a little about their lives, but they really were more interested in the work of the trinket boxes.'

Erica shook her head. 'It's beyond me.' She turned to her uncle. 'Didn't you think it strange that they should come to the shop at that time of day?'

'It didn't occur to me. I had other things on my mind.'

'Well, seeing that I'm not going to go any further than that I'll leave it until tomorrow. I'll have a word with the girls when they come in the morning and I shall make it quite clear that they do not come to the shop again without permission.'

'You're taking a lot on yourself,' Edward said disgruntled.

'I think I need to. I want to keep these girls working for me. Satisfied?' There was no reply and she left.

She climbed the stairs, aching inside, feeling as if she was no longer a part of the family. Her uncle, just standing there, had nothing to say. He would know that Charles and Edward were to blame. How could he help it? Yet he offered nothing. It was so unlike him.

She started to undress and was shivering. They were a team. Or supposed to be. Perhaps they didn't want her to be a part of the team any more. She felt that Edward had behaved atrociously, telling her that she was taking a lot on herself. Some one had to do it.

She pulled her nightdress over her head and got into bed. If only she could stop shivering...

She spent a restless night, tossing and turning and being hot then cold in turn. Pray heaven she was not going to be ill. She would have to talk to the girls in the morning.

About four o'clock she drifted into an uneasy sleep and woke at six as always.

Charles and Edward had gone to work

and her uncle was having his breakfast.

'It's not your turn, to stay at home,' she said.

'Sit down and I'll pour you a cup of tea. You look dreadful. I felt you would need some help today with the girls.'

'It's not your job. They work for me.'

'They work for all of us, remember. We're a team.'

'I thought you'd forgotten that.'

'I behaved badly last night. I was trying to work out what had happened. I wasn't there the first night the girls came but Charles assured me that they stayed no more than a few minutes that night. I was busy the second and third time they came. Charles said they got carried away. They liked the girls, they were good company. They had never been allowed the company of young men.'

'And Charles and Edward obviously thought they would supply it,' Erica said bitterly.

'Try and not be too hurt about it, Erica. They're sorry, they'll apologise this evening.'

'It's not necessary. I don't care any more one way or another.'

'Erica,' her uncle spoke gently, 'this is not like you. You're not well and I think you ought to go back to bed.'

'Not until I've seen the girls.'

'Try and have something to eat.'

'I don't want anything. I'm not hungry.'

'Come and sit nearer the fire. And don't say no.'

He more or less picked her up and put her in one of the armchairs and put a rug around her.

Erica dozed but was wide awake when the girls came breezing in at eight o'clock.

'It's cold this morning,' Angie said. 'So, what have we to do today, Miss Erica?'

Then she saw that Erica was not well. 'Shouldn't you be in bed? You don't look well.'

Margaret and Emily were concerned.

Her uncle put chairs for the girls and asked them to sit down, adding, 'We need to have a talk first.'

'What is it, what's wrong?' Margaret asked.

John let Erica begin.

'Your mother came to see me last night, to ask if you could do less night work, said you had not come in until eight o'clock and added that she and your father had been worried to death.'

They all suddenly wore a guilty look.

'We didn't think about it,' Margaret said. 'All we wanted was some freedom.'

John said, 'But you lied to your parents. Told them that Erica had asked for work to be done.'

The girls all looked at one another then nodded. 'Yes, we did,' said Angie. 'I think we know now how mean it was.'

'But we never have any fun,' declared Emily. 'Other girls have young men to escort them but not one of us have been taken out by a young man.'

'That's right,' Angie said. 'Papa and Mama once said that young men would be chosen as husbands for us. How old do we have to be before we meet any?'

Margaret asked if she could say something and John nodded.

'Well, it was real fun for us, talking to Charles and Edward. They didn't say anything that was out of the way. They were nice and we were enjoying ourselves so much, that we forgot the time. And I must say to Miss Erica how sorry we all are that she was blamed for keeping us late.'

'I shall take the blame that I kept you all late, it will make things easier, but you must never go to the shop again without permission,' Erica concluded.

They all promised and seemed relieved that their parents would never know they had misbehaved.

Erica gave them some work to do and afterwards John said, 'And now you must go back to bed, Erica. You look all in.'

Janet came in as John was about to see Erica upstairs.

She was all concern. 'You should have told me, John.'

Erica said, 'I wanted to give the girls some work.'

'Come along I'll take you up and I'll bring a hot water bottle. John, would you put the kettle on, please?'

Erica's whole body was aching by the time Janet had tucked her up in bed and brought another eiderdown.

'Now you must not get up again until you've got rid of this awful chill.'

'I won't,' Erica whispered.

John brought the stone hot water bottle, wrapped in a piece of flannel and Janet put it beside Erica.

They went out and they were both talking seriously.

At that moment Erica wished she could die.

A few hours later Erica was delirious and John went for the doctor.

The doctor announced it as a bad attack of influenza.

That night Erica had a nightmare in which some people were trying to push her over a cliff. She screamed and kept on screaming and the whole family were there trying to help her.

Then John took her in his arms and

talked soothingly to her and gradually she quietened.

Eventually she slept, tears still on her cheeks. Janet said she would sit with her and John said he would stay too.

John and Janet talked in whispers, wondering where she had picked up the influenza.

Janet ventured to say she felt that Erica had not been well for some time, thought that she was worried about something and John said it could be that she was worrying that Frank would never marry her, unless she gave up making trinket boxes.

'That isn't fair,' Janet said. 'They are a part of her life.'

John said that he felt Frank would not change his mind and added that he was inclined to agree with him. Children would suffer if any came along.

Janet said, 'Rubbish,' and explained that hundreds of children had mothers who worked and were none the worse for it. They began to get a little heated and John put a finger to his lips and changed the subject to talking about who else they could get to make more boxes while Erica was ill.

Janet said, 'I think the three girls will fill in very well. They are all good.'

Erica did a lot of sleeping, and as it was Charles' turn to be home the next day he took short turns to sit with her.

Poor Erica, he thought, she had not had the best of life. She was in love with Frank. Charles began to wonder if he would react the same and thought no, love should always come first.

He began to think of Margaret who he had been drawn to but, although he had enjoyed her company he knew she was not the kind of girl he would want to marry. There was too much mischief in her. A little mischief was all right, but not too much. She had spoken of never having been out with a young man, but he had known by the way she talked that she had been out with several young men. She had given herself away.

Erica stirred then opened her eyes. Charles said softly, moved by her weakness, 'Hello, Erica, are you feeling better?'

She nodded then whispered, 'It's time I was up and about.' She began to put the cover aside and Charles called to Janet for help.

Janet soothed her and covered her up. 'Perhaps tomorrow,' she said gently.

The next day it was Edward's turn to be home. He too sat with Erica for a while when she was sleeping. He too felt sorry for her because she was in love with a man who wanted her to give up making boxes. He had been in favour with Frank at the time, but not any more. He now knew what love meant. He did love Janet, in a way, but he had never known true love until now.

Could he have any peace in his mind if he walked out and left Janet? He must. It would be hell leaving her but without the girl he loved almost to distraction it would be a worse hell.

Three evenings later he left a note for Janet and went away with a girl who, he said, he had loved at first sight.

Chapter Thirteen

The next morning Erica got up for the first time and came downstairs.

All she could see were grim faces. Then Janet saw her and said, 'Erica, you ought not to be up.'

'I felt well enough to do so.' She looked from one to the other. 'What's wrong?'

There was a moment's silence then Charles said, 'Edward's run away with a girl.'

Janet, white-faced, said, 'He left a note saying that he still loved me, but with this girl he didn't know such a love existed.'

She screwed up the note tightly. 'I only wish I knew which one of the three girls he went away with.'

After another short silence Charles said, 'None of them are to blame. It was a girl who came regularly to the shop to buy trinket boxes.'

'You knew and you didn't tell me.' Janet was trembling with anger.

'I didn't know. I knew he liked her, but he never said anything at all about leaving you. I thought it would peter out. He made more fuss of the girls than he did of Irene.'

'Irene? So that's her name. I'd choke her if I could get my hands on her, ruining our marriage.'

Erica looked at her Uncle John. 'Didn't you know anything?'

'Not a thing. I think he ought to be brought back. He's a part of a team. Mother left him money because of this.'

Janet raised her head. 'Did he take it with him? I know where he kept it.' She ran out and went upstairs.

When she returned she tipped over an empty box. 'He never even left me a penny for housekeeping.' There was an utter hopelessness in her voice.

John said, 'You have no need to worry about that, Janet. You are a part of our family.'

'That's not what I'm worried about. It's his thoughtlessness.' Tears welled up and rolled slowly down her cheeks. John took her in his arms. 'We'll find out where he is.'

Janet's tears stopped. 'I don't want him back. Never. Nor do I want his money.'

While Janet put bacon in the pan, Erica said, 'Janet might not want Edward back, but she has a right to share the money. She and Edward were married when Mother was alive. I think a search should be made for him.'

John nodded. 'I agree. But where do we look? I doubt whether he'll stay in London with his—woman.'

Janet said in a cold voice, 'Edward had a great fondness for Guildford. He often talked about it.'

John said, 'It might be worthwhile going to take a look.' They all agreed. Then he turned to Charles. 'I can't leave you on your own. It means getting another man in the shop. Who can we ask?'

Charles said, 'We could ask that young man who comes in every Saturday. He's always saying he would enjoy having a job like ours. He's likeable, seems to have a lot of common sense. He comes from a wealthy family.'

'You mean Alexander Gilmorton?'

'That's it. I couldn't think of his name.

If he comes in this morning we could ask him.'

Janet said dryly, 'I think you would be wasting your time.'

'Well, I don't, Janet. It makes me livid to think that Edward would walk out with all the money. And who gets it? His paramour, that's who. He'll be buying her fancy things, jewellery.'

Janet's lips tightened. 'You're right. I'll agree to you taking on this Alexander, that is, if he comes in.'

'Well, he has come in every Saturday for about eight weeks. It would be a coincidence if he missed this Saturday.'

Erica said, 'I wish that I could help.'

John gripped her shoulder. 'You concentrate on getting well.'

'I can at least give the three girls something to do.'

John and Charles went to the shop and two hours later John was home. 'Alexander Gilmorton, came in. He said he would be pleased to come and help in the shop. I'm going to Guildford. It's a small place. I'll soon know if Edward is there. Do you want to come with me, Janet?'

'No, I don't, because I wouldn't be responsible for my actions. I wouldn't know which one to kill first. I hate them both.'

'I'm away, I'll see you later.'

Erica had gone upstairs to lie down for half an hour, feeling cross that she was not picking up as much as she thought she would be. No doubt she would have been feeling better if this awful situation had not arisen.

What could Edward be thinking about, getting involved with this wretched girl? And to take all the money. That was despicable.

When Erica got up again and went downstairs Janet was sitting huddled over the living room fire.

She scolded Erica. 'You've being foolish to come down again.'

'It's the only way to get my strength back.'

Janet sat back in the chair and closed her eyes. 'I never guessed there was a weakness in Edward.'

'Isn't there a weakness in every one of us, Janet? My weakness is the love I have for my trinket boxes. It's foolish to be so dedicated. Yet I can't stop wanting to go on with them.'

'I can now understand you being the way you are about them. What I can't understand is Edward loving this other girl. We had a close love. Especially after dear little Andrew died. Edward adored him. He was always gentle with me. He talked about his work. He shared everything with me. Then suddenly he wants this other woman. Actually saying, he had never known true love until he had met her. It hurts, Erica. I've never known such pain.'

She paused then went on in a low voice, 'I said I wanted to kill him, but I don't. All I want to know is what this love is that he has for this person. I thought I would have had his love for the rest of our lives.'

'So did we,' Erica said, wondering at the same time if the love she felt for Frank was the right kind of love. How could one tell?

It was half-past seven that evening before John arrived home.

'I came straight here,' he said. 'Knowing you would be waiting to know if I had found Edward. I did find out where he was boarding but unfortunately, I didn't see him.'

John looked weary. Erica said, 'Sit down, I'll make you a cup of tea.'

He sat in the wooden armchair and sighed. 'What a day. Their landlady told me that she had no idea when they would be back. I explained that I was Edward's uncle and asked if I could wait in the room. She hesitated for a moment then agreed.'

John paused. 'What I hoped for was to

218

find some money.'

'And did you?' Erica asked anxiously.

'Yes, I did, but not the money his mother gave him. I couldn't find that.'

Janet's head came up quickly, 'I can't believe it. Did you...?'

John held out a packet. 'Yes. It's not much, but he's your husband and he shouldn't leave you penniless.'

Janet took it and sat looking at the money. 'What a shock he'll get when he finds out it's missing.'

'I imagine so. And, of course he'll blame the landlady for letting me into the room.'

Janet gave a dry smile. 'We'll wait for repercussions.'

Erica wanted to know if Edward had passed the girl off as his wife and John said, 'Oh, yes, but I sensed the landlady didn't like her. Anyway, you have the money and no one can take it from you.'

Janet was silent for a few moments then she said, a break in her voice, 'I think you ought to know that I'm pregnant. Edward doesn't know. I hadn't told him.'

Erica got up and going over to Janet gave her a hug.

'He must be told.'

'No. If he comes back, which I doubt, then I shall tell him but I would stress it's for the baby's sake. I do not want him back if he has a feeling of reluctance.'

John shook his head. 'I don't know what to say, Janet. Is it right that you should bring up the baby on your own?'

'I'm capable and I wouldn't spoil it, not like I spoilt dear little Andrew.'

Erica ached for her. How terrible that this should happen now. Would Edward have left Janet if he had known? Perhaps not...

The next day the three sisters brought their boxes to show Erica. They were not finished but Erica was delighted with them.

'We hope to finish them this evening at home,' Angie gave a mischievous smile. 'We are truly dedicated. And Papa and Mama are very pleased that we are working for you.'

Emily asked Erica how she was feeling and she said, 'Much better. I hope that I shall be well enough to get on with some work tomorrow.'

'Take care of yourself,' Margaret said, speaking seriously. 'You are the boss of the trinket boxes and we would be lost without you.'

Erica smiled. 'Thank you for my title. I sometimes feel of little importance.'

'How could you. The firm would fail, I'm sure, if it didn't have these boxes.'

Angie and Margaret agreed with her and Erica suddenly felt a warm glow.

The girls might be mischievous, but they had a quality side. She began to feel a great deal better.

When Janet counted out the money she said, 'I wronged Edward. He's hardly touched it. I'm glad that he had not thrown it away on his...his woman.'

Erica said, 'I have a feeling he might come for it. He'll be furious that John brought a share of it to you.'

'We shall have to wait and see.'

Edward came that evening and he was in a vile temper. There was a big row. He wanted to know how John dared to have gone to his lodgings and 'robbed' him of some money.

'I didn't rob you,' John declared. 'Janet is your wife and you had no right to leave her penniless.'

'I can do what I like with my life,' he shouted.

'Not when your wife is expecting your child!'

Edward had his mouth open to say something and he paused, closed his mouth and stared at her. After a few seconds he said, 'Is this true?'

'Yes, but I don't want you back.' Janet's eyes were blazing. 'I can bring the child up and you can have your wretched money back to spend on your—your paramour.'

'She doesn't want my money, she just wants my love.'

'Lucky her.'

Erica realising that Janet was very near to tears, appealed to Edward, 'Don't you want another baby?'

'Of course I do.' He was still angry. 'I never got over the death of young Andrew. But what do I do? Give up the woman I really love? I can't help the way I love her.'

'You're a weakling, Edward,' John spoke in a disparaging way. 'You'd better go and take your money with you. We'll keep Janet and we shall all love her child. Now get out and don't ever come back here again.'

Edward hesitated just a moment then, turning on his heel, stormed out.

There was a bleakness in Janet's eyes for a moment then she said, 'I suppose I have to suffer because my mother is a witch. I only hope to God that I'll be allowed to keep this child safe.'

Both John and Erica declared she would. Both told her she had suffered enough, then Erica said, 'Tomorrow or the next day we'll ask the vicar if he will come and sanctify the house. He'll clear out any witchcraft or devilry.'

Janet raised her shoulders. The bleakness

was still in her eyes. 'I hope you are right.'

The next day it was Charles' turn to be at the house. Erica, feeling almost normal, asked him how Alexander Gilmorton was managing at the shop.

'Splendidly. He's a charmer and has promised to recommend his friends. He's popular with most people, and I think he might be responsible for increasing our sales.' Charles smiled. 'He has a good line of talk.'

'I'll have to meet him.'

'That's no problem, not if you're planning to come to the shop tomorrow.'

'Definitely. I can't stay away any longer.'

When Erica went to the shop that afternoon she met Alexander Gilmorton. Charles was right. He had a lot of charm. He was tall and slender and had curly brown hair which had gold streaks in it. She thought, however it was his voice that was so appealing. It was deep and soft. She did think, however, that he was a little boyish looking but when he shook hands with her he had a man's grip.

He seemed to know the price of everything in the shop by heart and talked in a firm way to the customers. She liked him.

He also appeared to like her. He said

he thought her very accomplished.

'Thank you. John and Charles and myself are very grateful that you've helped us out.'

He smiled. 'I hope your other brother does not return too soon.'

As Erica did not know what Alexander had been told about Edward she answered lightly, 'If he does return soon we might be grateful for a helpful hand.'

'And I would be grateful if such a chance arose.'

Erica decided she must in some way get the girls to meet him and wondered if they would be impressed or not. It depended on what kind of man they would be interested in. When she returned from the shop and they called with their work she would tell them about Alexander Gilmorton and see what response she got. She would not, however, rush at it.

A few days later the three girls seemed to be in a slightly depressive state. Emily was the worst, complaining how dull life was. 'When Edward was there he was always such fun. Now we have to have permission to visit the shop. There was always something so exciting about meeting customers, especially men.'

Margaret said, 'I know what you mean

but we could ask to visit the shop.'

'No, it's too early.' This from Angie. 'The parents wouldn't agree, you know what they were like when they found that we came home late. Erica was very good and took the blame.'

Emily gave a deep sigh. 'The parents have been talking for ages of us meeting our future husbands but nothing has come of it.'

'Will it ever?' Margaret asked. 'I don't think Mama wants us to get married.'

Angie looked up. 'I don't think I would be interested in getting married to anyone of the parents' choice anyway. They're sure to be the namby-pamby type.'

The girls were certainly unsettled. Yet they enjoyed their work. Erica had to admit that the house was like a morgue since Edward had gone. Janet had become a closed-in person and Charles was not much better.

Determined not to lose the girls Erica tried to think how she could cheer them up. Should she let them spend some time at the shop? No, their parents wouldn't allow them to go. That, in their opinion was a man's world.

Erica suddenly thought of Alexander Gilmorton. He would be an attraction to the girls.

Could she get the girls to meet him? He

came from the wealthy class which would at least please their parents.

Customers came in and Erica left the men to take off her coat. She knew nothing really about his life and he would possibly want to spend Sunday with his family. But at the same time she guessed he was a woman charmer and might quite readily accept an invitation to lunch next Sunday and, meet the three girls.

During the next two days Erica found herself fascinated by the new assistant. Although John had been angry about Edward's behaviour he had never looked as if he was living in a morgue as Charles had done. Now Charles was his own self and seemed very pleased with Mr Gilmorton's sales.

Both John and he seemed pleased too when Erica suggested asking their new assistant to lunch, but both were a little wary of asking the three girls.

Erica gave her reasons. 'They all seemed to be in a slightly depressed state. "Life is so dull," they say. So it is. Now I don't want to lose them as workers and thought if I asked them to lunch too it would give them a lift.'

'What about them getting permission from their parents?' John asked.

Erica smiled. 'I don't think that would be any problem. Mr Gilmorton does come from the aristocracy.'

John and Charles laughed and asked what she was waiting for.

Alexander accepted the invitation at once and when the girls were asked they were almost bubbling over with joy. They did say, however, they would have to have their parents' permission, with Angie adding, she was sure they would agree.

They did, but their mother became a pest wanting to know everything about Mr Gilmorton.

Erica replied firmly, 'I only know he comes from a good family, but if you have any doubts, there are plenty of other young ladies I can ask.'

'Oh, no, no. I'm satisfied. They shall be with you all. I give you my word.'

Even Janet seemed to brighten a little when she knew about the arrangements.

'It'll be a change,' she said. 'I needed something like this to perhaps get me back to normality. I'll see to the meal.'

The girls arrived first and were excited. They wanted to know about Mr Gilmorton, how old he was and what he was like. Erica told them they they would have to wait and see.

When he did arrive they were tongue-tied and Erica could read their minds. What a gorgeous man. What a wonderful husband he would make.

Janet had made a vegetable soup, cooked lamb chops, and for dessert she had made a fruit trifle.

During the meal Alexander drew the girls out about their lives and they all acted coyly.

He told them how he admired their work and the girls, to Erica's surprise, gave her full credit for their improvement.

John and Charles had got back to their normal selves and were both entertaining too.

Janet did not do much talking but seemed more pleasant than she had been recently. And when Alexander praised the meal she acknowledged it with a smiling nod, which all helped to make the occasion successful.

Alexander said he had to leave at three o'clock but they all sat in a circle with Alexander giving a brief talk on his life.

He said he liked riding, but hated fox-hunting. 'Why should they be hunted?' he asked. 'Isn't it more satisfactory for farmers to shoot them than have the animals torn to pieces by dogs?' He gave a shiver. 'It makes me curl up in shame.'

They all agreed with this.

'I like a game of cards,' he said, 'but I don't like playing for high stakes. I hate to see a man bet a high figure and when he loses he goes out and shoots himself. A life gone for wanting to win.'

While John got up to pour wine for the men Janet whispered to Erica, 'Just a bit too goody-goody, wouldn't you say?'

Erica smiled and nodded.

But when Alexander began to talk again the subject had changed. This time he talked about his childhood and how terrible he was at sums.

'Much to my parents' disappointment I never improved. I had excellent tutors but somehow I could never take it in.'

He smiled then, a lovely smile that encompassed them all.

'Do you know, it was not until John asked me if I would like to fill in with serving in the shop, that I found something I like doing.'

There were murmurs of amusement.

'Truly,' he went on, 'I found it quite intriguing to sell a customer an item that he or she had not even thought about. It was wonderful. I would like to go into business.'

John sat up. 'Please don't say you are going to leave us?'

'No, of course not. I wouldn't think of such a thing, not until your brother returns.'

There had been a slight panic in John's voice, now he said, quite calmly, 'We may be able to keep you on...when he does return.'

Alexander grinned. 'That would be wonderful. Then I could go on doubling your sales.'

Emily then said suddenly, 'Are you married, Mr Gilmorton?'

There was a small shocked silence and Emily obviously realising that young unattached ladies did not ask such questions, looked embarrassed.

'I'm, I'm sorry,' she said in a low voice.

Alexander smiled. 'No, I'm not married Miss Emily, and I won't be for many years. I want to live my own life, now I've found out what I want to do.'

He downed his drink then got up. 'And now I must go. I have to visit my family on a Sunday afternoon. I've thoroughly enjoyed myself. The meal was excellent.' He bowed to Janet. 'I know this was thanks to you, Mrs Curtis.'

Then he thanked the rest of them for being such a wonderful, warm and caring family. 'You are lucky,' he said solemnly, which had Erica thinking that his family were not so caring.

When he had gone John said, 'What a man. He seems so happy but I do wonder if his life is as wonderful as he tries to put over.'

'I don't think he tried to put that over. He's a man, who wants to live his own life but up to now has found opposition from his family.'

'Just as we have,' Margaret said solemnly, She got up. 'I think we must go.'

John said, 'I understand your mother was coming for you. Shouldn't you wait?'

'We do want to have a word with Emily, saying what she did. It was terrible.'

Erica said, 'Forget it. I hope you enjoyed the meal and the company generally.'

'Oh, yes, it was wonderful,' all three proclaimed.

And at that moment the front door bell rang, Margaret groaned. 'That will be Mama. Wanting to meet Mr Gilmorton.'

Erica went to the front door and met the beaming face of Mrs Lewis.

'I hope I'm not too early, Miss Erica.'

'No, the girls are ready to leave. Mr Gilmorton has just left.'

'Oh.' Mrs Lewis's disappointment was very apparent.

'Here they are.' The three girls came to the door fastening the buttons on their coats. Erica whispered to them, 'Smile.'

They smiled, very stiff smiles and their mother said, 'So you've had a lovely time.'

There was a dutiful response of, 'Oh, yes, wonderful,' and they left with the girls calling out their thanks to Erica.

Chapter Fourteen

There was another short silence after they left then Janet gave a sigh. 'What a shame that Alexander was adamant that he was not interested in marrying for some years to come. I think it quite spoiled the girls' afternoon!'

Erica shook her head. 'It was wrong to presume that he might be a possible husband. And yet I think it was in my mind. Perhaps I was at fault for asking them.'

'Not at all. They must lead very dull lives and heaven knows who they'll end up with. I don't think that their mother has any romance in her soul. All she'll be concerned with is finding men from a good background. And I don't suppose it will worry her if they are forty or fifty.'

'Oh, no, she couldn't be so heartless.'

'I don't think she'll want them to have husbands. On the other hand, she won't want three spinster daughters.'

'Well, we'll wait and see.'

Erica thought how awful it must be to be looking for a husband, which brought Frank to her mind. Surely there should be a letter from him soon. At that moment she longed to see him. Ached to be in his arms.

The following morning there was a letter from him and Erica tore the envelope open.

She started to read the letter then stopped and looked up.

'What the...?' She started again at the beginning and finished the sentence before stopping again.

What on earth was Edward doing in Durham?

Frank told her in his letter that he had been utterly astonished when Edward walked into the shop.

'He looked terrible,' he said, 'and didn't seem to know what to do. He eventually told me that he had left the shop and wanted work. We gave him some breakfast and when Bert and I went into the kitchen to try and work out what could be wrong, Edward walked out and we haven't seen him since. We drove round in the van and there was no sign of him.'

Then Frank wrote, 'Please can you let me know the full story...'

Her Uncle John was at home and Erica

took the letter to him.

He said the same thing as Erica had said, 'What the...?' and stopped.

Then he read to the end of the line.

By the time he had finished the letter he said, 'Come along we'll go and send a telegram.'

'What about Janet. Should she be told?'

'No not yet, we must know more of what's happened. Let's wait until we receive Frank's reply, then we'll tell her.'

They went to the post office and sent the telegram, explaining briefly that Edward had left Janet for another woman, and it wasn't until the next morning that they received a reply from Frank.

After John had read Frank's telegram he looked at Erica with a sigh. 'What a right mess! I would guess from what Frank's just written, that Edward's lady love has walked out on him...and stolen his money.'

'Oh, no!'

'Should Janet be told now, do you think?'

'I don't think we have a right to withhold it. But then there's the baby. What effect would this have on Janet?'

John said, 'Janet is a very strong person. I think we must tell her.'

'She did say a while ago that she still loves Edward, in spite of the way he's behaved.'

Janet was unpacking the groceries when they came into the kitchen.

'Sit down, Janet we have something to tell you.'

Her expression never changed while John was talking and when he paused near the end she said, 'I'll go to Durham and when I find him I'll knock some sense into him.'

Erica ventured to say, 'Do you think that's wise, Janet? You have the baby to think of.'

'It will be all right. I know it. I'll leave today.'

Erica glanced at John and he raised his shoulders.

Later when Janet was looking up train times Erica pointed out how long the journey would take and how tiring it would be.

'Nothing is worse than waiting for word. Edward needs me and I want to be there and hunting for him before he gets too far away.'

Erica wished she could have gone with her, but it was out of the question. There were not only meals to prepare but there were boxes to prepare for the three girls to work on. She quite definitely had to keep the work going.

Damn Edward and his lady love who had gone off with his money.

He deserved to lose it. At that moment Erica was sorry that Janet might find her husband and bring him back. They were better off with Alexander Gilmorton working for them.

Later she felt that she had been most uncharitable. Edward was her brother, and how did she know how strong love could be?

Her Uncle John saw Janet off at the station but said that she had refused to travel with a family. 'She told me she was not a child but a respectable married woman. I cursed Edward.'

'So did I. It's going to upset all of Frank's and Bert's plans. I only hope she won't expect Frank to travel with her searching for Edward.'

'I doubt it, she's not the type. Well, we can only hope for the best. I gave her some money for the train fares, so she should be all right.'

'I can only pray that she'll find Edward soon. Get the whole thing sorted out once and for all.'

The next day at midday there was a telegram from Frank saying, *Janet arrived safely. Gone in search of Edward. Will keep in touch.*

The following morning a letter came from Frank. It was quite long. He said that Janet had found Edward and that he

236

was sick and was in hospital. He had been found collapsed on the hospital steps. She said she would bring him home as soon as he was able to travel.

Frank went on: *'When I knew she was coming I prayed that you would be with her. Is there any chance of you coming to Durham, my darling?'*

'No chance at all,' Erica whispered, but oh, how she longed to see him. Was she being foolish in not giving up the trinket boxes? She would have to give it a lot of thought.

No sooner was she working on them, however, than she knew she could not give them up. They would always be a part of her life.

That day, Mrs Todd from the farm, came to visit them.

As soon as she saw Erica, she knew something was wrong. 'I can tell by the look on your face that's something's amiss. Tell me what's happened.'

So Erica told Mrs Todd the story of Edward and she was amazed.

'I just can't believe that Edward would do such a thing. He's always loved Janet. I always thought him a devoted husband.'

'Apparently not. Now we have another problem. This woman in his life has left him and apparently stolen his money. John gave Janet some money to travel with, but she is now paying for him to have private treatment in this hospital.'

'So Janet obviously found some of the money.'

'I just don't know what to think, Mrs Todd. I didn't know there was any left. It's a proper mix up and quite frankly, although Edward is my brother I don't really want him to come back. I feel that he will change all our lives.'

'That's up to you and to Charles and your Uncle John.'

'Yes, I know. Charles and John are strong personalities.'

'I've always thought of you as being strong too?'

'Am I? I don't think so.'

'You must be,' Mrs Todd said gently, 'when you refuse to marry Frank who loves you because you want to go on making trinket boxes.'

'It's difficult to make people understand. I've been making pipes since I was a child. I had to work. Now these boxes are something that I long to make. They're a part of me.'

'Shall I tell you something, Erica? Before I married I worked for a high class dressmaker. She made beautiful gowns. I wanted to have a business, I wanted to design gowns. My own designs. I would draw them whenever I had a minute to spare. Sometimes I would get up during the night and design a new one.'

Mrs Todd paused then went on. 'My mother found out and burned every one I had ever done. She told me I would get married and there would be no dressmaking business in my life. I wanted to die. Then Harold came into my life and we fell in love. He was a farmer. Was I to completely lose my dream? He wanted children. So did I. I gave up my dream and married him.'

'And have you ever regretted it?'

'No, but I still fashion dresses. I've brought some to show you.'

She took a bundle from her bag. 'I'll leave them with you and you tell me what you think of them. Will you be able to say with all honesty that I should have sacrificed my life for them?'

Mrs Todd got up, then leaned over and kissed Erica on the cheek. 'I'll call and see you tomorrow, my love.'

Erica sat for a long time after she had gone, afraid to look at the drawings, guessing at what Mrs Todd had sacrificed.

It was not until the evening when they had all gone to bed before she looked at them. Then she was full of wonder. How could she have given up such talent? There were exquisite styles of dresses that only monied people could afford to buy in today's world. Dresses studded with beads in various patterns, one with a short train that could be held over the arm. There were low-necked gowns and one with a high backed piece that had coloured beads with a beautiful pattern of flowers. Truly lovely. And her friend had sacrificed her art to marry and have children. Had she ever regretted it?

When Mrs Todd came the next day and Erica enthused over the designs, Mrs Todd said, 'I will still go on designing them, yet I have no regrets that I gave up my work to marry and have children. I wouldn't be without any of them, not for the world.'

Erica said, 'The difference is that you can go on designing them and could, I'm sure, sell the designs. I can't do that. My trinket boxes have to be made. I must admit I'm torn but I still haven't made up my mind.' She picked up the designs. 'They are utter perfection. Have you ever tried to sell them?'

Mrs Todd shook her head. 'No, I want to make the dresses. Selling the designs would give me no pleasure. I can understand how you feel but you are losing something so precious in your life. Children, babies. If you really love Frank, think again, Erica.'

'Yes, I shall, I promise. Perhaps when Janet has her baby it might help me to change my mind.'

'I hope so. Perhaps one day I shall make

dresses. When the children are older.'

'With a farm to tend to?'

Mrs Todd said, 'Harold and I might retire, let the boys have the farm.'

'And then your husband would want your company.'

She laughed. 'I can't win, can I?' She paused then added soberly, 'Do you know what I think sometimes? I think there must be hundreds of talented women who never have the chance of proving their talents. They go on slogging all their life to do the basics and never get any further than a pittance.'

'That's true.'

Mrs Todd's designs kept coming into Erica's mind most of the day. Mrs Todd had as much talent as she had with her trinket boxes. If she could sacrifice her work to have children then so should Erica give up the idea of making boxes.

It would be some time before she could marry Frank. Perhaps by then she would be able to make the sacrifice. She must make the sacrifice. She did love Frank and she did want children.

And now, she thought, she must put her problem from her mind and continue to make as many trinket boxes as she could.

When Mrs Todd came again, Erica was able to say she was going to marry Frank when it was possible.

'Oh, I'm so glad, Erica. You won't regret it. And never let yourself think that perhaps you can make some boxes during the day while your babies sleep. They must have your full attention and love.'

Erica's cheeks burned a little. That had been in her mind. Oh, dear, it was not going to be easy. Then she straightened her shoulders. If Mrs Todd could do it then she could. She would be firm.

Janet wrote a few lines to Erica every other day, telling her what news there was. One time Edward would be making progress, then the next time he had slipped back. She was getting worried.

A further letter said he was beginning to take an interest in work and she hoped that this was a good sign.

Erica had told her that both John and Charles were willing to have him back, but stressed that they were keeping on Mr Gilmorton. What she dare not risk was telling Janet that both men were worried in case Edward would want to leave a second time.

And this is how Erica felt about it. Because there was something missing in Janet's letters. She had never once said that she was sure it had just been a phase in Edward's life and that from now on everything would be all right.

Frank wrote to Erica every few days but said very little about Edward. It was always the shop he talked about. He described the shop and everything they had bought. They had been to Scotland to the factory which the people in the train had recommended and ordered a selection of shoes and boots.

They also had customers who had ordered suits and had top tailors to make them.

Frank also ended his letters, *I hope to see you soon in Durham, my darling. Write to me...*

And every time Erica ached to be in his arms.

Perhaps soon, when all this with Edward had been settled she would be able to go for a weekend.

It was another three weeks before John had a letter from Janet saying that Edward was now well again. Would it be all right to bring him back home?

John discussed this with Erica and Charles but Charles did add that Edward might not be willing to have Alexander Gilmorton stay.

'If Edward doesn't like it then *he'll* have to leave,' John spoke firmly. '*He* was the one who left in the first place.'

This was all agreed on, but Erica guessed that they were all uneasy...

Janet and Edward arrived at six o'clock on a Wednesday evening, having stayed overnight in Doncaster.

John and Erica went to meet them. Erica felt uncomfortable and thought this was awful. Edward was their brother.

She and John put on bright faces when they arrived and Edward who had looked sheepish at first, now accepted that he was welcome home.

He talked a lot and Janet helped him. He liked Durham. Would have liked to live there. A beautiful cathedral.

John said they would go to the shop first then Edward could see Charles and meet Alexander Gilmorton.

Alexander was very pleasant and polite to Edward but Erica thought that Edward was a bit surly.

John said he would take them home for dinner, then he would return to the shop.

On the way to the house Janet seemed to be doing all the talking.

They had hardly arrived home when Edward all but shouted, 'And who does Alexander Gilmorton think he is? The boss of the show? Well, he needn't think he's going to be my boss!'

Erica could see John was angry, but he was under control. 'I think I had better put this right straight away Edward. Mr

Gilmorton is an excellent salesman. He's increased our sales. He's an amiable man. You walked out on us in spite of being one of the family. Now you either accept Gilmorton and be pleasant to him or you leave.'

Edward pushed back a chair. 'I'm not going to stand for this!'

He started to walk towards the door then Janet said firmly, 'Edward, I've put up with a lot from you. If you walk out of here you can stay out. I no longer care.'

'You led me to believe you were on my side.'

'You imagined it. I wanted you back home for the sake of the baby, but you made my life hell constantly grumbling as you pretended to be ill.'

'I didn't pretend, I was ill.'

'No, you only thought you were because your woman walked out on you and took your money with her.' The awful bitterness was back in her voice. 'The baby will be better without you as a father.'

'Don't say that, Janet,' he pleaded. 'I adored little Andrew. I shall love this baby. Please let me stay.'

She hesitated a moment then with a sigh said, 'You would certainly have to change your attitude.'

'I will, I promise. I'll do my best to be pleasant to Gilmorton. I'll treat him as a boss, if you want me to.'

John said stiffly. 'That won't be necessary. There are no bosses in our business. Just treat him as you would any of us. He's a salesman, as we all are.'

'So I can stay?'

John looked at Erica. She said yes, but hoped that Edward had gone. He was no longer like a brother to her and she wished that she did not have to sit and have a meal with them.

John said to Janet, 'And you, Janet?'

'Yes, as long as he follows the rules.'

'I will, I promise.'

They sat down to the meal.

'Right,' John said, 'Charles and I will be home after nine.'

After he had gone there was silence and Erica suddenly noticed that there were tears in Edward's eyes. Then she felt sorry for him. Who was to know what he suffered? On an impulse she put a hand over his and said, 'Everything will seem better tomorrow, Edward.'

He gave her a wan smile and later did try and make some conversation. And when John and Charles arrived home they all sat talking about the business and how much it had improved.

The next morning it was Charles' turn to spend a morning at home. He told Erica how John had told him about Edward's attitude and how pleased he was that John had told Edward he had to fit in.

'Do you know,' he said, 'I was sorry at first that he'd come home when I saw his surly face. Later I felt sorry for him. And now I feel glad that's he's fitting in. We've never had such a to do before, have we?'

'No. I feel sorry for Janet, realising that she only wanted him back home for the baby's sake. I hope it works out.' She paused. 'I wonder what tale the girls will have this morning. They were talking of their parents finding prospective husbands for them, but not one of them was hopeful.'

'Do you know, when they used to come to the shop in an evening, I learned that they were not young ladies at all.' Charles grinned. 'They were little devils. Each one had been out, in secret, with a man.'

'I guessed that. They all seemed to know too much about men.'

Erica told Charles she was surprised that he and Edward had urged them on and he laughed.

'They didn't need urging on. I think their parents will have to watch them or they'll be finding the girls in trouble.'

'Pray heaven they don't. I certainly don't want to lose my workers.' Erica hesitated a moment then tried to ask casually if Charles knew who their Uncle

John's young lady was.

Charles stared at her. 'You know more than I do. I didn't know that he had a young lady.'

'Oh, he just mentioned it casually.'

'If he has a young lady I'll get to know who she is.'

'I wouldn't bother if I were you.' Erica picked up a trinket box and examined it.'

The doorbell rang and Charles said, 'Here are your workers. I must hear their news then get on with the meerschaums.'

Charles gave them a cheerful good-morning but they all looked miserable. He said, smiling, 'So why aren't there any nice bright faces this morning?'

'Bright faces?' Angie said, raising her eyes ceilingwards.

'We've all been introduced to our future husbands. The youngest is thirty and the eldest is thirty-six.'

'And I have the eldest one,' Margaret said. 'He could be my grandfather.'

Emily sighed. 'I have the plainest one.'

'I'm sure you're all exaggerating,' declared Erica.

'Exaggerating?' the three of them chorused. 'You should see them.'

'You don't have to have them,' Charles informed them.

'But we do. According to Mama, she

and Papa were careful in their choice.'

'They might be much better by the time you've got to know them,' Erica suggested.

'How do we get to know them? They've got nothing to say. They're like cardboard characters.'

Erica said cheerfully, 'Now I know you are all making it sound worse than it really is. I would accept one cardboard character, but not three.'

'Wait until you meet them, then you'll change your mind.'

'How am I going to meet them?'

'They are coming to visit us this evening at seven o'clock. Make an excuse. Perhaps bring a trinket box that you want us to see.'

'I'll do that. Now what have you brought me?'

Charles still smiling, said, 'And I'll go and get on with my own work. Oh, by the way, Edward's back.'

'Oh, he's fun,' they all said, looking brighter.

Charles grinned. 'Not any more. You'll see him one of these days when it's his turn to be home. But be careful, his wife will be here.'

The misery was back.

The girls as always produced some excellent work and were pleased that

Erica gave them some tobacco boxes to do next.

They would be a change. What was to go on them?

Chapter Fifteen

Erica searched her mind for a valid excuse to go the Lewis's that evening, but was unable to come up with anything suitable. Then she suddenly thought of a much larger tobacco box she had made some time ago and decided it could be a talking point between the men and the girls.

Each panel was edged by tracery but in the middle of one was a painting of mountains and where the mountains divided was a dying sunset. Erica had forgotten how beautiful it was. The sky tinged with red, orange and gold lighting up the grimness of the mountains.

She would take it and ask the girls if they would be willing to make a few similar. If the men were not interested then they were not men suitable for the girls.

With a feeling of satisfaction Erica put the box in her bag and took it with her that evening.

Mrs Lewis welcomed her with a beaming

smile. Erica offered to come another time after explaining why she had come, but Mrs Lewis insisted she come in and meet the girls' future husbands.

When she went into the cheerless drawing-room, with the girls sitting together and the men sitting opposite, her heart sank.

Not one of the six had a smile on their faces.

Mrs Lewis, still beaming, introduced Erica as the girl's artistic tutor.

Each man stood up and gave a slight bow to Erica and said they were pleased to meet her.

Mrs Lewis drew forth another chair for Erica and as she sat down she noticed that the men were not bad looking.

Before anything more could be said, she drew forth the box and said she thought that the girls might be interested in making one sometime, then started to put the box back into her bag.

Angie reached out a hand. 'No, don't put it away. The men might be interested in what we do.'

'Of course we would,' said one solemn-faced man. Then, as he examined it and passed it to the others, their expressions changed, became animated.

Mr Lewis came in and looked annoyed that the men and the girls had been interrupted in their meeting. He glared at Erica who got up and said she was sorry she had arrived at the wrong time, she must go. She reached out a hand for the tobacco box but first one and then the other two men wanted to examine it again.

In the end girls and men were all talking. Mrs Lewis looked very happy and soon her husband was taking an interest.

Erica could not make out which man belonged to who and simply could not make out who was the eldest. Each man was quite good-looking and their manners were perfect. Perhaps Mrs Lewis had been right in her choice.

Before Erica left an order was given to her for a tobacco box from Mr Lewis, and the girls asked her to make one each for the men.

She went home happy and looked forward to hearing what the girls would have to tell her the next day about their future husbands.

The next morning Erica awoke to a number of sounds. There was someone shouting and another person yelling. She flung back the bedclothes and getting up, grabbed her dressing-gown and went on to the landing.

John came out of his room. 'What's going on downstairs?'

'I don't know, I'm just going down to see.'

When they went into the kitchen, Edward and Janet appeared to be having a row. Charles was saying, 'Will you both shut up a minute and then I might find out what all this is about.'

Edward yelled, 'I'll tell you what its about. My wife has stolen what's left of my money!'

Janet's eyes were blazing. 'How dare you! Your wonderful girlfriend stole half of your money and ran off! And when I found you in the hospital the nurses handed over your possessions. I discovered what was left of the money, paid all your medical bills, and took the rest for me and the baby.'

'How dare you take it! That's *my* money and you had no right, you dirty rotten...' He tried to launch another attack on Janet but John stepped between them.

Janet said, 'I wanted you back for only one reason—so that the baby would have a father. What a mistake I made—you're disgusting and I want nothing more to do with you!'

'Well I can tell you now,' he shouted, 'I'll leave, but not until I have my money!'

There was a stubbornness about him that made John realise he would not leave until he had it.

John said to Janet, 'Give what's left of the money to him, and let him go.'

'I'll only give half of it, I have a child to bring up.'

'We'll attend to that,' John said. 'You are family, we'll look after you both. Go and get the money, Janet. Please.' He spoke gently.

She hesitated a moment then went upstairs. When she came down she threw a box at him. It fell to the floor. He picked it up, walked to the door and turned.

'And I'll tell you something else. When this baby is born, I shall have it from you.'

'If you dare to touch it I'll kill you, I swear it!' Janet's eyes were blazing.

He gave a bitter laugh. 'And I'll tell you lot something else: You can keep your Alexander Gilmorton!'

John said, 'Just get out and don't come back. Ever.'

'Don't worry. I wouldn't come back for a king's ransom. Good riddance!'

Edward stormed out, banging both doors as he left.

Janet stood a moment then went upstairs.

Erica found herself wondering what her mother would have thought of all this. There had never such a time as this when they were poor. And now, this upset because she had left them all this money. It was a tragedy.

John sat down and put a hand to his head for a few moments then he looked up.

'I can't believe all this has happened. But, there's one thing, he's best out of the way.'

'Yes, I know.'

Charles said, 'I must get to the shop. Sorry I wasn't much help.'

'It's a good job you didn't try to help. Heaven knows what point we would have reached.'

Charles went to the shop and Erica went upstairs to see Janet.

Janet had a suitcase out and was taking items from the drawers and putting them in the case. Erica went to her and started putting the things back in the drawer.

'You can't leave us,' she said gently. 'You and your baby will always be family.'

Janet began to cry. 'I know, but in spite of everything I still love Edward. That might be hard for you to understand but I've never ever loved anyone else. I think I even understand how he feels about Irene.'

Then her expression changed, became bitter. 'But if he ever tried to steal the baby from me I would kill him.'

'Come on downstairs and we can have a

talk.' But Janet would not be moved from her room, and so Erica went downstairs alone.

It was John's turn to be home for the day and he said to Erica as she came in, 'I don't feel I want to do a thing, but of course I'll have to. What do you suggest?'

'Well, I do have an order for the tobacco boxes. If you could perhaps do some tracery. You have done it before.'

'Yes, but I'm not so good at it as you are.'

'I'll do some as well. I won't go to the shop today.'

'You'll miss it.'

'Yes, but business comes first. Always.'

When the girls arrived about half-past six they were talkative and said that Erica was responsible for them liking the men.

Angie smiled. 'Apparently they are willing for us to continue with our work.'

Emily said, 'Our parents aren't happy about this. They want grandchildren, but as we won't be getting married for at least a year, we are contented.'

'What work do you want us to do?' Margaret asked. Erica had cut several of the larger tobacco boxes and she and John had done some of the fine tracery but she began to wonder if she was doing the right thing. It was delaying the trinket boxes and Emily was the only one so far who had tackled country scenes.

Well, now was the time to try it out.

She explained she wanted to see drawings first and they went happily away to try them.

John had been to the shop at lunchtime to relieve the men, who he learned had both been kept busy.

Charles had told Alexander Gilmorton that Erica would not be in the shop that day, that she was very busy at home and, according to John he had seemed very disappointed not to be seeing her.

'How nice to be missed,' she said lightly. And, felt a little more cheerful.

When the girls brought their drawings the next morning, Erica said, 'These are very good. Especially the sunsets. Try the work on the boxes themselves.'

They were again in a talkative mood about the three men, with Angie saying that actually, they each had the wrong man. She liked the one that Emily had; Emily liked the one that Margaret had, and Margaret liked Angie's man.

Erica said, 'Tell your parents this.'

They didn't dare, they complained. They had no idea how the men felt about it.

'Well, you won't know until you ask.

They might feel as you do and would like you to change.'

They said they would have to think about it.

The following day they were all smiles. Their mother had sat them at table with the man they wanted to sit with and it had worked. They were all happy.

Erica felt that she should be happy too, but she felt miserable.

Was it because she wanted to be with Frank? He was constantly in her thoughts. Should she ask if she could go to Durham and stay for two of three days. If she left say, on the Friday, she could spend Saturday and Sunday with him and come home on the Monday. This time it would be different. She could tell him that she would give up making the trinket boxes and tobacco boxes.

That is, in another year's time when they would marry; Frank and Bert were building up a business. It would take a year to do it.

Erica began to feel a little brighter. She would mention it to the family that evening.

Both John and Charles seemed taken aback. It would mean leaving Janet on her own.

'It's only for a weekend,' Erica stressed. 'You two will be here on the Sunday.'

Janet insisted it would be fine. 'I think it's time that Erica had a break. She's been working all hours God sends.'

John and Charles gave in. Yes, of course. They did spend more time at the shop than she had. 'You'd better write to Frank tomorrow and let him know.'

Erica laughed and shook her head. 'No, I shall go and surprise him. I'll write to Mrs Tyson and ask if I can spend the night with her. She did beg that I would let her know if I came up that way again and promised that she would travel with me to Durham and have another look at the cathedral.'

She wrote the next morning and had a telegram the next day, *Delighted to be seeing you. Let me know time of arrival...*'

Erica felt so excited she kept packing a case then replacing what she had packed. 'I just can't wait to get away.' Then she said to her brothers, 'And don't either of you dare find some one for me to travel with.'

Erica said goodbye to Charles and Janet at the house and John drove her to the station.

She noticed that John was eyeing everyone on the platform and when the train came in, he put her into a carriage where there was an elderly couple. But he did refrain from asking them if they would look after her.

There was mischief in his eyes when he said, as the train was about to leave, 'They are going to Doncaster.' He gave her a hug. 'Let us know as soon as you arrive at Durham.'

'I promise.'

The couple were pleasant companions. And from Doncaster she travelled with a family. When she arrived she felt silly with excitement when she saw Mrs Tyson waving to her from the platform.

They hugged one another and got a cab outside the station.

They talked non-stop to the house and Erica laughed as she reminisced how she had fallen asleep as she undressed for bed the last time she stayed with her.

They both had so much to tell one another and it was late when they did get to bed.

The next morning Erica gave Mrs Tyson a trinket box and two for her friends and refused to take payment for them.

On their way to Durham Mrs Tyson asked if Erica would be giving up her work when she married Frank.

'Yes, I must, but it will probably be another year before we get married.'

'I thought you were both madly in love.'

'We are, but Frank and his friend have

to have the shop paying before we can even think of marriage.'

They talked about this on the way and Mrs Tyson was all for Erica and Frank getting married and struggling together.

'But there's a partner involved in the business. Frank would never have had this business had it not been for Bert.'

'Well, you know what's happening, I hope it turns out all right for you.'

They had to be directed to the shop and Erica realised it was in a good district.

The shop was in a tree-lined square and there was a narrow lane at the back where there was a van.

Seeing a young lady stepping out of a cab Frank opened the shop door. The next moment he was staring at her and for a second Erica had the feeling he was not pleased to see her. Then he was hugging her and demanding to know why she had not let him know that she was coming.

She laughed. 'I wanted to surprise you.'

Then Frank was aware that Mrs Tyson was smiling from the inside of the cab and he practically lifted her out.

By then Bert was outside and hugging Erica.

The shop was quite big and well stocked. The men ushered the ladies into their back room, with Bert saying, 'Our kitchen.' Chairs had to be cleared to give Erica and Mrs Tyson a seat. Then a young man came in and he was introduced as Wilfred, their assistant. He made the tea while they talked.

'What a surprise Bridget will get,' Frank said.

'I don't expect her to put me up,' Erica replied.

'What, she would never forgive you if you went anywhere else,' Frank said.

Mrs Tyson said she had come with Erica to have another look at the wonderful cathedral, then she was going home again. Both Frank and Bert tried to persuade her to stay but she said to Frank, 'No, this is yours and Erica's weekend, and I wouldn't have it any other way.'

Bert told her he would walk her to the cathedral, but would then have to leave. They had an appointment at eleven o'clock.

'A wealthy man is ordering some suits,' Frank said smiling. 'We can't miss it. Actually we're doing very well.'

Bert and Mrs Tyson left, with Mrs Tyson promising to call for Erica early on Monday morning.'

After they had gone and Wilfred had left to go into the shop Frank took Erica into his arms and kissed her passionately. 'Oh, my darling how I've longed to do this. If the business goes on the way it's doing we won't have to wait a year to be married. More like six months.'

Erica felt startled. A year seemed a long way away. Six months seemed only weeks away.

Frank stroked her cheek. Then he said softly, 'But we won't even need to wait six months to make love, will we?'

The shop door opened and a woman's voice said, 'Shall I go into the kitchen Wilfred?'

'Just a moment, Miss Latimer, Mr Frank's fitting.'

'Oh, dear, tell him I'm here, will you?'

The female voice was a cultured one. Frank was already going to the door. The next moment Erica saw him walk into the shop and go to the counter.

Through a slit in the kitchen door Erica could see a well-dressed attractive young lady smile at Frank and put her hand over his.

'So you have a fitting session, darling. How long will you be?'

'About half an hour.' He drew his hand away. 'I must go, it's one of my wealthiest customers.'

'Papa is your wealthiest customer, darling.' Although the lady was well spoken there was an irritation in her voice.

'Of course. I shall see you in half an hour,'

263

'I don't know whether I shall be here then.'

'Then Monday perhaps. Bye.'

Erica saw him draw away and eventually Frank came in through the door that led into the kitchen. She sat up straight.

'Sorry, my darling,' Frank said, 'An awkward customer. Miss Latimer's father is a very wealthy man and she seems to think that she owns everyone she knows.'

Erica felt a relief.

When Bert came back Frank said, 'I'll run Erica to Bridget's.' He smiled. 'I can't wait to see her face. She'll just be so delighted.'

They were soon at Bridget's and Frank marched into the living-room saying, 'I have a surprise for you Bridget.'

She struggled to her feet. When Erica came into view she exclaimed, 'Oh, my love!' and burst into tears.

Frank said, 'Well I'll leave you both to discuss news.'

Bridget was full of talk of the shop and Bert and Frank's clientele.

'They've done extremely well,' Bridget said.

Erica, trying to speak casually, asked about Miss Latimer.

'Oh, her family are rolling in money. I don't like her and never will. She's been spoilt since she was a baby. She seems to think that every man she meets falls in love with her.'

'I saw her today, but didn't exactly meet her.'

'She wants to get her claws into Frank but he sensibly stays clear of her.'

'Good for him.'

'Oh, he's certainly in love with you, Erica,' Bridget spoke softly. 'He's always talking about you, and is waiting for the time you'll get married.'

Erica tried not to think that the time had been reduced to six months. How would her family take it?

She put that firmly from her mind. She would enjoy the time she was able to spend with Frank.

Which turned out to be very little during Saturday.

She was allowed, however, some time during that day, at the shop, and sat in the kitchen while the men fitted clothes or sold some ready-made.

Erica was interested in the stock and felt they must be heavily in debt with all they had.

Bert waved debt aside. Nearly everyone in business had debts, they would never get stock without it. Then he added, 'The wealthiest people are the worst payers. It's like getting blood out of a stone.'

Erica said, 'Can you both honestly say

that you were not better off with the market stall?'

They both agreed they were, but they both said they didn't want to be stuck with a market stall for evermore. Frank explained that there would be much more profit in the long run by going up in the world.

'It's what we both want,' Bert explained. 'I hope to marry some day and I want my wife and children to live comfortably. So does Frank.' He grinned. 'That's right, isn't it, boyo?'

'Definitely.'

Erica was allowed in the fitting-room and could see all the expensive patterns of material.

She walked around the shop and studied the high class boots and shoes. The neckties, the fine cotton shirts and the beautiful silk ones. There were expensive silk pyjamas and ready-made overcoats.

Erica said, 'I do think you need a time for payments of goods that have been made. They ought not be allowed to wear clothes that have not been paid for.'

The men looked at her horrified. They would lose all their trade. It was out of the question.

Bert suddenly laughed. 'We would soon be bankrupt if we used those methods. I bet some men are wearing clothes that have never been paid for. But, those same men have brought other customers.'

'And do these other men recommend other customers?'

'No,' Frank said firmly, 'they do pay and get a discount if they can recommend other people.'

Erica sighed. 'I suppose I shall have to let you run your own business. I'm used to being paid for goods that I've made.'

Frank was laughing, 'I think that would be a good idea. Ah, a customer. I think you had better nip into the kitchen.'

It was a middle-aged, well-dressed man who wanted a pair of riding boots.

The young assistant was out delivering a suit and both Bert and Frank attended to the customer.

It took them half an hour before the man was satisfied but Erica was pleased to know that he paid cash for them.

'So, who says we don't get paid?' Frank teased her.

He gave her a hug and Erica wondered if this was to be the order of the day. She had hoped that Frank could have taken time off but now saw the drawbacks.

By the time they had had their dinner that evening she would only have one more day left.

She decided to go back to Bridget's house.

The assistant was back and Frank said, to Erica's surprise, 'I'm coming with you, we'll have a walk by the river bank.'

Her heart gave a small leap. At least they would be spending some time together, even if it was just for an hour.

The afternoon was cold but Erica felt excited as Frank said in a low voice, 'We must find somewhere where we can make love. I need you, Erica. I must have you. I've been waiting too long.'

So had she. Delicious little shivers ran over her body. There were not many people about and Frank said, 'We'll find a seat among the bushes,' and his voice was not quite steady.

They went down one of the slopes and they came eventually to a seat tucked inside a ring of trees. 'How about this?' Frank said, emotion in his voice.

'It's too exposed,' Erica said. 'Someone could come suddenly and what chance would we have?'

'You're right. We'll go further on. There are some seats hidden among the trees.'

They found what seemed to be the perfect place for lovemaking. Frank took her by the hand and they went along a narrow path that eventually led to a small space that seemed perfectly hidden by thick bushes.

Frank took off his jacket and spread it

on the ground. Then he laid Erica down and she was sure he would hear the beating of her heart. He undid the buttons of her coat and the buttons on her dress. By this time, delicious anticipation was running all over her body.

Frank had just put his hand under her skirt when there was the sound of children laughing. They were quite close and Frank jumped up and pulled Erica to her feet. He managed to get his jacket on and she quickly fastened two buttons on her coat by the time three or four children arrived in the spot where they were.

The children stopped and stared then backed away. The next moment they had gone and were heard laughing.

'Oh, God, that was close,' Frank said. 'I wouldn't like children to learn the facts of life from us. Come on, let's get out of here.'

He pushed a way through the bushes and came out at a spot where there was a seat. 'Not here,' he said. 'It's too close.' Erica was still trembling. Frank stopped and held her close for a moment before releasing her. 'I think we need to find an empty house.'

Trying to speak lightly, Erica inclined her head and said, 'Do you know of one?'

Frank grinned. 'As a matter of fact, I do. A perfect one. Let's go.'

Chapter Sixteen

The house that Frank had spoken of belonged to a couple who had moved abroad.

'I have a key to the house,' he said. 'We could go there this evening.'

Erica shook her head. 'No, not to the house of someone you know.'

'I don't know them. They came into the shop and asked if I would have a key and look in now and then. Just to see that everything was all right.'

'I couldn't, Frank. They're trusting you.'

'I'm not going to steal anything.' He lowered his voice. 'I do know there's a lovely big settee. It's such an opportunity and I want to make love to you, Erica. Don't deny me. Please. I'm aching to love you.'

'I'm aching for you too.'

'Then say yes.'

'Can I think about it?'

He smiled. 'If you refuse I'll never forgive you.'

Erica knew when he took her into his arms and kissed her passionately that she would not deny him.

They walked along by the river, his arm around her waist. He said, 'I can't help wondering if it wouldn't be better to get married than being so far away from one another. It's a torment at times.'

Erica went rigid for a moment. 'I couldn't, Frank. I do have orders to complete. And things are in a bad way at the moment.'

She told him about Janet and Edward parting, but not the whole story.

'That's bad, isn't it?' he said.

'Janet is expecting a baby so we have to look after her too.'

'Good Lord, what is Edward thinking about? Do you think they might get together again?'

'They could,' she lied. 'So you see I'm under an obligation at the moment.'

'And we could make love while we have the chance.'

'Yes,' she whispered, and knew she would go to the house.

Frank took her to Bridget and left, saying they would close a little earlier that evening.

Bridget called, 'I'll have the dinner ready for half-past seven. Bring Bert with you.'

Erica was still trembling at the thought of what she had promised Frank. But then she thought, other couples must make love. Was she wrong to think otherwise? She

271

must be sure though, very sure that there was no chance of her becoming pregnant.

Frank and Bert arrived at Bridget's prompt half-past seven.

They were laughing. 'How's that for a prompt delivery?' Bert asked. 'He's plagued me the whole afternoon that I must be prompt. And here we are and no dinner on the table.'

'It will be by the time you've pulled your chairs up,' Bridget teased them.

And it was, with their help.

Erica always enjoyed the meals that Bridget made. But this time she was not conscious of having eaten anything. Was it because of the way her body was acting? She remembered once asking one of the older girls who had told her about sex how she would know when she wanted to make love and the girl said, 'When your body tells you, you daft thing.'

Well, her body was certainly telling her now.

It was as though Frank had his hand on the secret parts of her body that made her squirm. No, that was the wrong word, it would be better to say, made her nerves leap.

That was not even right. She must stop thinking about later when they would go into the couple's house.

She tried to concentrate on what the

men were talking about.

It was the shop, of course; both of them delighted that they had had a good day.

How much were they in debt? It must be an awful lot of money.

She suddenly wanted to laugh. Here she was, one minute thinking only of sex and the next wondering what debts Frank and Bert had.

Then she began to wonder what time they would be leaving.

How long did it take to make love? No one had ever told her that. Ten minutes, half an hour, an hour?

Frank said, 'Well, we better get these dishes washed then Erica and I are going for a long walk, and a talk about the future.'

Bridget laughed. 'Don't you dare touch a plate. I'll see to them. Off you go for your walk.'

Bert started to clear away and she told him to go and do what he did every Saturday night: go to the market then have a drink with the boys.

Frank held out her coat for her. Erica thrust her arms into it and when Frank closed it around her he whispered, 'Not long now.' Which set her heart thumping.

If only she knew what to expect.

She had heard girls say that they didn't really like it but if they didn't give in to their boyfriends they would be thrown over for someone else. So they had to pretend to like it. How could one like it if it hurt? If only she had listened a little more. But she had always found the subject embarrassing. She might have listened a little more closely if she had been older. But then she had only been about eleven.

It was the only time in her life when she had had a few girl friends. Her mother, however soon put a stop to that. 'They're scum,' she had said, 'They're rude and they swear. You'll leave people like that alone.'

Erica reflected now that if she had slipped out some times to meet these girls she would have learned a great deal more.

They had all married young, had several children and worked at a job, leaving their mother or an aunt to look after the children.

She knew of quite a lot of young mothers doing work at home and looking after their children.

No, she must forget all that. Frank would never marry her if she kept on with the trinket boxes. She was sure he would make a good father.

'You're very quiet, my love,' Frank said suddenly. He had left her for a few moments and now came in with a scarf. 'It's cold outside so wear this. Come, let's get going.'

They hurried, laughing towards the house which Frank had pointed out to her.

It was a large house, surrounded by a small park of trees. There were railings all around it. Frank unlocked the gate, locked it again after them then walked up a path to the front door. Then Frank unlocked the massive oak door, held out his hand and led her into the hall. She stood looking around her and felt her heart beating wildly.

This was luxury and all wrong for their purpose. There were statues of soldiers around the walls, wide shallow stairs that led up to landings that branched off.

Erica said in a whisper, 'It's too luxurious. I wouldn't enjoy making love here.'

Frank put a finger under her chin and tilted her face.

He was smiling. 'Would you rather make love in a summer house?'

She nodded, 'Yes, I would.'

'Then it can be done.'

He took her by the hand and led her out to the back garden. There was a lightness here too. Then Erica realised that the moon had come from behind a cluster of clouds.

Frank had a key for the summer house too. He unlocked the door and drew her inside. There was a strong smell of new wood.

The only furniture was a long settee covered with cretonne, two chairs and a small wooden table on which were some blankets. 'How's this?' Frank asked.

Erica smiled. 'It's made to order.'

He relieved her of her coat, put a folded blanket on the settee for a pillow and took off his own coat.

'There we are,' he said, 'now start undressing.'

She stared at him not sure she had heard right.

Frank had his collar and tie off and had started to take off his shirt.

There was something all wrong about this. She remembered being told that men would tear the clothes off the girls and Erica had thought it all exciting. She no longer felt any emotion.

'Erica, take your clothes off. I'm winning.'

'I don't want to take them off.'

Frank groaned. 'Don't say after all this that you don't want to make love.'

'I don't like the way you told me to take my clothes off.'

'Because I felt I couldn't wait another minute to make love to you.'

'You might have made love to dozens of girls but I've never made love before. It's—it's the first time.' There were tears in her voice.

'Oh, my love, forgive me. I'm sorry. I was too keen. Come along, I'll help you.'

'No, no, I can do it.'

She managed to get the buttons of her dress undone and let the dress slip to the floor. She was being a complete fool.

She took off her camisole then her petticoat but when she removed her vest she held it in front of her. Frank was already naked. He took the vest from her and let it fall to the floor. 'Don't be afraid, darling, I'll try not to hurt you.'

It was he who undid the tapes of her white knee-length knickers and got her to step out of them.

And it was then that emotions began sweeping her body.

He picked her up and put her on the settee and lay on top of her. Erica only wished she knew what happened next.

She tried to say, 'Tell me what to do,' but Frank whispered, 'Shush,' before claiming her mouth.

He then found the secret part of her body and when he entered her carefully she tensed at the pain, but it was a pain that made her experience an agonising pleasure, a pleasure that increased as he began to move. She gasped.

Frank whispered, 'I'm trying not to hurt you.'

'Go on, go on,' she urged.

Seconds later it was all over. She had lost the wonder of her seduction.

Frank apologised. 'I'm sorry, my darling, I couldn't wait any longer.' There was a trembling in his voice. 'Just give me a few minutes.' He rolled away from her, his head resting on her shoulder.

What had happened? Why had he rolled away from her. Was this then lovemaking?

His breathing became easier. 'You were throbbing with me,' he said softly. 'It'll be better the next time for you.'

So there was another time. How long did this go on?

She saw from the small window that the moon was sailing along in a clear sky.

Were they governed by the moon? She wanted to ask but found she was unable to.

It was only minutes later that he was fondling her body and excitement began to rise in her again. So it was not all over.

When he entered her this time his movements were more quick and the agonising sweet pain kept on increasing until she was calling out, 'Don't stop, don't stop!'

Myriads of lights began to burst in her

brain, then she knew it was all over. She knew now what ecstasy meant.

She felt an exhaustion she had never before experienced and they lay panting, then Frank suddenly exclaimed. 'Glory be, my darling! You were perfect. Absolutely perfect.'

She wanted to say something and was unable to. But she felt a great joy.

Erica soon found out that this night was not yet over.

They lay together in a semi-sleep until a clock somewhere began to chime. The tenth chime had Erica sitting up.

She shook Frank. 'Frank, it's ten o'clock. Bridget and Bert will wonder where we are.'

Although Frank did get up he made no move to hurry. 'I wish we had been staying all night.'

'Well, we're not. Come along. Get ready.'

She was trembling.

He locked the door behind them. 'I think we'll have to get married,' he smiled.

Erica, worried, said, 'We'll talk about that tomorrow.'

Instead of Bridget and Bert being worried about them they both seemed quite relaxed, both reclining in an armchair each and Bert with his feet up on a stool.

Frank said, in an easy way, 'Hello, Bert, you're home early this evening.'

'Early? It's nearly half-past ten.'

'Is it? We did a lot of talking and a lot of walking.'

There was a wicked, mischievous gleam in Bert's eyes. 'I thought you would.'

Bridget said, 'I'll make us all a cup of cocoa.'

Bert got up. 'You sit still. I'll make it.'

As he pottered about Bridget said, 'Well, Bert and I have had a lovely talk about the past. I quite enjoyed it.'

Frank said, 'So what time did Bert come in?'

Bridget answered, 'He hasn't been out.'

Both Erica and Frank were staring at him, knowing how Bert liked going out on a Saturday night.

Frank said, 'Don't your pals make you welcome now you've gone up in the world?'

'It's not that. My ex-fiancée's husband has joined the gang and I don't want any back-chat from him.'

'That's not like you, Bert.' Frank shook his head. 'You can always get the better of any one if you make your mind up.'

'I know, but I wasn't in the mood tonight.'

Frank left it at that.

280

Chapter Seventeen

When Erica was in bed that night all she could think about was Frank making love to her. It had been so different to what she had imagined.

What had she imagined? She had been unprepared for Frank's movements. This had brought the final glory. Just thinking about it sent small nerves tingling in her body. She would have to stop thinking about it. She would be back home on Monday and there would be no Frank to pleasure her.

Frank had suggested they get married and she had been the one to make excuses. *Should* she give in and arrange to get married?

No, that wouldn't work, not with Edward having left them.

There would come a time when she would have to leave, that is if she was to have a life of her own, and then the men would have to find someone else to do the work that she did. Erica, however, did not dwell on it. That was somewhere in the future.

She slept an uneasy sleep, eventually.

They had a leisurely breakfast with the men talking shop as usual, and with Bridget very interested in the subject.

She said once, 'I've heard it said that it takes three years before you'll make a profit.'

Frank laughed at this. 'We're making a profit now.'

Bert shook his heard. 'Not yet, old son. Bridget is right. We'll start making money in our third year. I reckoned it all up the night before last. Don't forget we are using borrowed money now.'

'I think we'll have to go over this.'

So books were brought out, the men studied them and Bridget raised her eyebrows.

She said to Erica in a low voice, 'I said the wrong thing.' Then raising her voice she added, 'I should be asking Frank where he's taking you for your last day.'

Frank heard and looked up. 'Oh, Erica, forgive me. I forget everything when we start talking shop, I can go into this next week. You get ready, it won't take me long to be ready. A quick shave...'

When Frank and Erica were outside, Frank said, 'You seem preoccupied this morning, my love. Is there anything on your mind?'

'You know what's on my mind—I couldn't stop thinking about last night.'

'Nor me. But I don't think we'll be able to go to the house today without being seen. It is Sunday, and people go for walks. I think perhaps we'd better wait until this evening.'

'Oh, no, why should we wait until this evening?'

Too late Erica realised that Frank had been teasing her again.

'Are you desperate, my love?' He was laughing as he said it.

'No, of course not,' she snapped. 'It was just that I was thinking how little time we have and that it will be months before we can be together again.'

'I know,' he spoke softly. 'I desperately want to make love to you, Erica.'

But there were still quite a number of people out for walks. 'I'm beginning to think it would be sensible to wait until evening,' Erica said.

'I think so too. We'll walk by the river.'

It was a beautiful morning and Erica was glad they had decided to walk. She felt they had achieved something. There had to be something more in their lives than making love. And there was still the evening.

During the afternoon Frank again talked about the business but she was pleased that he had discussed so many sides of it. She would now understand if he wanted to talk to her in his letters about a certain aspect. She would be involved. He described materials, the most expensive ones and why they were the most expensive. She learned that a certain material would never crease. And that was all to do with the weaving. Frank would have liked her to have gone to the mills to see them made but there was not the time, she had to go home tomorrow.

There were moments when she would wonder if the evening would ever come and was disappointed to find that she had no feeling of excitement as she had had the night before. Perhaps they needed to be in the summer house before this would happen.

It was surprising how many people were still in the area that evening. Frank and Erica strolled backwards and forwards past the house then, as they reached the gates for about the fifth or sixth time Frank said suddenly, 'We'll get in now.'

He had the gates opened in seconds, had them locked then they stood behind some bushes, Erica's heart beating madly.

In the next few seconds they were hurrying along the path that led to the summer house and it was then that Erica began to feel the waves of excitement.

This time Erica needed no help to get prepared for their lovemaking. She began to undress and so did Frank.

He swept her up in his arms and icy little shivers ran up and down her spine. He put her on the settee. This time, however there was no love play and it was all over in seconds.

Frank said, 'I'm sorry, my darling, I couldn't wait. It will be all right for you the next time.'

It was, and for the following time too, then excitement for Erica petered out. They lay, Frank's arm around her, with Frank wanting to know what he was going to do without her.

She said in a low voice, 'Don't you dare bring anyone else here when I'm gone.'

He laughed softly, 'I wouldn't dare, they would want luxury.'

'Oh, they would, would they?' Erica drew away from him. 'I suppose you mean by that it would be the monied people you would want to be making love to.'

'Of course.'

Erica knew that Frank was just teasing her, but she felt a little angry. Had he made love to anyone else? That woman who had come into the shop and put her hand on Frank's in a possessive sort of way?

She drew away from him.

285

Frank protested. 'Erica, what's wrong? I was teasing.'

'I know, but what I don't know is how many women you could have. You're an attractive man.'

'Thank you very much, but I don't want other women. You are the one I want.' He got off the bed and started to dress. 'I've wanted girls since I was sixteen. I could have had them, but I waited until the right person came along and that was you. But if you can't trust me then it's over.' There was anger in his voice.

'I'm sorry, Frank. It was just that I love you so much.'

'You don't love me. You never have, otherwise you would not be accusing me of wanting a wealthy woman. You had better get dressed and we can get out of here. To me it was a place for love. To you, it was nothing.'

Erica got off the bed and started to get dressed. She felt suddenly dried up inside. She had never thought of him in this mood. It would never have worked.

He put the settee as it had been before then after putting on his coat he walked to the door.

'Are you ready?'

'Yes, I'm ready. And I'm glad I've found out what type of man you are.'

'Oh, and what sort of man am I?'

286

'Petty, unforgiving. I'm glad I found out now before we had gone any further.'

'Petty, you say. Do you think I'm petty because I try to protect myself from you, who thinks I'll go with other women, wealthy women when you've gone home.'

'I just thought—'

'You didn't think very far.' He opened the door. She walked past him into the dark night. The moon was behind a cloud. Why had she not realised before what type of man he was.

'Yes,' he said, coming up to her, 'you are the petty one. I expected you to trust me, but you immediately accused me of wanting other women, rich women. That hurt me.'

They walked in silence through the garden then Frank paused while he looked up and down the road to see if anyone was coming. Everywhere was quiet. He unlocked the gate and locked it after they were in the street.

Erica walked a little ahead of him and he made no move to catch her up. Was this then the end? She had given herself freely to him, expecting the time to come when they would be married. With a sudden stab she realised she could be pregnant.

She had asked him every time they had made love if he had used something to prevent her becoming pregnant. All but the last time.

Should she ask him? She had a right to know. No, she wouldn't lower herself. The pain of his rejection of her was unbearable. She would never in a million years have thought it would end like this. What would her family have to say about it? But then, of course, she couldn't tell them the reason.

Oh, God, what could she say? Tell them that he had found someone else. No. That wouldn't do. She could say they had both found that they didn't love one another enough to marry.

But what if she was pregnant? She just had to know.

She plucked up courage and let him catch her up then asked him if had used something the last time they made love.

There was a was a moment's silence then he said, in a cold voice, 'No, I didn't, but if you were pregnant I would marry you.'

'I wouldn't marry you now if you were the last man on earth.' Her tone was scathing.

'We must think of the child.'

'There would be no child. I would have an abortion.'

'It's wrong to destroy the child.'

'No more wrong than having parents that hate one another.'

'Erica, I don't hate you. It's just that—'

'You've made it very plain that you want nothing more to do with me.'

'No, you've got it all wrong. I wanted you to see how you were treating me. I don't want wealthy women. I wanted you. But I knew you would never believe me.'

There was a pause, then Frank said, 'Look, there's a seat further along. Let's discuss it, shall we?'

They sat down and were silent for a few moments then Frank said hesitantly, 'I had been waiting for years for the right girl to come along. Then I met you and fell in love with you at once. It didn't seem wrong to me that I should want to make love to you, knowing that eventually we would be married. But then I behaved badly when you suggested that I might make love to wealthy women.'

'I was at fault for saying what I did.'

'Can we make it up again, Erica? I do still love you and you are the only girl I shall ever want.'

'And you are the only man I shall ever want, Frank.'

He held her close and there was no longing for him to make love to her. Erica was only sorry that they could not have stayed in the summer house for longer.

The one thing that worried her later was the fact that she could be pregnant.

It would be two weeks before she would know. Well, if she was, she would tackle it if it had to be.

Mrs Tyson arrived early to take Erica to Newcastle on the Monday morning and she realised what a kind person she was to do such a thing. She wanted time while she was travelling to think about the future.

As it happened she had pleasant companions but she had plenty of time for thinking. And in that time she knew it would be difficult, if she was pregnant, to leave home and marry Frank.

The family could buy trinket boxes and tobacco boxes but she knew they would not be like her own work. And she would be letting the family down.

Oh, why did life have to be so difficult?

All the family were there at the station, including Janet, and Erica had such a warm welcome that she felt like crying.

They all, of course, wanted to know how Frank was doing with his shop and she had plenty to tell them. But all the time there was this nagging at her. What if she was pregnant?

When she was in bed that night she made up her mind that if she was, she would have an abortion. She was not yet ready for marriage.

Frank had stressed on her that she must

write to him every day and was glad when she was able to say that she had not felt sick, or different in any way.

But on the day when her period was due nothing happened and it was then she felt sick.

How could she possibly kill Frank's baby? Oh, God. That this should happen to her now. She felt ill all day and at last Janet asked her what was wrong.

Erica told her and added that she was not yet ready for marriage.

Janet sat down and talked to her. Told her it was wrong to take a baby's life. Who was she to say it should be killed? But she gave her a hug and told her that the holiday could have made her period a little late.

And this turned out to be the answer. The next day her period started and Erica cried so much that Janet explained to the others that she was having a lot of pain.

Erica kept telling Janet that she felt she had killed the baby and Janet told her it was all nonsense. It was simply that her period was late.

By the next day Erica had accepted this. 'Never again,' Erica said, but knew if she could only see Frank again she would take all the love he could give her. And made up her mind then that her brothers would have to start looking around for someone to make her trinket boxes and tobacco boxes.

She had become quite friendly with Alexander Gilmorton and told him how she felt about Frank. 'I want to be married to Frank,' she said. 'My life is empty without him.'

'Don't rush into anything,' he answered gently. 'Take your time. You have to realise that he is struggling to get a business on it's feet.'

'Yes, I know but we're very much in love and hate being apart.'

'You do as you want, of course, but give your brothers a chance to get the right firm to make the boxes. The ones you make of course are unique. You really put some beautiful work in them.'

'The girls are very good too.'

'Yes, but your work is exceptional. You are an artist. Perhaps if you are married you can take up artistry.'

'I—well, I don't think that Frank would want me to work at home.'

'But that would be wrong to drop a gift like that. Not many people have it.'

'No, I suppose not.'

Erica began to think that Frank was wrong. Why should she give up this precious work? She was good. Why should she waste such talent. It was God given. She began to change her mind. She had not yet said anything to him. He would be at the shop all day and she would be tied to the house doing nothing. No, it was wrong.

When Erica told Janet what Alexander had said, Janet said, 'Alexander has nothing to do with your lives. You and Frank should decide what you want to do.'

'I know, but at the same time he's right. I don't want to lose what talent I have. Frank wants me to sit at home all day, waiting for him to come home. I would go mad with nothing to do.'

'You should have thought of that.'

'I know, but it was not until Alexander put it to me that it hit me. I must write to Frank, and tell him I would like to do some small paintings.'

His reply was short. He wanted a wife not an artist.

Erica was furious and wrote an equally short letter back.

She had agreed to give up making trinket boxes but she wanted something to do at home.

Frank's reply to this was, *'Other wives look after their husbands and their homes and wait for babies to be born.'*

Erica was so incensed at this attitude that she wrote, *'I'm not your slave. I no longer wish to marry you.'*

And with this written she had a

wonderful feeling of freedom.

Whether this would last she had no idea. What she was sure of was that she no longer wanted to be married. She had worked since she was a child and wanted to go on working.

When she told Janet what had happened Janet was all for it. 'I don't think you were ever in love with Frank. If you had been you would have given in to him at once. You would have been longing to be with him all the time, whereas you were worried that you would have to stop making trinket boxes and were unable to even be allowed to paint pictures. I know it's easy to talk but I do feel that in time you will meet the right man.'

'And I don't think I will. I think I'll end up being a spinster.' There was a dryness in Erica's throat. Could she bear it not having children and a home and a husband? She needed to love and be loved.

Then she decided she would give her love to Janet's baby. Yet knew at the same time that this would not be the same as having one's own family.

When she told John and Charles they were both shocked. She must think it over carefully.

She told them she had and would not change her mind.

It was three days before she heard from Frank.

This was a longer letter and he showed no remorse that they would not be getting married:

'I don't see how you regard me as behaving like a slave driver. A man must be master of his household. You had already agreed to give up your work when we got married, and then you suddenly change your mind.

All I wanted was for you to be a warm and loving wife and I was well satisfied when we were together for those few days when you came to be with me.

What made you change your mind? Have you found another man you want to be with? I still love you and I always will. But...I must be master and could never allow you to run the house. That would be wrong.'

Erica lowered the letter. Frank must be the master, he said. Why could he not see her point? She could be at home for a year before she even became pregnant. Was she to sit at home twiddling her thumbs and not make anything at all? No, it would never have worked. She had no regrets.

The letter she penned in return explained there was no other man in her life, it was

just that she could not be idle. She thought
he would understand this. She had a talent
that she couldn't bear to lose. Which she
would if she married him.

She was sorry that it had ended in
this way but she wished him well in the
business.

There was no reply to this letter from
Frank, but two letters came for her, one
from Bridget and one from Bert.

She read the one from Bert first. He said
how upset he had been to hear from Frank
that there would be no marriage between
them:

'He truly loves you, Erica, but he has
a stubbornness in him that won't make
him budge. I'm so terribly sorry and so
is Bridget. She is heartbroken, having
thought of you both as a son and
daughter.

I know exactly how you feel and
understand that Frank should allow you
to carry on with your work until children
come along. But Frank is Frank and
he won't change. Bridget and I are so
sorry and do hope that you both can get
together again.

With love from Bert.'

Erica was tearful after she had read
Bert's letter and it was some time before

she could read the one from Bridget.
Bridget wrote:

'My darling Erica, how upset Bert and I were when Frank told us that you would not be getting married. We could hardly believe it. I had expected the marriage to take place quite soon. The trouble with Frank is that he's so determined to have his own way. I told him so, but it didn't make him change his mind.

You are a very talented young lady and if only Frank had been sensible you could have done some lovely pictures while he was working at the shop. But no, he wouldn't have it. He wanted things his way. Yet I know he's still in love with you.

Oh, my darling girl, I know you are right not to give in to him. He can't have all his own way. I do hope that he might come round to your way of thinking and that I shall be still hearing of the wedding to come. Do let me know if he changes his mind. With much love to you, Bridget.'

Erica wept some more, knowing that at least two people knew she was doing the right thing.

Once she was over the tears she no longer worried. Her talent was one of

God's gifts. She would be able to help her family. That was why it had been given to her.

Although John and Charles had been worried about her at first they began to find the benefit.

John did have a long talk with her one evening, saying she was not to think of them, they could find people who would do the work that she did. 'I know that your work is exceptional Erica, but if you are still in love with Frank and want to marry him, then do so.'

She shook her head. 'No, that's all over. There might come a time when I don't want to do any more work, but while I'm in this mood I'll do it. Think no more about it.' She paused a moment then added, 'I thought you agreed with Frank?'

John shook his head. 'Not any more. I thought about it a lot, and can see the selfishness in his attitude. But when you want to give up working on trinket boxes and the tobacco boxes tell us at once, Erica. You deserve a rest.'

'Yes, I will, Uncle John. I promise.'

Erica went on working at home in the morning and went to the shop in the afternoon. John and Charles took turns helping her in the mornings, which meant that Alexander Gilmorton was always there all day with either John or Charles.

He was an excellent salesman and was always cheerful. Erica kept to her own section but quite often she needed some help and it was always Alexander who came to the rescue.

He would spend time with a customer pointing out the beauty of a painting on a box and he never failed to sell it.

The girls came to the house every morning with their work and they seemed to be improving every day.

They always stayed for a chat and Erica always enjoyed hearing about their men friends.

'They're full of fun,' Angie said one morning. 'There are times when we have to stifle our laughter in case Mama should think they were not serious enough.'

Margaret said, 'They all think it's time we should be making plans to get married but we want to keep on making the boxes. It gives us money of our own.'

Erica felt a moment of panic. 'I thought that the men folk had said that they would allow you to go on making them when you were married?'

'Yes, they did, but it's not what they say. It's Mama and Papa who says what happens. If they want grandchildren, well that's it. The orders will be given to our husbands and there will be no more making trinket boxes.'

'Oh, dear. Just when you are all doing so well.'

'I'm sure you'll be able to find someone else to do them.'

Erica was not so sure. The trouble was that trade was increasing every day...

Chapter Eighteen

Then another thing cropped up to put that matter out of her mind for the time being.

John arrived home one morning and asked her if she would like to own a bigger shop. She could see he was excited.

'Where?' she asked.

'Further up the road. Do you know that shop that sells a lot of old rubbish? Well, the owner has died and the sons want to sell it. We have first choice. It's double-fronted. You can have one side and we can have the other. What do you say, Erica?'

'It must need an awful lot doing to it. I noticed that one of the floor boards were missing. What else needs doing to it?'

'Whatever needs doing can be repaired. It's cheap. The sons have a big business in

Chicago. They want to get back to it.'

'That old man had no family here. One of the customers told me a while ago. She said that at times he didn't know what he was doing.'

'Well, the poor soul's dead now and Charles and I would like to have the shop. Get your coat and come and see it. The sons want to be rid of it and it's now or never.'

They looked into their shop on the way and Charles and Alexander were also excited. Charles said, 'You must say yes, Erica. Don't let us down.'

She had a struggle to get her breath. 'We'll go now.'

And off they went at a quick pace up the High Street.

When they arrived it was worse than she had imagined. She was introduced to the two sons who seemed to be very respectable. The elder one said, 'Father wanted to hang on to the shop. He left everything to us. Our solicitor will handle everything. We could go now and see him if you like.'

Everything was not settled that day but nearly a week later they had bought the shop with all the rubbish and also there were many boxes upstairs in three rooms.

'Heavens knows what's in them,' Charles said, 'but they're sure to be rubbish. The sooner we get rid of them, the sooner we can get the repairs done.'

Erica, however, had looked inside one and after having found a plate, which turned out to be Dresden porcelain was quite determined to look into every box.

'This is ridiculous,' said Charles. 'It's holding up the work on the shop. It's just one piece.'

'But there could be a whole dinner set. And just think what that would be worth. I don't care how long it takes but I'm going to examine every piece. Janet will help me. She knows a little about antiques. Her grandmother had quite a few.'

When Charles started to argue John said, 'Let them get on with it. They won't be happy until they've gone through every piece. It won't take all that long.' Then he added, 'But I hope you'll get rid of the stuff downstairs first. That at least will be a start.'

There was nothing of value in the boxes downstairs. The pieces were also all dirty too. Erica and Janet washed them all and charged coppers for each one. There were some odd cups and saucers, some ashtrays, nothing matched. But they were all soon sold.

Erica was surprised to find when she added it up that there was nearly five pounds.

'Not bad,' she said to Janet, 'for just a little bit of trouble.'

They started emptying one of the boxes upstairs. Each piece was wrapped in old newspapers and they were so dirty Erica guessed they had been there for years.

The first pieces they had brought out after the Dresden had been of no value but then Erica found an ornament which had her saying to Janet, 'Oh, look, Janet, isn't this lovely? I feel it should be worth a few shillings, perhaps more. What do you think?'

'I would say we might get as much as a pound for that. It is lovely.' It was a tall jug, covered in raised flowers and with a gilt handle and rim.

They really started in earnest after that and from the one box came a beautiful inkwell stand, a bowl with a scene of London painted on it, an exquisite teapot which Janet was sure would fetch five pounds, two silver candlesticks, that although they were tarnished Erica found out they sparkled with some rubbing.

By this time she was convinced they should be seen by an antique dealer. She decided she would suggest asking Mr Taylor from whom they had bought the first shop.

John and Charles understood their enthusiasm but did suggest seeing first what was in some of the other boxes.

They had as many worthwhile pieces in three more boxes and when Alexander Gilmorton saw what had been produced was as excited as the girls. He named two paintings that he said he was sure were worth twenty pounds each at least, and John wrote to Mr Taylor and asked him if he could come to the new shop and have a look.

He came a few evenings later with his sons, after their shops had closed, and all three men were more than interested.

They made a note of what they took away that evening and offered to come again the next evening. Erica and Janet worked like Trojans and in the evenings the five men worked too.

That evening they had a fine pair of porcelain vases, two inkstands with the glass beautifully carved and painted, four Wedgwood tureens, all on a fixed stand, two clocks, one gilt and brass with an enamelled timepiece in the form of a ship's wheel and the other a brass elephant clock, the elephant royal blue and gilt.

Erica and Janet had them arrayed for the Taylors' inspection and they all drew a quick breath that evening when they saw them.

'My goodness,' Mr Taylor said. 'They're worth quite a sum. Why did the old man hoard all of these? He could have been selling them.'

'He probably didn't know he had them, or, he just felt like hoarding them,' John said. 'Who can tell?'

They came every evening and when the list was made it seemed to Erica to be quite a long one.

After the sums had been totted up Mr Taylor beamed at them. 'Well, I think you'll be pleased to know that it adds up to eight hundred and fifty pounds. I have, of course to allow a profit for our own business.'

'Eight hundred and fifty pounds.' Erica whispered the amount then she said it aloud and they were all laughing.

'Amazing!' she said. 'And to think John and Charles wanted to throw them all out.'

John smiled. 'I think this calls for a celebration. But not here, we'll go home.'

They had champagne and Erica thought it was one of the most rewarding evenings she could ever remember.

They talked, they laughed, they sang.

The next morning she felt terrible for a time but she soon recovered and was full of joy.

This, of course, set Erica thinking. The girls had kept doing the trinket and tobacco boxes but now she had an urge to collect antiques.

But when she mentioned this to John and Charles they were not agreeable. John said, 'The shop is essentially a tobacconists and Charles and I want to keep it that way. You must also remember that it was not until the Taylors moved to the West End that they began making money. They do deal with more expensive pieces, but don't think because we've had this fantastic luck that this sort of thing will be happening every day.'

'No, I know it won't. I did think, however, that it was worth trying.'

Charles said, 'Get a shop of your own, Erica, but don't bring us into it. We are not money mad.'

'Oh, aren't you? I notice that you accepted your share of the money that we got from the goods and you wouldn't have had that if I hadn't pressed to open every box.'

'You can have it back if you want to.'

'I don't want it! I simply made a suggestion and you call me money mad.'

She was near to tears and John said quietly, 'Just let's calm down. Think this over, Erica. Think it over carefully. It's up to you to do what you want to, but don't forget that you broke up a prospective marriage because you wanted to go on making trinket and tobacco boxes.'

'That had nothing to do with any of you.'

'All right I won't say any more.'

'No, I didn't mean that. I tried to plan my life to fit in with the family.'

'You shouldn't have done, Erica.'

'Can't you see I had to? We each had a share of Mother's money. She would expect us to share it. I felt I couldn't let you down.'

She burst into tears and John took her into his arms and talked soothingly to her. 'Although we all had a share of the money we were all individuals, my love. We each must do what we want to do.'

'We all helped Janet,' she sobbed on, 'and I—I liked it that way. I—don't want to be on my own...'

'No, of course not. Dry your eyes and we can have a cup of tea and a sensible talk.'

John took out his handkerchief and started to dry her eyes.

'There, there. Is that better?'

She nodded and found herself thinking how it was always John who did this sort of thing. She had wanted more money. Wasn't it natural? Now she was not sure what she wanted.

Charles made the tea and while they drank it John talked. 'I can understand you wanting to make more money, Erica, but Charles and I don't want to change our lives. From being children we've made pipes. We improved them and we were glad when you made the trinket and tobacco boxes. We were still in our own line, but now you want to start another line altogether and neither of us want that. Do you understand how we feel?'

'Yes, I do. I just thought, well, it would be good to try something else.'

Charles said, 'We won't stop you, Erica. But remember this. Edward wanted to change things and it all went wrong.'

'But that was different. He fell in love with someone else. I'm not in love with anybody at the moment. I don't think I ever want to marry.'

'You will in time,' John said. 'I think at the moment you don't quite know what you want to do.' He gave a brief smile. 'Do any of us know?'

The talk got lighter and Erica began to feel she had been through a dark tunnel and was coming out of it.

She did say, 'When are you two going to get married?'

Charles smiled. 'I do have a young lady in mind. One of these days I might pluck up courage and ask her out.'

'And what about you, Uncle John?'

He tilted his head. 'And I too have someone in mind. We'll both give you a surprise one of these days and invite you to our weddings.'

'Oh, not too suddenly,' she said and tried to force a smile. Erica hated the thought of her Uncle John marrying again.

'We'll let you know in good time.'

John took Erica's hands in his. 'Do you feel better?'

'Yes, a great deal better. At the moment I'll stick to my trinket and tobacco boxes.'

'Good.'

Chapter Nineteen

Every day before she went to the shop she went to the new shop to see how the workmen were getting on. The floor had been repaired and the men were stripping the walls. John had asked her if she wanted the walls painted or hung with wallpaper.

She said she thought that wallpaper would be more classy and she and John and Charles decided on a pale gold wallpaper with a narrow stripe of a deeper gold. They also decided that skirting boards and the front door should be a warm brown.

The men were busy papering when she called and she stayed only a few minutes then left.

When she reached the old shop the men were all laughing.

'What's so amusing?' she asked.

'It was Alexander telling us a joke,' Charles said. 'Not suitable for a lady though.'

She took off her coat and hat and Alexander took them from her and hung them up. He said, 'Did you like the paper now it's on the walls?'

'Yes, I did.'

'It won't be long before we'll be in the new shop. I'm looking forward to it.'

'So am I,' Erica said.

There were more women coming into the shop these days and Erica was sure that Alexander was the draw. He was the same to every woman but some of them acted coyly. They supposedly came in for tobacco for their husbands but Erica was sure that husbands liked buying their own.

Odd times when Alexander was helping Erica sell a trinket box or a tobacco box they would come over and admire them, but to Erica's surprise Alexander would end up selling one of the boxes. One time he grinned. 'That lady did not really want a trinket box.'

Erica laughed. 'You are the salesman here.'

The next day Erica had the morning

310

off, and the three Lewis girls came to show their wares. 'The new shop should be finished in another week,' Erica said. 'It was in such a mess, with so much rubbish to be cleared out that was why I had to let you all get on with your work and you've made a very good job of them all. And how are your future husbands?'

There was a short silence then Angie said, 'Mama and Papa are wanting to arrange for us to be married by the end of January.'

Erica's stomach gave a quiver. 'So soon? And after that there'll be no more work from you.'

Margaret spoke up. 'The men say there will be. As we told you before they all say they'll stand up for us and demand that we be allowed to go on doing our work.'

'But you know Mama and Papa,' Angie replied.

Erica said, 'Do you know what, I still think that your men will win the first round. They are all strong men with ideas of their own.'

When the Lewis girls had gone home, Erica went to sit with Janet, who was doing some sewing in the kitchen. 'It'll be good to move into the new shop next week,' she remarked to Janet.

'Yes, it should be heaven for all of us. So much more room. I was just thinking last night that we might be able to do without this house. There are an awful lot of rooms above the new shop. It's three-storeyed.'

'Yes, I know. But the third-storey rooms are attics.'

'Have you seen them since they've papered and painted? I wouldn't mind one as a bed-sitter.'

'Too many stairs, Janet, with a baby on the way.'

'I suppose so. It's just that they're so light and they each have a fireplace.'

'I hadn't noticed that. I was in and out of them when all the boxes were in. Then they seemed gloomy.'

'Well, they're not now. Take another look at them. One of them, the largest, is nearly all windows. They overlook the city.'

'You'll have to stop or I'll be wanting to run down now.'

Janet laughed. 'Wait until tomorrow.'

Erica liked the idea of having a bedsitter of her own. There was a sitting-room and another big room they called the lounge. Neither the sitting-room or the lounge had been furnished yet. Erica felt she could hardly wait for the following day.

She went early to the new shop. The workmen had not yet arrived. Erica went from room to room and became more intrigued with every one.

She knew before she left that she would definitely have the largest attic room, and had even furnished it in her mind's eye.

While she was having breakfast with John she told him where she had been and the room she wanted and he said quietly, 'I'm glad you are staying, my love. I thought you were thinking of leaving. We would have missed you terribly.'

She reached out a hand and laid it over his. 'I was a bit of a fool. I wanted the sky.'

She then withdrew her hand and told him about the Lewis girls and their marriage plans. 'Don't worry if they're not allowed to work anymore, I can get people if you need them from Handlebury's. They're closing down next month. They're not doing the trade. They'll be pleased to be able to get work for some of their women. Mind you, they're not up to your standard. They'll need some training.'

'Splendid,' she replied.

The day they moved into the new shop Erica had a feeling of having lived there all her life. They all agreed to her having a bed-sitter and John talked about getting furniture for it as soon as possible.

Erica thought it strange. She had not really felt very much different when they had moved into the small shop, but felt a very big difference when she moved into this shop.

She had gained a new confidence.

The next day they were open and they were all surprised at the custom they had. Quite a lot of new customers.

Again there were a number of women who bought trinket boxes and tobacco boxes.

Everyone who came in praised the shop, said how sizable it was, and now Erica could hardly wait to have her bed-sitter furnished and to move in.

Chapter Twenty

Erica had her bed-sitter furnished more quickly than she expected. John and Charles told her that furniture from a mansion was going to be auctioned that very day and, they decided they would keep the shop closed and John would go with Erica and see what they could pick up.

As soon as Erica went into the mansion she saw what she wanted. She called it the Blue Bedroom. The carpet was deep-piled, there were blue velvet curtains, a chintz cover on a neat brass bed, a cupboard and two chairs.

John told her they might be costly and to this Erica said recklessly that she was prepared to bid high. She had the money.

She got them all for less money than she had expected and was absolutely delighted.

They also got furniture for the lounge. In this case the carpet was a deep rust and so were the velvet curtains. The three piece suite was in brown velvet and John also bid for chairs, three small tables and several pictures.

In another room Erica got a pale beige three piece suite in velvet and a drop leaf table.

There were a lot more things that Erica would have liked to buy but John suggested they should be satisfied with their bargains.

They hurried back home, with Erica full of excitement and Charles and Alexander congratulated them. 'You did well,' Charles said and Alexander teased Erica and asked her if she was going to throw a party when the room was furnished.

'Most likely,' she said. 'I won't have my own shop but I will have my very own living-room. I think it's wonderful.'

The furniture came the following day and men laid carpets, and hung curtains. The rest of the things were put into place and Erica felt she had never been so happy.

Two days later she was in the depths of despondency. She had had a letter from Bridget telling her that Frank had become engaged to a wealthy young lady.

'I'm so terribly sorry, Erica,' she had written, 'I had always thought you would get together again and get married. I feel heartbroken, you were so right for one another. Bert is upset too. He'll be writing to you. We've both tried to tell Frank he's doing the wrong thing but he won't even listen. He's said it has nothing to do with us. You know how stubborn he is.

'He's supposed to be getting married in two months time but whether he'll change his mind before then we don't know.

'Oh, my darling girl both Bert and I both love you and we are both hoping that Frank will change his mind.

With much love to you, Bridget.'

Erica sat a long time with the letter in her hand, wondering if Frank was marrying wealth because he needed money for his business. If so, he was a fool. That would not bring him any happiness.

But then, hadn't she behaved in the same way? She wanted a business on her own. She was not willing to give up making her trinket and tobacco boxes. What she wanted was a shop of her own. She was now paying a price for being persistent.

Deep down she knew she had been hoping that Frank would change his mind.

Well, he had, but in the wrong way. Frank would no doubt pay a price if he wanted money for his business.

It was impossible to snap out of her misery that day and she had not only told John and Charles about the letter from Bridget but told Alexander too.

John and Charles were of the opinion that she was well rid of Frank, but Alexander was sympathetic towards her.

He said, 'How do we know when we are right? From being a child I wanted to be born of poor parents.'

Erica stared. 'Why, in heavens name?'

'Because it seemed to me that they could do as they wanted. I was always ordered to do something.'

'We were never allowed to do as we wanted. We were told by our mother what we had to do and we did it.'

'But you were working. I had nothing to do. When I was older I had a tutor. I hated him. But my parents knew what was right for me.'

'I don't think you've have been badly done to.'

'I was. I was an only child. Everything

was arranged for me. My parents are furious that I came to work with you all. But I stuck out for it. I was working. It was wonderful. They did insist that I live at home and I agreed.'

'I think you are very lucky, Alexander.'

'You don't know the half of it. I'm expected to marry a girl they chose for me.'

'Tell them that you will choose the girl you want to marry.'

'I can't. It's not allowed. It's the class I was born into. Don't you see how tied I am?'

'No, I don't. But then that's probably because I was born poor.'

'But look how far you've come. You have freedom, you have money. You can do as you wish.'

Erica wanted to say that he could have done the same but realised how tied he was with convention. It must have been drummed into him since he was a young child that he had to do this and had to do that. But when she came to think about it, how much better off was she?

She would probably end up being a spinster, with no man to love her.

Erica was unhappy for a while then she came to her senses. She knew now she would have loved to be married, had a husband and home and children, but she had spoiled all that. It was her own fault. Her work had seemed the most important thing in her life.

Now, looking back, she guessed that Frank had been stubborn because he had wanted wealth for his shop. Well, he was welcome to it.

She would go on with her boxes. Until she was sick to death of making them. Then what?

No, she would go no further than that.

There were the weddings of the three Lewis girls to look forward to. There was the new shop with so many new customers and the birth of Janet's baby, plus the pleasure of her lovely bed-sitter. That really was a special treat to her.

John came with three women who were looking for work when their factory had closed down. None of them were young, but Erica explained what she was looking for and they were all very interested and said they would like to try and paint the trinket boxes.

They were quite good but needed some practise. Erica said she would pay them while they were practising. The three of them thought it was very kind of her. They were all widows with children.

There was a slow improvement but at last Erica felt she would take them on. They were grateful and she was sure they must have worked long hours to do what they had done.

During the next few days more women came looking for work. They were not young either. Their clothes were darned but they were clean. Erica decided to take them on too.

They were slower than the others but they began to improve and one of this lot proved to be excellent.

Life became interesting again.

They were selling more trinket and tobacco boxes and could do with all she was getting from the Lewis girls and from the new women she had taken on.

Janet would often come up and sit with Erica in an evening and most of her talk was about the baby. She never mentioned Edward but Erica often thought he was on her mind.

They were both knitting for the baby and Erica wished on occasions that it was time for the baby to be born. But it was not due for a good few months yet.

They decided that this year they would have a proper Christmas and they had a Christmas tree with tinsel and baubles on it. They also had a turkey and a Christmas pudding.

Several people called, including the Todd

family. John poured drinks for them and they all thoroughly enjoyed it.

The Lewis girls called too and they whispered to Erica that the end of January was to be their wedding day.

The end of January was supposed to be Frank's wedding day too but so far there had been no word from Bridget.

Then a Christmas card came from her and one from Bert.

Both said that the marriage was not taking place. They would write in the New Year.

Erica's heart skipped a beat. So what had happened? Had Frank changed his mind or had his fiancée changed hers?

When would she know? She kept the news to herself.

It was on Boxing Day that Charles brought his lady friend to meet them all. She was small with dark hair and terribly shy. Her name was Nadine.

Impulsively Erica said, 'Oh, what a beautiful name.'

She smiled. 'It was my grandmother's name.'

'Do take your coat off and sit down.'

Janet came in and she and Nadine were introduced and soon they were all talking.

Nadine stayed for tea and lost some of her shyness.

They left after tea so that Charles could go and meet Nadine's family.

After they had gone Erica turned to her Uncle John and asked why his young lady was not here.

He grinned. 'Because they've all gone to relatives for the Christmas season.'

'And will we meet her after the Christmas season?'

'I'll think about it.'

Erica picked up a cushion and threw it at him. 'I don't believe that you have a young lady.'

'Oh, you'll meet her, all in good time.'

Erica had a lot to think about. She wondered if Frank had drawn out of his wedding or if it was the bride-to-be.

Strangely enough it didn't mean anything to her. She wouldn't want him now, not even if he begged her to marry him and told her that it didn't matter about the boxes.

Why was this? She obviously had not loved him as she had thought. How did one know true love?

Three days later she knew.

John had come up to her room and was sitting reading a book. She was knitting. She put down the knitting and sat watching him. What a handsome man he was. So very good-looking.

Then suddenly it came to her. She was in love with him, always had been. She wanted him, wanted to be his wife, live with him have his children.

Oh, God, how impossible it was. She would have been willing to give up making boxes...but there was no way, not even if he loved her. It was considered a crime to marry one's uncle.

And he had a lady friend. He had promised to bring her to meet them.

He sat pulling at a strand of hair. Then he closed the book and looked up. 'Well, that's all for tonight. Are you tired of knitting?'

'No, yes. I mean I've done enough for this evening.'

He got up and coming to her ruffled her hair. 'I think you are ready for bed. I think I'll have an early night too. Charles is out with Nadine.'

She wanted him to stay but what could she say? She had to say something to keep him.

'Do you think that Charles will marry Nadine?'

John sat down again. 'Yes, there's no doubt about that. He was talking about it the other night, said he didn't want to wait.'

'And is—Nadine willing for an early marriage?'

John smiled. 'Oh, definitely. Have you seen the way she looks at him at times?

323

She adores him. Lucky man.'

'And will...you have an early marriage?'

'Now that I don't know.'

'What's her surname?'

'You'll know when I introduce her.'

'Why make such a secret of it?'

'Because I don't know whether she's in love with me or not. I'm going to bed. See you in the morning.' He ruffled her hair again. 'Don't stay up too late.'

She heard the door close quietly behind her.

How could she go on living in the same house?

Erica knew then the real pain of loving, knowing that nothing could ever come of it.

How was it that she had not realised this? All these years.

But then she had known she had loved him, but not in this way. She had thought of herself as his niece. He had always helped her over troubles, had sorted things out for her.

He had often sat with her for a time in the evening, since she had had the bed sitter. Sometimes Janet would be there and they would talk about business, sometimes if Janet was out visiting friends John would come in and pick up a book, never reading for very long. She had been conscious that he missed Charles.

But never for a moment until this evening had she ever thought of him as a husband.

It was a fiasco. She should leave the house. No, that was impossible. She wanted to be near him. Oh, why had this to happen?

She must pull herself together. Be sensible. She would have to be.

The days went by and Erica steeled herself to talk to John in a natural way. Perhaps she would get used to it in time. Other people had had tragedies in their lives. Then came the day when the girls were due to be married.

On the morning of the weddings Erica sat at the back of the church. It was a packed church. The organ was playing and suddenly Erica was aware that the brides had arrived. They were all heavily veiled. She saw Mrs Lewis smiling and when the organ began to play the Wedding March everyone stood up. Each bride had a child holding the trains.

It was the organ playing that brought tears to Erica's eyes.

The grooms stepped out and took place at the sides of the brides.

Erica stayed to see the photographs taken, saw tears of joy in Mrs Lewis's eyes and then left to go home.

Erica was aware of a big hurt inside her that she would never be a bride.

Janet said, 'I thought you were invited to go to the reception?'

'I was, but I wanted to come home.'

'Why, Erica?'

'Because I know I'll never marry.'

'Nonsense, of course you will. I think that Frank will come to his senses.'

'I don't want him. Not even if he asked me on his bended knees. We would never have been happy.'

'There are other men.'

'Yes, there are other men,' she said, and went to take off her coat. Poor Janet had lost her husband. She did, however, have her child to love, in time.

Erica learned later that the honeymooners went to different places. Angie and her husband went to Eastbourne, Margaret and her husband went to Bath and Emily and her husband went to Blackpool. The places were their own choice.

When they returned they shared a large house but had their own apartments.

The girls came to see Erica and they were all excited. They had come for their usual work and she was told that their parents had nothing to do with what they wanted to do.

'There's such a change in the parents,'

Angie said. 'If we have babies then we shall have a house of our own. I'm not bothered about children but Margaret and Emily can't have them soon enough. I shall be auntie to them.'

Although Erica was delighted to see them all she couldn't help but think that she would never have children of her own. And it was something she now longed to have.

The weeks went by and John had got into the habit of coming up to sit with her on the nights that Charles was out with Nadine.

One evening he said, 'Erica, do let me know if you would rather be on your own. I just plonk myself down.'

'I love having you, John, in fact I think I would miss you if you didn't come and sit with me.'

'Well that's good to know.' He sat hesitant for a moment then he said, 'I don't know whether I told you that I had put in for a divorce from Hesther.'

Erica put down her knitting. Her heartbeats had quickened.

'No, John, you hadn't told me. When did you put in for it?'

'Several months ago. Hesther raised no objections.'

'She would have had a nerve if she had objected.'

Then it suddenly struck Erica that perhaps her uncle had put in the divorce so he could perhaps marry this woman he talked about.

When she mentioned it he said no, that had nothing to do with it and, at that moment Janet came in.

'Any room for another visitor?'

'Yes, of course,' Erica said. 'Every one is welcome.'

John jumped up and drew up another chair. 'Do you know, this is a very comfortable room. I have a feeling of belonging here every time I come in.'

Erica felt a rush of pleasure. 'John, you couldn't have said a nicer thing. Come any time. And you too, Janet.'

Janet gave a deep sigh. 'It might seem a very strange thing to say but every time I come into this room I want Edward back.'

There was a short silence then John said, 'If you had the chance would you have him back?'

'Yes, I think I would. I know he behaved badly but I still love him. I was furious at the time, but how do I know? I could have fallen in love with someone else.'

This brought another silence. Then John said, 'We don't know where he is, of course, and we don't know what Charles would think about having Edward back.'

Erica said, 'Charles is in love. He may think differently now to what he thought when Edward left.'

John nodded. 'That's true. I can try and find out where Edward is.'

'Oh, I know where he is.'

Both John and Erica looked at her with surprise. 'You do?'

'Yes, he's working on a farm at the other side of the Marshes. He didn't see me. He looks thinner and looked very unhappy. That was when I knew I still loved him.'

'You have a strength, Janet,' John said quietly.

'I think most women have.' She got up. 'But here I am spoiling a lovely evening.'

'Not at all,' John said. 'There must be all sorts of things to discuss in this beautiful room. What do you think, Erica?'

'I agree. I too hated Edward for the way he had treated Janet, but I don't now, not any more, not after she had said, that *she* could have fallen in love with someone else. That had never occurred to me. Edward may not want to come back but I do think it's worth finding out.'

Janet said, 'If he has no wish to come back I'll accept it and get on with my life.'

She was the first to leave that evening and after she had gone John said, 'I've learnt a lot this evening.'

Erica looked up. 'Such as?'

John grinned. 'Haven't you learned a lot too?'

'Yes, I have.'

'Such as?'

Erica laughed. 'I think we best keep our secrets.'

'I agree.'

John, more serious said, 'Please don't ever stop me from coming to your room, Erica.'

'I won't, I promise.'

After John had gone Erica thought there was a lot that had not been said that evening and she wanted to know what it could mean. She felt bewildered. It was as though he had been trying to say he was in love with her.

No, she was exaggerating. Building up something that was only in her mind. It was something she longed to happen. But what good would it be if it were true. They could never marry. It was against the law.

She must put it from her mind and never think again in that way.

But she did know one thing that pleased her immensely. John loved to come to her room and talk to her. Pray heaven that that would never stop.

Chapter Twenty-One

The next day Janet went to the farm where she had seen Edward and came back very quiet.

She said, 'He wants nothing more to do with me. He would not come back to the house to be an underdog.'

'Did you explain that it wouldn't be like that?' Erica asked.

'I did but he wouldn't even listen. He's like Frank. Stubborn. He wants to be the boss.'

She dropped her handbag on to a chair. 'On the way back I called in at the shop to tell John what he had said. He was more hopeful than I was. Told me to give him two or three weeks to think it over. Edward looked terrible, Erica. He'd lost quite a bit of weight.'

'That's natural. He's not used to carrying heavy loads. Which he must do at a farm.'

'I suppose so. I'm not going to grieve over him. I have the baby to consider.'

She took off her coat and hat, hung them up and turned slowly. 'I promise you this. If he attempted to take the baby from me at any time I'd kill him, and that is no idle threat.'

She looked grim. Not a bit like the Janet she knew.

Erica hoped that John was right and that Edward would change his mind when approached the next time.

The days became colder. At times there was ice on the roads. When the girls and the women brought goods for Erica to examine she always made them a hot drink. They seemed grateful for this little kindly touch.

Sometimes Erica would imagine herself as a spinster then would shake off the image. Time enough when she was a spinster!

She wore brighter clothes and one day decided to change her hairstyle. She built her hair up and let stray curls fall to the side of her face. Usually her hair was tied back and it was hair that curled naturally.

John was the first one to notice the change at breakfast.

'You've changed your hairstyle, Erica. It makes you look younger than ever. You'll have all the men in the shop falling for you.'

She forced a smile. 'Good, I could do with a lift.'

Charles remarked on the change and so did Janet.

Erica began to feel a little excited. She had changed it for one person only. Yet knew at the same time that even if she looked glamorous it would make no difference to John's feelings for her.

But it was nice.

The girls raved over the change and even one or two of the other female workers passed remarks.

She looked forward to going to the shop.

The first customer she served was an elderly man who always teased her. Today he beamed at her and asked the men who the beautiful new assistant was.

Alexander gave a bow and said, 'Miss Erica Curtis, your honour. She meets the Queen today.'

Erica laughed. 'A little exaggeration, sir. All I've done is change my hairstyle a little.'

'Well, all I can say is, keep on doing it that way.'

'I shall.'

It was a rewarding day to Erica, but when she got home that evening she felt a little flat. What had she achieved? Nothing really, except some flattery.

But the next evening she felt she might have achieved some thing. She was aware that John would sit a few moments watching her, then read his book for a while then watch her again. Her heartbeats quickened. She began to day-dream. Supposing he had fallen in love with her? Was it possible that they could get married and go and live in another town?

But then what about children? They would be of the same blood and often suffered physically. No, she could not do that so really she was no further forward. She would have to stop day-dreaming.

She went on knitting but was careless for once and kept dropping stitches. She kept picking them up when John said, 'Are you in trouble, Erica?'

'Yes, I keep dropping stitches.'

'Is it a difficult pattern?'

'No, it's just that I—I, well, I'm in love with someone else.'

John closed his book, put it on the table beside him. 'Do I know the person?'

She forced herself to smile. 'I'll tell you his name when you tell me the name of your lady friend.'

He smiled too. 'Oh, it's like that, is it? One of these days I'll let you know.'

'Good, and I'll let you know the name of my man friend.'

'Do I know him?'

'I'm not telling.'

'Spoilsport.'

'You can talk.'

John began to chuckle. 'We could go on all night if we wanted to.' He picked up his book, opened it at a page that had a bookmark in and started to read again.

At least he tried to appear to be reading but not a page was turned.

Did it worry him that another man could be in her life? She doubted that it would...not unless he had fallen in love with her.

This time her heart began a mad beating. Was it possible? The more she thought about it the more possible it seemed. But where could they go from there?

She kept dropping stitches and John never turned one page. She put the knitting down and asked him if he would like a cup of tea. She had a feeling that her voice was not quite steady. John closed his book and got up, saying that he would make it.

He made small talk as he filled the kettle. Where was Janet this evening? Was she out visiting?

Erica said yes, she had gone to Mrs Todd's. John asked Erica if she thought that Edward would weaken and want to come home, something he had asked her earlier.

She said she thought it possible. Then she got up and started putting the cups out. John told her to sit down, he would see to the tea and she knew he was agitated. Why?

She went and sat down again, but was watching him all the time. He was not agitated about making the tea, he was agitated wanting to know who the man was that she was in love with.

And there could be only one reason for this. He was in love with her.

Should she ask him? No, what a fool she would feel if he told her no.

Oh, God, if only she had never fallen in love with him...

Then Janet came in and the talk became general.

The following evening Charles came up to Erica's bed-sitter to talk to her and John. He told them he had been talking to a man who worked at the farm where Edward worked. He said that Edward was a good worker but never mixed with anyone. He went out at night on his own but didn't drink.

Janet came in and they discussed it but agreed it would be sensible to wait a while then Charles or John would have a few words with Edward.

The following night when John came in, Erica was aware once more that he kept watching her. She managed to pluck up courage to ask him why he kept looking at her.

To her surprise he grinned. 'Because you're a very attractive young lady and I keep wondering who it is you've fallen in love with.'

With a fastly beating heart she said, 'It's you, of course.'

'But you've always been in love with me. You always kept telling me that I was your favourite uncle.'

Erica said in a low voice. 'But this is different. I want to marry you.' When she glanced at him she saw a frozen look on his face. He got up and walked around the room. 'That's impossible.'

In desperation she said, 'We could live in another town.'

'There are blood ties, Erica, which make it impossible.' He spoke gently.

'Do you love me?'

'Yes, you're my niece.'

'No, I mean could you love me if I were your wife?'

'That can never be. You must understand. If you start pressing me I shall have to leave.'

'No, please, never do that. Please stay. I won't bring it up any more. Come and sit with me in an evening.'

He ran his fingers through his hair. 'This must stop, we would never be at peace.'

Erica drew herself up. 'We would. We can be friends. Please don't deny me this.'

337

John was a long time in answering and when he did he spoke firmly. 'It would be in friendship only.'

'Yes, I promise and I won't go back on my word.'

'I think in time you'll realise, Erica, that there is a love between us but it's an uncle and niece relationship. I think that you are hurt over Frank's attitude.'

'Possibly.'

He talked about Frank. He would be hurt because she wasn't willing to give up making the boxes.

Although she knew she would never go back to Frank she agreed, not wanting to lose John's company.

John left shortly afterwards and did not come to keep her company the next night in spite of the fact that Charles was not seeing Nadine that evening.

Janet came in and talked all the time about Edward, of how they had first met and also of the fact that his mother had ended up agreeing to her staying.

'Do you know, Erica, the more I think of your mother the more I think there's a lot more we don't know about her life.'

Erica raised her head. 'In what way?'

'I don't know. I just feel there couldn't be only one secret.'

'I think it must have been terrible to keep it to herself all those years.'

Janet sighed. 'I think so too. Saving all that money, even when there were times when there was no food in the house.'

'Yes, I've thought of that often. But there, as Uncle John says, it takes all kinds to make a world.'

It worried Erica that John had not come to sit with her that evening and she wondered if he would break off the visits gradually.

The next evening he came in and said, 'Sorry, I didn't get to see you last night, but I wanted to get in touch with Edward.'

'Did you see him?'

'Yes, the woman at the farm told me he always went for a walk in the evening and told me where he went. I found him after a while and he was not a bit aggressive. He apologised for his behaviour to Janet and had thought things over since then. He told me he would like to come back home. He wanted to be with Janet and wanted to be there when the baby was born. He seemed genuine enough. I told him I would tell Janet how he felt and let them sort it out.'

Erica was so pleased that he had not stayed away from her for the reason she had thought, and was glad they had a good talking point.

She asked John if he had spoken to Janet and he told her yes and she seemed quite amenable to Edward returning home if they were all willing.

'I'm willing,' Erica said.

John said that he was willing and also that Charles was too.

'Janet will be coming up with Charles later so that we all know what to expect.'

'Good.' Erica could not help feeling how well things had turned out. It would have been awful if John had stayed away. A few minutes later Charles and Janet came in together to discuss Edward's attitude and they agreed that he should at least have a chance to come back home.

'It isn't going to be easy for him,' John said. 'He had no love for Alexander, but he did say he was willing to apologise to him.'

Erica said, 'There would be quite a few of us working in the shop, but now we are not so cramped as we were.'

They all agreed on this and Charles did say, 'I don't fly into tempers as I did before I met Nadine. I suppose that will help too.'

They agreed.

So it was settled that Edward would come and they would all have a talk together.

Edward had said that he would like to be working in the shop and that they needn't worry, he was a changed person.

He had learned a lot of things since casting Janet aside.

He would never again fall for another woman. He loved Janet and would look forward to the baby coming.

It was finally settled that Edward would be back at the house the following Sunday. He wanted to give the farm some notice to be fair to them.

When Edward moved in all went well. He apologised to Alexander and seemed to get on all right with him, and he was pleasant to the customers.

On the day after New Years Day Erica had two letters, one from Bridget and one from Bert.

Bridget wrote:

'Darling girl. It was Frank who broke the engagement, but when I asked him if it was because of you, he said that he still loved you, but he would not marry you if you refused to give up making your boxes...'

Erica was livid. What a nerve. Still taking it that she would rush to marry him if she did as he said.

She finished the letter:

'Won't you think about it, Erica dear?

341

You make such a good pair. Think it over carefully. With much love, Bridget.'

Bert's letter was totally different. He said he hoped that she was no longer in love with Frank. What a big head he had become:

'Still says he'll marry you if you'll give up making the boxes.

'I don't think you will be such a fool as to want to marry him under these conditions. There are heaps of men who would be very willing to marry you without having to give up your work. Let me know if you are in love with anyone else. I'd like to impart this news to him. Get him off his high horse.

With love, Bert.'

Erica laughed at Bert's letter. He was always so down to earth. She would write and tell him that she was in love with someone else, a man who had no objections to her making the boxes.

It was more difficult to write to Bridget, who had so much wanted her to marry Frank. But she would know too what a big head he was. It would do him good to find that he couldn't have all his own way always.

Edward would come sometimes to her room in an evening with Janet and they would sit and talk about things in general. Edward was a very much changed person to the brother she had known.

Janet seemed quietly happier than she had been and was so looking forward to the birth of her child. So, apparently was Edward.

John and Charles would come in some nights too. There were very few nights when Erica was alone. She didn't want to be alone. It had her thinking too much.

Then one evening Janet came in on her own and seemed fidgety.

When Erica asked her what was wrong she said, 'John told me not to tell you, but I feel I must tell you.'

Erica felt emotional. 'Is he...getting married?'

'No. He wants to leave the family.'

'Why?'

'Because he's—because he's in love with you, Erica.'

Relief flooded over Erica. 'I've wondered at times.'

'But don't you see, you can't marry. If there were children—'

'I know that too and I promised John I would never make things awkward. We would just be friends.'

Janet sat down and took Erica's hands in

hers. 'Look, Erica, John can't bear living in the same house knowing that he's in love with you. He has to leave.'

'No, there's no need. Explain to him. I'll never make any demands on him.'

'He wants you and can't have you. It wouldn't be right. Also, he...he was the illegitimate son of your mother.'

Erica stared at her. 'Of mother? Oh, God. He told us that the illegitimate baby had died.'

'I know. He felt a terrible shame. Wouldn't we all? You'll have to let him go, Erica.'

'No.' Tears sprang to her eyes. 'I would rather go.'

'That wouldn't be right either.' Janet got up and walked about the room. 'You remember I told you a while ago that I felt that Faith had other secrets, but I couldn't think at the time what they could be. Now I have a remembrance of your Aunt Rebecca coming to the house one afternoon and your mother telling her that she had no right to come to the house. That she must go. I was in the next room but I remember your Aunt Rebecca shouting, 'You've had all your own way with your secrets, it's time they were made known. Other people are involved.'

'The next thing I heard was a scuffle

and I remember your mother pushing her out of the front door by her shoulders and slamming it against her. I remember I was trembling.'

'What—what happened after that?'

'I don't know. Nothing was said about your aunt's visit. I told Edward about it and he said to let it drop. The only thing they knew about their Aunt Rebecca was that she and your mother were always quarreling and eventually when you were all young they fell out.

'Your mother, of course, knew I was in the house when your aunt called and she told me if I told anyone what had happened she would put both Edward and I out on the street. I had no choice at that time. I was expecting the baby.'

'What other secrets could my mother have?'

'I don't know. It's just that it seemed to me that if a person keeps a secret so persistently that there are other secrets in their lives. I could be wrong. We don't want to lose John out of the business. We've just got Edward back and he's settling down nicely.'

'Does he ever talk about the woman he left you for?'

'Only once. He told me he hated her and that there would never be another woman in his life and, I believe him.'

Erica began to plead with Janet. 'Can you persuade John to stay? I won't be any trouble to him. He needn't come to my room in an evening. I would rather be the one to leave, not that I want to leave. But he must stay because of the family.'

'I'll see what I can do. Of course he'll be annoyed that I told you, after I promised that I wouldn't.'

She went out of the room and it was a long time before she returned. 'John won't have you leaving. He agreed that he would stay out of your room, but did mention that you would see him every day in the shop.'

'I think that would work out. We're always too busy to talk in the shop and I'll steer clear of him as much as possible.'

Janet gave her a hug. 'Why do these things have to happen? I'll have a word with him.'

John agreed on this score and Erica wondered how she would continue to live without having John nearly every night in her room.

It worked reasonably well. He didn't stay out of her way at the shop. Sometimes he teased her and she always responded.

As time went on, however, when Erica was alone in her room she would find herself thinking about her aunt who had talked about other secrets and wondered what they could be.

She must have been very young when her mother and her aunt were friendly. She asked Charles and Edward about their aunt and they could only remember her vaguely. At the time, Charles said he thought that their aunt had lived only two streets away, but did remember that they were not allowed to visit her.

The more time went on the more she wanted to know what other secrets her mother could have been hoarding and in the end decided she would try and find her aunt. She may not even be alive but at least she would try and find her.

On the Sunday morning she told Janet what she was going to do and Janet tried to persuade her not to. 'What purpose would it serve?' she asked.

'I only want to know if there are any other secrets in the family and I won't get to know if I don't ask.'

Janet sighed. 'I hope you won't regret it.'

Erica set out to find the house they had lived in at the time. She knew where it was but had no idea of the number. Perhaps her aunt had a family.

To her dismay all the houses had been pulled down and new ones built. A bad start. She knocked at the door of the nearest house and asked the woman who answered the door if she knew of a woman called Rebecca Green, and told her where she thought she used to live.

'Oh, yes,' she said, 'Becky Green. She started a bread and cake shop a few years ago, but now she's crippled with rheumatism and had to give it up. If you go the end of this street and turn right then turn into the third street, it's the first house on the right. A young girl comes in to look after her.'

Erica thanked her and felt she was in luck. But would her aunt want to know her? Well, at least she would soon find out.

A girl of about sixteen answered the door and when Erica asked if she could speak to Mrs Green the girl asked her name.

Erica hesitated a moment then said, 'Tell her it's her niece Erica Curtis who's calling to see her.'

The girl went into a room and came out smiling.

'Mrs Green will be delighted to see you. Follow me.'

They went into the living-room and a woman, who was sitting in an armchair with a stick at either side of her, gave her a beaming smile.

'Forgive me, I can't get up easily. Come and give me a kiss. What a surprise!'

Erica leaned over and kissed her on the cheek.

'Take your coat off and sit down. Would you like a cup of tea?'

'No thank you, it doesn't seem long since I had my breakfast.'

The girl, who looked to be sixteen said, 'While you have a visitor, Mrs Green, I'll just nip along and see how Mr Dunn is this morning.'

'Don't hurry back. My niece and I will have so much to talk about.'

When the girl had gone Mrs Green said, 'She's a gem. Don't know what I'd do without her. Now tell me, Erica, is your mother still alive?'

'No, she died a few months ago.'

'We never did get on. Then we fell out eventually. Well, she always had her own way. Always after making money. I never had any children and she would never let any of you come and see me. She was a mean woman, a secretive woman.'

'She was a worker. She taught us how to make clay pipes. It was she who built up the business. Now we are in quite a big way.'

Her aunt sat looking at her, as if weighing her up then said, 'Tell me, Erica, why did you come to see me?'

'It's rather difficult to explain. You said that my mother was always after making money.'

'Oh, she was, there was no doubt about

that. And she was secretive too.'

'Secretive in what way.'

'Now this is difficult for me. I don't know how much you know of your mother's life.'

'We didn't know anything about it at all, until she died.'

'How much did you know about your father?'

'I hardly remember him. My mother would never talk about him. I used to think that it would upset her to mention him. I feel now that I want to know more about her life. I feel that she had secrets that we were never told.'

Mrs Green nodded slowly. 'She had a lot of secrets that I felt ought to be told. What exactly is it you want to know?'

'There's one important thing. We have a young uncle who has lived with us and worked with us. I've loved him since I was a child.' Erica sat silent for a while then went on.

'Then I came to realise that the love I felt for him was the kind that made me want to be married to him. I told him one evening how I felt, yet knew that it was illegal to marry a close relative because children could be affected by the blood. We knew that my mother had had an illegitimate child and John had told us that the child died.

'Then when I confessed to loving him I found out that *he* had been the illegitimate child and that he was terribly ashamed about it. He wanted to leave the house.

'Then my sister-in-law told me she thought my mother had other secrets, but had no idea what they were.'

'I want to help you, but I wish I knew where to start. I never had any children and your mother would never let any of you come and see me. It hurt.' She looked up. 'But I'll tell you what I know.'

Chapter Twenty-Two

Mrs Green sat silent for a moment then gave a deep sigh. 'Your mother was barely sixteen when she gave birth to John. Both her parents were shocked by this and eventually, our mother agreed to pretend to have given birth to the baby. They had a big family and John was known to the children as their baby brother.

'Faith was a good-looking girl and had men wanting to marry her. She refused because she was having an affair with one of the upper crust.'

Mrs Green paused. 'There were plenty of such secret affairs going on in those days. And, I suppose still are.' She sighed again. 'Your mother and I never got on and eventually we fell out. Then a layabout called William Curtis heard about this man who was keeping Faith and he tried desperately to find out who he was, guessing she would be paid for her favours but, he had no luck.

'Although he was a layabout he was a good-looking man and had a lot of charm. He courted her and eventually asked her to marry him. And she agreed, which I couldn't understand. She must have known what he was.'

Again Mrs Green paused. 'I hope you can understand this.'

'Yes, go on.'

'Well, Curtis was still trying to find out who this man was. But he could never find them together. He did know, however that she had some money because he saw her hiding it one day. She told him it was her wages and he was not getting any of it. He could get himself a job.

'When Curtis told her he would tell everyone about her affair she replied sharply, "Go ahead, but if you do you won't have long to live." This shook him and he left her and sought some one else that would help him to live free.

'He found a widow with a child whose sea captain husband had been drowned at sea. He was kind to her and eventually made love to her.

'Two months later the widow and he were killed in an accident. No one claimed the baby and Faith, who had always wanted a little girl, adopted it.'

There was a silence then Mrs Green said quietly, 'And that little girl was you, Erica.'

Erica's heart began a quick beating. This meant that there would be no blood ties between John and herself. They could be married! When she told her aunt this she said, 'I'm glad I told you the secrets.'

Unfortunately this made no difference to John. He told Erica he could never marry her. He was too ashamed of his birth.

She pleaded with him. 'John, you are not responsible for being illegitimate. Your parents were responsible.'

He still would make no move. 'We can't ever be married, Erica, I'll never have children and put that dreadful burden on their shoulders.'

'Kings have illegitimate children,' she said.

'I'm not a king,' he spoke coldly.

'We won't have children. We can share other people's offspring.'

'No.' There was a hard line to his jaw and Erica gave up.

Edward said to her one evening when he was with Janet in her room, 'Give John time, Erica. I needed time to come to my senses.'

'But your case was different.'

'It was the same in a different respect. I refused to see sense. And this is what John is doing. He will realise in time what he is missing. Be patient. You couldn't be married yet anyway. He won't be free until his divorce is through.'

Pray heaven that Edward was right and John would feel more free when this was settled.

Erica went to see her aunt from time to time and learned about her family. 'Quite a few of them are dead,' she said. 'They're spread all over the place. I do get a few lines from one or two now and again and I write back. I wish my life had been different. I longed for children and had three miscarriages, but never a birth. Faith would never allow any of the children to come and visit me.'

'I wish I had known.'

Her aunt patted her hand. 'Well, you're here now. There are times when I wonder if I was right, wanting to probe into Faith's life. Perhaps I was a little jealous of her. She always had a man. And she had money to leave you all. I always thought of her

354

as mean, and secretive. You told me the last time you were here that she said in the letter she left that she loved you all and couldn't show it. Poor Faith. We can always learn something in life, even if we are nearing the end of our days.'

Erica scolded her, 'Don't say that, Aunt Rebecca. You've got years to live yet.'

'I don't know that I want to live much longer, being in pain all the while.' She smiled suddenly. 'But it's been lovely having you to visit me. Like a bit of sunshine in my life.'

So little to give, Erica thought when she left, and so much appreciated. From now on she wouldn't grumble any more about John being so stubborn.

A week later Janet came into her room on the Saturday morning and said in a low voice, 'Frank's downstairs. He was searching for you. I left him talking to the men, do you want him to come up?'

'Frank? I—I don't know.'

'I think you should see him when he's been searching for you.'

She squared her shoulders. 'Well, all right, but give me time to change my dress.'

'*I will.*'

She had made up her mind she would be quite brusque with him, but when he came in, smartly dressed, hat in hand she felt a weakening.

'Hello,' she said. 'What a surprise.'

Janet left them and Frank came forward. 'I came to London to do some buying and felt I couldn't leave without seeing you. You have a splendid shop. It was good to see your brothers and your sister-in-law.'

'I'm glad you called. Sit down, won't you?'

She thought he looked as if he had walked out of a Bond Street tailors. 'How's business?' she asked.

'Splendid. We're having the shop enlarged.'

Erica was not at all sure of her feelings. He looked more handsome than ever and so well groomed.

He said suddenly, 'You've changed your hair-style, Erica. It suits you.'

She had to admit that flattery was pleasing.

'Thank you.'

He said, 'I wondered if you would come and have lunch with me?'

She hesitated a moment, wanting to know about the girl he had been expecting to marry then thought, what was she letting herself in for? Did he want them to get back on the old footing? No, that could never be. Not even if he told her that she could go on working after they were

356

married...as if he would.

'I'm so sorry,' she said, 'but we're much too busy.'

'What a pity. Perhaps another time?'

'Yes.' She asked quickly after Bert and Bridget and was told they were both well.

'Bert is a perfect salesman,' he said. 'Carries it off so well and Bridget is fine and sends her love. I wouldn't want to go anywhere else to be looked after. She treats us both as children one minute and as rather royal gentlemen the next.'

'Give her my love,' Erica said.

They talked about the business for a while then Frank said he thought he must be going.

Frank called out to the family that he would see them again. They sent him greetings and told him he would be welcome.

Outside the door Frank paused. 'If you are ever anywhere near Durham I hope you will call.'

There was a yearning in his voice. Erica replied softly, 'Yes, of course.' Then she went quickly back into the shop, not quite sure how she felt at that moment.

It seemed to her that love was a fickle emotion. Frank had been the first man she had fallen in love with. But then he had been at fault wanting to dominate her, then getting engaged to someone else.

Erica went upstairs to her room. It was strange how he had changed. When she first met him he seemed an ordinary young man. In fact, at first she was not sure whether she really liked him. And it was not until she had gone to see him at Durham that they first made love.

Later she had fretted that she might have become pregnant. Was she any better than her mother? Yes, she had not taken money to let Frank make love to her.

But Frank was a totally different man now. Well dressed, well mannered, polished. What should she do?

John came up during the evening to ask about her meeting with Frank.

'He's not bossy like he used to be. It's as though I had just swopped roles with him,' Erica said.

'Well, that's not very flattering.'

'It's not meant to be. I'm caught up in my own little world where I've made myself aloof. Just as you have done. How could we ever marry? I've been known all this time as your niece.'

'It's because I love you that—'

'No.' Erica spoke quietly. 'If you had loved me you would have done anything so that we could both be together. I'm sorry John. You have to know the truth.'

He got up, stood a moment then left the room.

Tears filled Erica's eyes. feeling sure she had lost him.

Janet came in about ten minutes later and asked what was wrong with John. 'He put on his hat and coat and went out.'

Erica told her what had taken place and Janet said she thought she had been a little hard on him.'

'He wants to enjoy being illegitimate. He's revelling in it. Quite frankly I don't want to be married to anyone.'

'You will in time because you want children.'

'Yes.' Erica sighed. 'So what do I do? Marry Frank?'

'No. You were flattered by his attention. That won't make for a happy marriage. You said yourself that you wanted John because it was the right kind of love you had for him. I thought you were right to see Frank, to let John know that another man wanted you, but it went the wrong way.'

'And it can stay that way. I don't care.'

'You do, why lie about it?'

'But John should be sensible.'

'He will be in time. He'll tell you when he's ready.'

But John never came to her room and when she went into the shop he always found a reason for going out, or for being busy.

This went on for over a week and Erica began to despair that they would ever be friends again and she ached and wondered if she ought to apologise.

Then she thought, no, why should she? She was not to blame. Perhaps she had been a little hard on him, but she had done right to tell him how badly he had behaved.

A letter came from Frank saying how good it had been to see her and told her he still loved her. Was there any chance they could get together again...?

It was not his usual loving letter, but it stirred something in her. She wanted to be loved.

That evening John knocked on her door and said he had come to apologise for his behaviour. Erica hesitated a moment then said, 'You had better come in.'

He told her that he had behaved badly, and she nodded. 'Yes, you did.'

'Can you forgive me?'

'I can forgive you if you've lost the attitude of grieving that you are illegitimate.'

'Yes, I have, but I would still find if difficult to ask you to marry me. That is, of course, if you still wanted to.'

She gave a deep sigh. 'Oh, no, we're not going through all that palaver about it being a crime.'

'I love you very much,' he replied

earnestly, 'but we would definitely have to leave the country and I know what a trial that would be, Erica, not only for me, but for you.'

'Don't make excuses, John. If you really loved me you would marry me and not care where we lived. We know there are no blood ties between us. Isn't that enough? Do we have to shout it to the world?'

He gripped the back of a chair. 'No, but I do think that we need peaceful minds. You say it doesn't matter that we marry and live together but what if someone set the news going that we were married and it was a crime. How would you feel then? And don't say you wouldn't mind because you would. It would hurt.'

'No, John. You still can't get it out of your mind that you are illegitimate.'

'That has gone. Supposing we had children. Would you want them to know that their father was illegitimate?'

'They wouldn't need to know.'

'I never thought that I would ever learn such a thing. As I've told you, I've accepted it.'

'Very well, can we forget all this and remain friends?'

'I think that would be sensible.'

'So, you wouldn't mind if I married Frank?'

His expression changed, became cold. 'Is

that what you plan to do?'

'I feel he wants to marry me and I want children. There have been many times when I thought I would end up being a spinster. But why should I? There are quite a few men who want to take me out. I refused because of loving you. Frank has changed quite a lot. He's not so dominating as he used to be.'

'Erica, please, please, don't marry him. He hasn't changed. He became engaged to marry a wealthy young lady and she threw him over because she came to realise this.'

'That's not true!'

'Find out the truth before you even think of marrying him,' John said quietly. 'I'm sorry we can't be friends.' He turned to leave and Erica called to him.

'John, wait. I would like to be friends with you. If you do agree it would take some of the coldness out of my life. I miss our talks, hate it when I go to the shop and you go out or become busy.'

'And I would welcome your friendship, Erica. I miss our talks too.'

'Will you stay for a coffee?'

'Yes, I would like that very much.'

She smiled. 'Then sit down.'

It surprised Erica how quickly they got into the old footing. It was business they talked about, but with quite a lot of enjoyment.

When Janet came up later she smiled with pleasure when she found them arguing about a piece of business.

'It's like old times,' she said.

When John left she said, 'Well, Erica, when is the wedding taking place?'

'I'm sorry to say there will be no wedding,' she said, a sadness in her voice and she gave the reasons that John had mentioned.

'Give him time.'

'No, I don't think that time will make any difference. He seems set in his ways. He's dreadfully stubborn. I told him that I may as well marry Frank, but he didn't like that. I told him that I wanted children, that I had thought of ending up a spinster then decided that other men wanted to take me out.'

'And what did he have to say to that?'

'He pleaded with me not to marry Frank, said he hadn't changed, and hinted that the girl he had been going to marry gave him up. I think I could get the truth from Bridget or even Bert. I'll write to them both tomorrow.'

Erica got the letters off early the next day and had replies by return of post.

Bridget was a little cautious, saying that

she had always hoped that the two of them would get together eventually. She told her how pleased Frank was when he came back from London and told her he had seen her and the family and what an excellent business they had all built up. Then she told Erica scraps of news and said she hoped to see her soon.

Bert was more straightforward. He told her that Frank's rich young lady had thrown him over. He couldn't really blame her, he was taking other young ladies out on the side. Frank had changed; was getting a bit too big for his boots and he wouldn't take any advice from him. At the same time he was a good business man. He seemed very impressed with her family's business. He wished her the best of luck.

Erica sighed. Well, now she knew the truth. She would forget Frank and get on with her life.

It was not easy. She still had a little secret liking for him. He was a man and liked the company of women. What she did not want to be denied was children. They became a minor obsession with her. She longed for the time to come when Janet's baby was due.

Then Angie came one morning with the news that she was pregnant. She was greatly excited. Her husband was in the seventh heaven of delight.

Margaret and Emily were terribly disappointed. They had both being praying for a baby. 'Isn't it typical,' Margaret said, 'our Angie and her husband weren't a bit particular about having a child and now they are the first.'

'What do your parents say?' Erica asked.

'Mama's over the moon, and Papa seems very pleased too. Mama keeps telling Emily and I to hurry up.'

This made Erica long more than ever for a child.

There were times when Frank was very much in her thoughts, their very passionate lovemaking and she would feel all emotional. She would then want to have him make love to her.

But then John would come into her mind and she would remember how, when he just touched her hair or ran his fingers down her cheeks she would have the same reaction.

How could one tell the difference?

She knew the difference, knew that his was a different kind of love. She had known it weeks ago when she knew she wanted to marry him. There would be a certain peace with John. At least she had thought so then. Now she was not so sure. There was a torment in him because of being illegitimate. Frank did not have this worry. His fault was wanting to have a number of women that he could rule over. Would her life ever go the way she wanted it to go? Yes, she was mistress of it. She wanted children more than anything in this world. Frank would give them to her. She would write to him, see how he responded.

It took her a long time to write the letter that evening. She did not want to bring love into it. She told him she had been thinking about him quite a lot. Nothing would please her better than having his children. She would try and get to see him soon. That was, of course, if he still wanted her.

She ended the letter, *'Let me know soon,'* and signed it just *'Erica.'*

After the letter had gone she was in a torment.

It was wrong to want to marry someone just to have children. They must love their father, he must love them. She had never known her father but had often thought how nice it would have been to have known him. She had loved her grandfather. He had been so good to them all, seeing they all had a sweetmeat from him every time they met. He took them for walks, had taught them about the countryside, about animals. When he had died she felt that she wanted to die too.

Her mother had scolded her, slapped her once because she couldn't stop crying. Her mother might have loved them but she had never once showed it.

If she married Frank would he be so involved with other women in his life that he would show no love for his children? This would be unbearable. Why, oh why, had she been in such a rush to get the letter posted?

She knew why. It was because she wanted John to come to his senses and to tell her that he would marry her.

What a fool she had been. Would she ever grow up?

Chapter Twenty-Three

Two days later a letter came from Frank:

'Oh, my darling,' he wrote. 'What lovely news that you want to come and see me. I'm praying that you'll make a marriage date, soon. I've never stopped loving you. I think we were destined to be together. We shall have a wonderful honeymoon. Perhaps go to Paris. I can't wait. I shall have to get all my orders out so that we can spend the time together.

'Bridget is over the moon, so is Bert. He says I don't deserve to have such a beautiful wife, but I do know how lucky I am, my darling, and I promise you I shall never let you down. With all my love, dearest Erica, Yours for always, Frank.'

Erica sat, wondering if she could refuse to go. She would talk to Janet first.

After Janet had read the letter she raised her head slowly. 'You could not have had a more loving letter, but I do think you will have to have a long talk before you decide anything. Don't forget this is for life.'

'I know. What will John say about it? As soon as I had sent it I wished I hadn't.'

'It has to be answered.'

'Yes. I'm very much aware of that.'

'I know you want children, Erica, but is Frank the right person to give them to you? I feel he's in need of money.'

'That's unkind. I'm sorry you said it.'

'It has to be said, Erica. There are hundreds of people who have a way with them and are perfect on saying the right words. Look at the man that Faith married. A good-looking, charming layabout. Wanting only money from his wife. She got wise to him and refused to give him any.'

'Frank isn't like that.'

'Are you sure? He told you he was enlarging the shop and talked glowingly of ours.'

'I don't want to listen any more to what you have to say.'

'I shall only say it once more. Think it over carefully. Edward thought he had found the right woman and all she wanted was his money.'

'That was different.'

'There was no difference. I'll leave you to think it over.'

She went out and closed the door quietly behind her.

Erica sank into a chair. Was she to be in another torment again because of what someone had said? Janet didn't know the full story. She knew that Frank had made love to her, but she had no idea how tender he could be. This was important.

John had turned her down, sure that it would not have worked if they married. He had no confidence. One needed confidence to marry.

Erica went over and over all the times that she and Frank had been together and they didn't add up to very many. Whereas she had lived with John from being a baby. Then she thought, after all, it was her life, no one else should have any say in it. Her head went up. She would go and see Frank, have a talk with him. She had worked hard. Also she had more people making the boxes.

John came up to her room that evening and said, without preamble, 'Janet tells me you are planning to go to Durham to see Frank.'

'Yes, I am, any objections?'

'No, I think you are being sensible getting everything sorted out before you do marry.'

Erica was completely taken aback. 'So you approve that I want to marry him?'

'If that's what you want.'

'A short time ago you didn't think that.'

'Janet has talked me into it.'

'I see. Couldn't you make up your own mind?'

'I think talking to someone helped. Janet is a sensible person. She told me you wanted children. I can understand it.'

Erica felt annoyed. 'You seem to have it all cut and dried.'

'Not really. The family agree with me.'

'Oh, so they've been informed.' Her anger grew. 'So I can be dispatched to Durham without any of them caring a damn?'

'Of course they care.'

'And you want to make it easy for me too, I presume?'

'Yes, seeing that I have no real interest in the matter.'

'Thank you. Thank you very much. I was in love with you, wanted to marry you, but you refused. Determined that it was impossible.'

'It wasn't that it was impossible, Erica.' He spoke gently. 'I wanted what was best for us.'

'And you decide it's best for me that I'm pushed up to Durham to marry Frank.'

'I'm sorry, I understood it was what you wanted. Janet said you want his children.'

'I did. But—I—don't know for sure until I have a long talk with him.'

'No, of course not. I hope it works out for you.' He got up and Erica gripped the arms of her chair.

He didn't give a damn for her. He wanted to be rid of her so he could settle down to his single life. That's all he cared about. Well, she would go to Durham and talk to Frank. She got up too. 'There will be plenty of boxes ready. I don't think you will be short with all the people we now have working for us. I'll have a word with the rest of the family.'

'Do that. I'll bid you good-night.'

When he had gone Erica sank back into the chair. Her throat felt dry. She could hardly believe that she had been so keen to marry John. He just didn't care.

Nor did the family care. Well, she would start getting prepared to go to Durham the day after tomorrow.

When she told them the next morning of her plans they all seemed satisfied and she found it hard to believe.

What was the reason? Did they prefer not to have a woman serving in the shop?

Alexander was the only one who said, 'I shall really miss you, Erica. I hope you'll be very happy.'

She said shortly, 'None of the family seems bothered that I'm going to be married.'

He stared at her. 'What makes you say that?'

'They all seem to agree that it's a good idea.'

'Erica, it's what you want that's important to them. They're all upset. And especially John. He's very upset.'

'He didn't seem upset when he spoke to me last night.'

'He too wants what's best for you.'

'Rubbish. He's glad that I'm leaving, then he can get on with his own life and wallow in the fact that he's illegitimate.'

'Oh, Erica, how terribly wrong you are. It's because he's thinking of your happiness. You've always been so wrapped up in your family.'

'I know but—'

'Believe me when I tell you that they're all upset that you might be leaving them.'

'Well, I'll think about it.'

'Good.'

Erica thought about it for the rest of the morning then made up her mind that she would have to see Frank, talk with him, even if it was just a quick visit.

She sent a telegram that afternoon saying, *'Be with you, Thursday morning. Erica.'*

And she had one back saying, *'Wonderful, can't wait to see you. Love, Frank.'*

She packed her bag that night and told the family she would be leaving early the next morning. She knew that her friend at Newcastle was away and she would have to have accommodation for the night then travel by carriage to Durham.

She was quite calm the next morning when she said goodbye to the family. Edward and Janet were seeing her to the station.

She had said goodbye to Alexander the day before and when she said goodbye to Charles and John, Charles gave her a hug and a kiss, but John just gave her a light kiss on the cheek and wished her well.

John's expression haunted her when she was in the train.

Although he had smiled he was pale and had a distressed look in his eyes. She knew then that he did care about her, but it was not enough to make her wish she had stayed at home.

She had to talk to Frank. And it would have to be a heart-to-heart talk.

Erica had refused to travel with anyone and she was glad she had done so. Her fellow passengers were pleasant and did not talk all the time. It left her with her own thoughts now and again which was necessary. She only wished she could forget John's expression but this was bound to go in time.

The people she had been travelling with were only going as far as Doncaster, but to her pleasure the next passengers were going back home to Newcastle. They not only asked her to stay overnight with them but knew of a friend who was going to Durham the following morning and would give her a lift.

A load was taken from her mind.

The people who had brought her to Durham left her at Bridget's door. To Erica's surprise it was Bridget who opened the door. She looked distressed.

Erica put her arms around her and asked her what was wrong.

'Come in, my love. Take your hat and

coat off I've made a pot of tea.' She poured the tea then they sat down.

'Oh, dear, I don't know where to start. Bert and Frank had such a row last night. Bert was furious because he found out that Frank was going to ask you for some money to pay for enlarging the shop.'

Erica went tense.

Bridget paused a moment then went on. 'Frank had foolishly let Bert think that he had the money to pay for it and was furious when he pinned Frank down and found he was hoping to get some from you.' Bridget leaned forward. 'Don't get me wrong, Erica. Frank does love you, but I know how Bert felt. Bert is the real businessman of the partnership. Frank needs the glory of owning the biggest menswear business in Durham.'

'Tell me, Bridget, did Frank finish with the girl he was engaged to or did she give him up?'

Bridget pulled at the hem of her handkerchief then looked up. There were tears in her eyes. 'You know that I love you both but I have to be fair to you. She gave Frank up.'

'I see. Where is Frank? We'll have to have a long talk.'

'He won't be long.' She dabbed at her eyes. 'And I don't want him to know that I've told you.'

'I won't tell him, Bridget. I promise.'

Ten minutes later Frank arrived. He was smartly dressed and looked amazingly happy.

'Darling, I can't believe you're here.' He kissed her. 'Are you coming to the shop with me?'

She forced a laugh. 'I must have some fresh air first. I've been travelling since yesterday.'

'Of course you have. We'll have a walk along the river bank. Where's your coat and hat?' To Bridget he said, 'We'll be back for lunch.'

Then they were outside and he put an arm around her. 'I can hardly believe you're here. I hope you've come to make a marriage date.'

She smiled up at him. 'We must have a talk first.'

'I'm dying to show you all our stock. You'll be amazed at how much we have.' He talked about having the front window brought forward to make more room in the shop.

'That must be very costly,' she said. 'In one of your letters you were talking of us having a honeymoon in Paris.'

'Of course we will. Marriage is once in a lifetime.'

'Where would we live?'

'With Bridget at first, but we'll soon

have a home of our own.'

He was helping her down the steep path to the river.

'Frank, won't it cost a lot to have the shop enlarged?'

'It'll pay dividends.'

They came to a seat on the bank and Erica said, 'I think we had better sit down and discuss it.'

'We don't talk about money at a time like this.' He put an arm around her and drew her close.

She drew away from him. 'We must. If we marry I want a house of our own. I want a glorious honeymoon in Paris.'

The river was in full spate and Frank sat gazing at it for a moment then he said, 'And we will.' He paused. 'I did think if you could perhaps lend me a little, you would get it all back in time. It won't take long. We have orders for suits and—'

'It won't do, Frank.'

'What do you mean it won't do?'

'I've worked hard for my money.'

'A husband always takes charge of his wife's money when they marry.'

'Well no one will have charge of mine, I want to have a business of my own. That's what I've been striving for.'

'You can't run a business and have children. Who told you I was going to ask you for money? Bridget?' His face was flushed with anger.

'No one. It's common-sense. I want a business but I would put someone in to run it.'

He had calmed down. 'Then that's all right.'

'No, it isn't all right. If I put any money in your business I shall give it to Bert to handle.'

Frank jumped up. 'You what?' He was livid.

'Bert is the business head, Frank. You must admit to it. He always has been, even when you had the market stall together. Now you've been doing the buying and letting your head run away with you.'

He paced up and down in front of her. 'If you imagine I would hand over the buying side to Bert, you have another think coming.'

'It's up to you.'

'Well, I've told you how I feel.' He stopped pacing. His face was taut.

Erica said, 'Let me tell you something, when I was small we were poverty-stricken. My brothers and I made clay pipes. My mother was boss, she knew what had to be done and we did what we were told. We eventually progressed. We built up the business bit by bit. And that's what you must do. It's up to you whether you accept it or not. You must be heavily in debt as you are.'

He made no answer to that.

Erica got up. 'Go bankrupt, because that is how you will end up. I shall go home tomorrow.'

'I need time to think,' he pleaded. His anger had all gone. In the next breath he said, 'But I do want you to know, Erica that I love you and always will. Do you still want that walk?'

'No, I'll go back to Bridget's.'

They walked in silence and when they reached Bridget's door Frank said, 'I'll go to the shop and tell Bert what you've decided.'

Erica thought wryly. And she would go back to making her boxes.

Would she ever be rid of them?

Charles, Edward and Janet met her at the station. Erica said, 'The marriage plans didn't work out. We'll talk about it later.' She looked about her. 'Didn't John come with you?'

'No, but he's done a lot of fretting over you.'

She talked about the journey on the way home, but when they arrived home she told them about Frank expecting money from her. 'He's heavily in debt. I told him no.' Then, after a pause she added, 'I decided to give some to Bert.'

There was almost an uproar at this. Was she mad? Putting money in a shop that looked like going to the dogs? It was utterly ridiculous. Charles had a lot more to say but Janet gave a sigh and said, 'Well, it's your money, Erica.'

'Yes, and it no longer means anything to me. All I wanted at one time was as much money as I could get. Now I can see myself ending my days as a spinster.'

Charles said, 'It's foolish to think in that way. You'll have to talk to John, He's beginning to see some sense at last.'

'In what way?'

'When your telegram came telling us you were coming home, he said he didn't know whether you liked him any more but, if you did, he thought he could overcome the marriage problem.'

'How?'

'I don't know, we were interrupted.'

Erica raised her shoulders in a weary way. 'I don't know anything at this moment. I feel like a washed out rag. I don't even want to talk to him tonight.'

'Then don't.'

Erica slept well that night but felt drained in the morning. Janet, who brought her up some breakfast, suggested she try to go to sleep again but Erica said no, She had things to face up to.

The strange thing was that she no longer felt at peace in her own room.

A long stretch of misery loomed before her.

'You know, Erica,' Janet said gently, 'I've gone through the same mill and know what you're suffering. I came to realise that in spite of the way Edward had behaved I still loved him. None of us are perfect.'

Erica wondered if she was wrong in letting herself get so low. Should she talk to John? Find out what he had in mind. If she didn't she would never know.

That evening when he knocked on her door she called, 'Come in,' and her heart was beating fast.

'Hello, Erica,' he said softly. 'I'm glad you've agreed to talk to me. I may not have solved our problem, but I do feel near to it, if you are willing.'

'Sit down, John.'

'I don't know if you still want to marry me and, if you don't I can't blame you. I doubt that any of our customers have heard you call me Uncle John. It's always been just John. I also doubt that any of them know that Charles and Edward are your brothers. We could all be assistants as Alexander Gilmorton is. You were right when you accused me of being possessed by being illegitimate. I certainly was. Then I thought why should we both be suffering from my mother's sins?'

He paused then added earnestly, 'Could you love me, Erica? I love you dearly.'

'Yes, I could, John. I've been a fool in thinking I was in love with Frank. It'll be a long time before you and I could be married but I'm willing to wait.'

He took her hands in his. 'It will, however, come eventually.'

After hesitating a moment he drew her to him and kissed her and Erica wondered how she could ever think she was in love with Frank.

This was a different kind of loving. There was a passion in the kiss, but it was a gentle passion that brought a strong emotion, not a wild, frantic passion.

It was later, after the family had been told and celebrated that Erica wondered how Hesther would take it when she knew that eventually she and John would marry.

Well, that was in the future, it was no use worrying now.

There were times when Erica longed for John to make love to her but he never attempted it. She would get a good-night kiss but that was all.

The weeks went by until it was time

for Janet's baby to be born. Janet tired easily and Edward was impatient for it to happen.

Erica still had to see to the people who made the boxes and also to Margaret and Emily who also still made them. Angie had two months to wait for her baby to be born and her mother had stopped her making the boxes. She must look after herself.

Then Margaret called one morning, all excitement, to tell Erica that Angie had given birth to a premature baby.

'He's only seven months and quite tiny, but he's a lovely little thing.' She laughed. 'And has a surprising powerful pair of lungs. Angie and Michael are crazy about him. So is Mama and Papa.' Then Margaret's smile died. 'And here are Emily and I longing for a baby and can't get pregnant.'

Erica said cheerfully, 'It'll happen any time. Don't worry.'

But when Margaret left Erica was solemn. How long would it be before she would have children?

The person that Erica worried about the most was Janet. She was due to have her baby in ten days. She bulged a great deal and was very lethargic. The family wondered if there could be twins.

Then the very next day she was delivered

of a beautiful baby girl weighing eight pounds twelve ounces.

Janet said that they were going to call her Lilian because Edward had said when she was born that she was like a lily.

And so she was. Her hair was fair and curled slightly. She also had big blue eyes. But she had a temper. She hated to be bathed. When Erica bathed her, however, she never even gave a whimper.

This, of course pleased Erica no end. Also she was the only one who could get Lilian off to sleep at night by singing lullabys.

Janet said one time, smiling, 'You'll make a good mother, Erica, but I'll be glad when you have a baby of your own and I can have Lilian to myself.'

Erica said softly, 'I can't wait for that time to come.'

Two months later when Margaret and Emily called for some work they were over the moon. They were both pregnant.

Margaret said, 'And our husbands are as daft as we are.'

For Erica it was a treat to see their joyous expressions, and she could only pray that she would have children when the time came for her to marry.

Charles' lady friend Nadine was always talking about when she and Charles were married, but Charles did not seem to be in a hurry.

One day Erica mentioned it to him and he said, 'One has to be sure.'

'And you are not?'

'You know why, don't you? It's because of the way Edward behaved. He thought he was in love with Janet and went off with another woman. I'm afraid that could happen to me.'

'I don't believe it. You either love her or you don't. You and Edward are not a bit alike. You have no right to be courting Nadine.'

'But I love her.'

'You can't really love her or you would never question it.'

'Might I just say something, Erica? You thought you loved Frank then found it was John you truly loved.'

She was taken aback. 'Yes, I did, but there were a lot of other things that came into our lives. If John should change his mind I would stay single.'

'Well, I'll think about it.'

Erica began to wonder if they all took after their mother and wanted changes. But then their mother was not her mother.

Oh, Lord, she prayed, help Charles to sort himself out.

It was not long after this that Charles told Erica he and Nadine were going to be married in three months time. He added smiling, 'Don't look so worried, I've come to my senses. I've had long talks with John.'

'Oh, I'm so glad, Charles.'

'Nadine's parents are giving an engagement party next Saturday. Our family are being invited.'

'Lovely, something to look forward to.'

The wedding followed the party and it was when Charles and Nadine were back from their honeymoon that things began to go wrong.

Charles and Nadine were in the shop and all were laughing and talking when the shop door was flung open and Hesther came storming in. She began shouting at John.

'How dare you plan to marry Erica when the divorce comes through!'

John said quietly, 'Who told you that?'

'Never mind who told me. I know what your game is and I'll tell everybody about you both. And I'll tell the police too. You'll both be put in gaol!'

'Hesther, calm down,' John spoke sharply. 'Faith told me that I was illegitimate and that Erica was adopted. There are no blood ties between us.'

'And you believe it,' she sneered. 'Faith lied to you. You are her son all right!' she yelled. 'And Erica is her daughter. Get her birth certificate and you'll soon find out. You are *brother* and *sister!'*

She turned on her heel and went rushing out. She left the pavement and fought her way through all the traffic. They all stood staring. Then just before she reached the opposite pavement a horse-drawn carriage appeared. The driver quickly reined and shouted, 'Whoa!' but they were too close. Hesther fell under the horses' hooves.

Erica felt herself swaying. Janet grabbed her elbow and sat her on a chair.

There was a great commotion outside. People shouting.

The three men went across the road. Erica was trembling and she was ice cold. She looked up at Janet and said, with eyes full of despair, 'Who is telling the truth?'

'John. I feel sure of that. I'll get you a drink of brandy.'

It was only minutes before the men were back, but it seemed a lifetime to Erica.

'How is—is Hesther?' she asked.

John said gently, 'They are taking her to hospital. I must go and see how she is.'

Edward went with him and Erica sat in an agony until they returned.

Hesther had died.

Erica was silent. She felt that all the life

had left her body. Was this the ending of her dreams?

John tried to talk to her but she whispered, 'Not now.'

Chapter Twenty-Four

The next morning they were still worrying as to how Hesther had got to know that John and Erica were planning to marry when the divorce came through.

As Erica said, 'None of us have mentioned it to a soul.'

Janet looked at the men. 'Did either of you three perhaps mention it while you were in the shop?'

John shook his head. 'The shop would be the last place we would talk about such a thing.'

Then Erica suddenly realised that she was the culprit. Colour rushed to her cheeks. Oh, heavens, how careless she had been. She had told her Aunt Rebecca.

Although she hated to admit it they must be told.

They all stood staring at her then John said, 'What made you tell your aunt?'

'I was probing into the family and I never guessed even for a moment that she knew Hesther. I shall have to go and see her this morning and find out if she was the one.'

Rebecca looked grim when Erica called.

'I'm glad you called, Erica. It saved me writing to you. I had a visit yesterday from John's wife Hesther. She was shouting and raving. You've never heard anything like it.

'What excuse did she make for calling?'

'She didn't make any excuse. She wanted to know, no, she *demanded* to know if I knew that you and John intended to get married when the divorce came through.

'I told her yes I did and asked what it had to do with her. I didn't know then, of course, who she was.'

'She said, and she was slavering as she spoke, did I know that you could be both put in prison as you were brother and sister.'

Erica's mouth had gone so dry that she was unable to speak. Rebecca went on, 'I told her at once what your relationship was but she wouldn't have it. She said yes, it was true that John was illegitimate but it was all lies about you, no one had adopted you. You were Faith's daughter. She shouted at the top of her voice. "They are brother and sister!"

'I shouted back at her that she better

get out out of my house or I would have her put out. Fortunately, at that moment my next door neighbour came in, he has a key. He's a big burly man and when I told him that I wanted her out of the house he marched her to the door and put her out.

'Oh, Lord, what a to do! I could hear her going down the street shouting out about you and John. No one would make head nor tail what she was on about, of course, but I only hope she won't come back again. It shook me up a bit.'

'She won't come back,' Erica said, in little above a whisper. 'She's dead.'

Rebecca stared at her. 'Dead? What happened?'

Erica managed to get the story told and Rebecca said, 'It was all lies, of course. John wouldn't lie to you.'

'He's going to try and find out the truth. I can't help but feel sorry for Hesther.'

Rebecca sniffed. 'You've no need to feel sorry for her. She was just a bitter, vicious woman. There's one good thing about it. At least you won't have to wait until the divorce. You and John can be married soon.'

Erica shook her head. 'I would have to have proof that we are not related. Faith could have lied about me being adopted. I think she must have known how much

I loved John from being a toddler.'

'But she would not have lied, not have allowed you two to marry if you had been brother and sister. Definitely not. She might have liked having men, but she did have some principles.'

Tears sprang to Erica's eyes and she was unable to control them. In seconds she was sobbing.

'Oh, don't my love.' Rebecca reached out her hands to her. 'I know that feeling, my love. That is how my life has been at times. But I always get over it.'

Erica got up and dried her eyes. 'I'll make some tea.'

When Erica got back to the shop John came upstairs right away. 'Well,' he said, 'did Hesther visit Aunt Rebecca?'

'She certainly did.'

She told him all that had happened and he looked angry at the end of it.

'I'm terribly sorry that all this had to happen. One thing I'm sure about is that Faith would not lie about her having adopted you. We'll have to try and find your birth certificate. I'll go to Somerset House.'

Janet came in and she had to hear Hesther's story. She said, 'I think it's a good job she died. She didn't do any good when she was alive. A miserable, bitter woman. I know that I was bitter when Edward walked out on me, but I didn't start yelling at people.'

Erica said, 'I've just been thinking. If my name Erica Curtis is in the birth certificates at Somerset House then Faith is my mother.'

'And if it isn't?' John asked.

'Then it's hopeless because I don't even know the surname of my parents.'

Janet looked up. 'There's no one we can ask?'

'What puzzles me is,' John said, 'why Faith went to the trouble to tell me that I was illegitimate and not mention the name of Erica's parents.'

'Because we are obviously brother and sister.' Erica sounded forlorn.

'No. I feel it in my bones that we are not related. We'll find a way eventually. Everything else has fitted in. It seemed to me that Hesther was doomed to die. There must be a way to find out. We won't be beaten. Curtis and the sea captain's wife were killed in an accident. They—' He stopped. 'That's it! It would be in the newspapers. I'll go to the newspaper office and look through the old papers. They keep them for years.'

Erica said quietly, 'I think it would be wise to go to Somerset House first.'

There was a silence for a moment then

392

John said, 'Yes, it would be sensible. If there's nothing there I'll go on to the newspaper office. When Charles comes in, tell him where I am.'

It was the longest day that Erica could ever remember.

But at the same time it gave her hope. John was not back by seven o'clock, which meant that her birth certificate was not in Somerset House.

It was nearly eight o'clock when he came in and he looked drained. 'There's something I'm missing,' he said and dropped into a chair. 'Is it possible, Erica, that you are younger or older than we think and I've been looking at the wrong papers?'

Erica raised her shoulders. 'I don't know. At the moment I feel about a hundred.'

'Me too. There are plenty of accidents but none with a married man and a sea captain's widow. The whole gory details would be in.' He gave a deep sigh. 'I'll go again tomorrow and hope to find something.'

Janet came in with a cup of tea for him.

He sat up. 'Oh, that's very welcome. I'm parched. Thank you Janet.'

When Charles and Edward came in they got down to studying the position. Edward asked if the papers went in rotation.

John said he looked at each date at first but then went over them automatically.

'One could be missing,' Edward said. 'And could be the very paper you wanted.'

John groaned. 'I just couldn't go through them all again.' Then he sat up. 'Of course I could. I'll feel more like it tomorrow.'

'You go to the shop tomorrow. I'll go to the newspaper office.'

But John wouldn't agree to that. 'It's my problem.'

Erica thought she had never had any luck. Then she straightened up. No, that was wrong. It was foolish to think in that way. She had helped to make a success of the business.

It was other things that had gone wrong. Not knowing whether she was really in love with Frank. Not being able to give up making the boxes. She was at fault. But could she change? Time would tell.

All she could do now was to pray that John would find the name of her parents.

John came back late the following afternoon. He was smiling. 'I found the accident. Part of the paper was missing but the one with the accident in was with another paper. There were big headlines. It said, "MARRIED MAN AND WIDOW KILLED". Then it explained what had happened. A cab they were in had dropped

394

into a part of the road that caved in. They were both dead when they got them out.'

'How terrible,' Erica said. 'Was I mentioned at all?'

'Yes, there was quite a big piece. Mostly, of course, about the state of the roads and how they needed attending to.'

'Had my parents called me Erica?'

'Yes. Your parents' name was Ramsay. Your mother's Christian name was Marian and your father was Sea Captain James Ramsay.'

Tears filled Erica's eyes. 'And to think that I never knew them.'

'Fate governs our lives, Erica. If you hadn't been adopted I would never have met you.'

Her tears stemmed. 'I had never thought of that. Oh, John, I'm glad we can get married. Not now but in a few months time. I'll give up making my boxes. I want children.'

'And so do I, my darling.'

He kissed her in the gentle passionate way that Erica thought so beautiful.

John said, 'Shall we tell the family?'

She nodded slowly. 'I think it might be a good idea.'

The publishers hope that this book has given you enjoyable reading. Large Print Books are especially designed to be as easy to see and hold as possible. If you wish a complete list of our books, please ask at your local library or write directly to: Magna Large Print Books, Long Preston, North Yorkshire, BD23 4ND, England.

This Large Print Book for the Partially sighted, who cannot read normal print, is published under the auspices of

THE ULVERSCROFT FOUNDATION

THE ULVERSCROFT FOUNDATION

. . . we hope that you have enjoyed this Large Print Book. Please think for a moment about those people who have worse eyesight problems than you . . . and are unable to even read or enjoy Large Print, without great difficulty.

You can help them by sending a donation, large or small to:

**The Ulverscroft Foundation,
1, The Green, Bradgate Road,
Anstey, Leicestershire, LE7 7FU,
England.**
or request a copy of our brochure for more details.

The Foundation will use all your help to assist those people who are handicapped by various sight problems and need special attention.

Thank you very much for your help.